For my family. I love you with all my heart.

Chapter One

Like the well-oiled machine she'd become, Emma Westlake wrapped her hand around the Limoges teapot and counted down silently in her head.

Ten ...
Nine ...
Eight ...
Seven ...
Six ...
Five ...
Four ...
Three ...
Two ...

"Your tea, Dottie."

At the single nod she earned in return, Emma filled the matching cup atop the matching saucer to within exactly a quarter inch of its gold-trimmed lip and followed it up with a single splash of cream and two pinches of sugar.

She waited exactly three beats for the *Lovely, dear* that always followed, and then made her way around the linen-topped table to her own seat and her own cup. "Biscuit?" she asked, even as her mind filled in the answer she knew she'd get—the same answer she got every Tuesday at three o'clock . . .

"Why, yes, I think I will."

She held the basket out as the octogenarian helped herself to one, kept it hovering in place just north of the table's center point for the three-Mississippi-seconds' worth of hemming and hawing that invariably followed, and then firmed up her hold as the woman's frail hand reached inside for the *I really shouldn't* second biscuit.

"Thank you, Emma."

"Thank *you*, Dottie." Retrieving her napkin from the table, Emma unfolded it across her lap and smiled at the wheelchair-bound woman she'd grown to love in spite—or maybe because—of the weekly ritual.

The fact that the weekly ritual came with a steady paycheck was simply the unnecessary but always appreciated cherry on top of the cake. Especially now that—

"Aren't you going to have a biscuit, dear?"

Like clockwork, she swallowed back the instinctual urge to retch and, instead, nodded as she'd promised Dottie's husband she would during his deathbed phone call eighteen months earlier. After all, as per the unwritten script that never varied, never faltered, there would be a moment—fleeting, certainly, but still a moment—when the elderly woman would close her eyes in memory of dear old Alfred. And when that happened, the tail-wagging garbage disposal Emma had added to the weekly get-together six months earlier would be ready and eager to help bury the proverbial cardboard-flavored treat.

Leaning back in her chair just enough to afford herself a view of the golden retriever sitting faithfully beside her feet, Emma dropped her hand to her lap and flashed the get-ready signal she'd taught him. Sure enough, Dottie lifted her cup, glanced at the ceiling, murmured her husband's name, and then closed her eyes. In a flash, Emma snatched her lone biscuit from her dessert plate, pulled it down beneath the table's edge, and handed it off to—

"He doesn't like them, either, dear."

Emma sat up tall, her eyes meeting and then abandoning Dottie's. "*Them?*"

"Don't play dumb," Dottie said on the heels of a snort. "I may be old, and I may be confined to this cumbersome chair with wheels, but I'm not stupid. And that dog of yours is nothing if not consistent, as evidenced by the pile of twenty-three now-stale biscuits my cleaning lady found in the corner of Alfred's study."

Clamping back the urge to question the use of the word *now* in relation to *stale*, Emma hung her head in shame and—"Wait!" She snapped her full attention back to Dottie. "You said twenty-*three?*"

"Today's would've made twenty-four."

"But . . ." The rest of her protest faded away as the adding and multiplying part of her brain kicked into high gear. "I've been bringing Scout with me for the last six months now. Every Tuesday. Making this tea his"—she pulled up the edge of the tablecloth for an uninhibited view of her dog—"*twenty-fourth* and . . . Scout, you *traitor!* You didn't even eat *one!*"

"Now, dear, don't scold Scout for being the only honest one of the three of us."

She felt her mouth gape, rushed to close it, and then let it gape again, unchallenged. "The *three* of us?"

"Yes, three. You. Scout." Dottie pointed at each of them before landing her finger on herself. "And me."

"*You?*"

Dottie said nothing.

"Wait. You're telling me, after all this time—"

"Eighteen months," Dottie interjected.

Emma paused. Regrouped. "You're telling me, after eighteen months, that you don't like these biscuits?"

"They're dreadful."

"Dreadful?" Emma echoed. "But Alfred instructed me to buy them. To make sure to have them in that exact basket each week. And to offer you one—and then another—after I was seated with my own tea!"

"That was *his* part of the tradition. The tea part was *mine*. Tuesday at three o'clock sharp was *ours*."

She tried to make sense of what she was hearing, but it was difficult to hold a thought, let alone process it. "But you eat them every week," Emma argued.

"I do. For Alfred. It's the least I can do after he moved heaven and earth to make sure I still have my Tuesday afternoon tea by hiring you."

"Wow. I don't know what to . . ." Emma sat up tall. "Wait. Did Alfred *know* you didn't like them?"

Dottie took another, longer sip of her tea and then lowered her cup onto its saucer. "No. But that was okay. It mattered to him, just as the tea mattered to me. He knew that, which is why you're here. And as for the biscuits, there is no one else I would eat cardboard for every week."

It was Emma's turn to snort. "*Two* pieces, no less!"

The elderly woman's answering smile, along with the hint of tears that accompanied it, disappeared as quickly as it came, replaced instead by an eye roll to end all eye rolls. "It's clear I need a new housekeeper."

"Why is that?" Emma asked, draining away the rest of her own tea.

"Six months to find a growing pile of biscuits? You tell me . . ."

"Oh. Right." Flopping back against her chair, Emma fiddled with her spoon, her empty cup, her—

"Out with it, Emma."

She pushed her empty cup into the center of the table and then pulled it back again. "Out with what?"

"You're drooping on the inside."

"I'm . . ." Too tired to protest, she simply gave up. "It

doesn't matter. I'll figure it out. Today is about you. The way I promised Alfred it would be."

Dottie waved at Emma's words with her age-spotted hand. "The reason Alfred asked you—as opposed to one of our good-for-nothing children—is because we grew to care about you during all those nightly walks that took us past your great-aunt's old place. He liked watching you transform her weed-infested flower beds under his tutelage, and I liked picking you apart all the way back to the house."

"Picking me apart?" she parroted.

"In a *caring* way, of course."

Emma laughed. "Right. Of course."

"I suspect Alfred thought I could help you navigate life, and that you could—I don't know . . . Be something for me to look forward to, I suppose?"

"You look forward to our teas?"

"I look forward to *my* tea," Dottie corrected. "I look forward to *your* company, pathetic and otherwise."

"Pathetic?"

"Yes. You look like someone took your favorite toy."

"How? I smiled when I walked in . . . I smiled through every correction you made of my place setting . . . I smiled when I poured your tea . . . I smiled when you suggested I take a biscuit even though the very thought of those things makes me nauseous."

"Your mouth may have been smiling, dear, but your eyes weren't. And they haven't been for a while now."

Like a balloon on the receiving end of a pin stick, Emma deflated against her chair. "I . . . I don't know what to say except I'm sorry."

"For what? Being sad? Being worried? Please . . ." Dottie shifted in her wheelchair. "Save the martyr stuff and just tell me what's bothering you."

Glancing down at her lap, Emma drew in a breath and released it slowly. "It's really not a big deal. Nothing you need to be worrying about. I'll figure it out. Really. Somehow."

"You're fired."

Her head snapped up. "What did you say?"

"You're fired."

"But . . ." Emma stopped, gathered her breath again. "Please, Dottie, my company is in its death throes and—and I need that weekly check from Alfred's estate more than ever right now. Especially until I figure out what on earth I'm going to do next."

Dottie smiled triumphantly. "Now we're getting somewhere . . . You're not really fired, dear. I just needed you to cut to the chase so we can get to the business of fixing it."

"I'm not sure it *is* fixable. Not in the way I want it to be, anyway."

"Try me."

"The last of my corporate clients have finally pulled all of their travel bookings in-house. I knew it was inevitable—they've been dropping like flies for the past few years—but I really thought the last two were going to hold solid and . . ." She propped her elbows on the table in very un-tea-like style and dropped her head into her hands. "Yeah, I haven't booked a trip for anyone in months. Zip. Nada."

"So do something else."

She didn't mean to laugh, but she couldn't exactly stop herself, either. "Now you sound like my parents."

"Oh?"

"They want me to give in. They want me to sell the house and come back to New York. They want me to run one of their tutoring centers like my sister Trina does. But I don't want to step into *their* dream, Dottie. I want my own. I want to be my own boss in a business that *I* built from the ground up."

"You did that. With your travel business."

"My travel business that ultimately *failed*, sure. But just because it did doesn't mean I'm ready to give up on myself or this place yet. I love my little house. It really feels like mine now instead of just some place I inherited from my great-aunt. And Scout loves it there, too. It's our *home*."

"So what now?"

"*That* is the million-dollar question," Emma said, popping up her head. "I'm thirty-four, Dottie. I have no desire—and absolutely no money—to go back to school to learn something new. And while my family thinks the world starts and ends with the border of New York, I-I just can't go back there with my tail between my legs. I won't."

Dottie took another sip of her tea, another nibble—albeit pained—of her biscuit. "Who said you have to learn something new?"

"My phone line that never rings, and my checking account that has a higher number *after* the decimal point, that's who." A bark from underneath the table sent her head back onto her hands with an accompanying groan. "And, apparently, *my dog*."

"Why can't you just do more of *this*?"

"Trust me, I'm doing way more whining when I'm home. Ask Scout. He'll tell you."

It was Dottie's turn to groan. Only hers was accompanied by a hooked finger and a not-so-gentle shove upward of Emma's chin. "I'm not talking about *this*"—Dottie swept a dismissive hand at Emma and then widened the gesture to include the table and the teacups. "I'm talking about *this*."

"I don't get it."

"I'm talking about you being my friend."

Emma stared at the woman, waiting. When no further explanation was forthcoming, she pushed back her chair and stood. "Being a friend is not a business, Dottie."

"Do you not get paid to be here every Tuesday afternoon?"

"I do. But the *friend* part? That's just happened. Over time."

"Talk around it all you want, dear. But the simple fact is that you receive payment to be my friend each week."

With hands that knew the drill by heart, Emma stacked the saucers on top of the dessert plates and draped the linen napkins across her arm. "I don't really like the way that sounds. It sounds . . ." She cast about for the right word. "Fake. And there's nothing fake about this. Not for me, anyway. Not after all this time."

"That's why you should do this—because you're good at it, and you look the part."

"I *look* the part?"

"With that long brown hair you insist on parting in the middle, your cute, perky little nose, and those big brown doe eyes, you've got the whole girl-next-door thing down perfectly."

"Girl next door?"

"In other words, you'll make the perfect sidekick for others just like you do for me."

"Sidekick?" She was starting to sound like a parrot even to her own ears. "Oh, no. No, no, no. I'm not *your* sidekick. It's more like *you're mine.* Every Tuesday. Three o'clock sharp."

"It's my house, my teatime. *You're* the sidekick, dear." Dottie released the brake on her wheelchair and followed Emma down the hall and into the kitchen, Scout close on her wheels. When the plates and cups were in the dishwasher and the napkins in the laundry room hamper, the woman stopped all further movement with a splayed hand. "Anyway, back to my point. I'm not the only person who lives alone, Emma. Look at you!"

Craning her neck so as to catch a glimpse of herself in the antique mirror above the wall-mounted telephone, Emma took in her poker-straight hair . . . her lightly freckled nose . . . her plain-Jane—albeit thickly lashed—eyes and then spun around to find Dottie smiling smugly. "I can't hire myself, Dottie. I'm broke."

"My point is that lonely people come in all shapes, sizes, and ages. Some are doing fine in the friend department, I'm sure. But some, like me, just need someone every once in a while."

"That's what social media and dogs are for," Emma quipped, ducking her way around the woman and the wheelchair and heading back toward the living room.

Dottie followed. "There's a time and place for that kind of interaction, sure. Just as there's a time, a place, *and a need* for human interaction once in a while, as well. Focus on the latter. You'll make a killing."

"By being a hired friend?" Emma pulled the tablecloth off and balled it up in her arm. "That sounds awful."

"I think it sounds rather profitable to me."

"Who is going to hire me to be their friend?"

"I can think of someone off the top of my head right now." Dottie backed her chair up enough to clear the table and then wheeled herself over to her old-fashioned rolltop desk. "Maybe even two people."

Emma carried the tablecloth through the kitchen and into the laundry room, grabbed her purse off the coatrack where she'd hung it, as per ritual, and then rejoined Dottie and Scout at the front door. "Look, Dottie, I appreciate your encouragement, your ear, and your willingness to overlook a"—she dropped her gaze to Scout's—"certain someone's inability to cover for his owner. I really do. You're the best, and you're a blessing. To me, and to Scout. Truly."

"Why do I feel like you're brushing me off?"

"Maybe because I am?" Emma bent down, planted a kiss on the softly wrinkled cheek, and then watched as Scout followed it up with a jaw-to-hairline lick. "I'll be back next Tuesday for my weekly insult."

Dottie drew back in her chair. "I don't insult you, dear."

"Does the word *sidekick* not ring any bells?"

"I'm right about this, Emma. Just wait and see."

"Goodbye, Dottie." She stepped into the late-afternoon sun and snapped for Scout to follow. "Call me if you need anything."

"And *you* call *me* when you finally realize I'm right. Because you will."

With one last wave, Emma turned and headed down the walkway and onto the sidewalk, Scout's tail happily thumping against the side of her leg. "You know, you really kind of sold me out in there today, mister."

Scout's tail wagged faster.

"You're supposed to feel *guilt*, Scout. Not—"

A vibration in the vicinity of her hip had her reaching inside her front pocket and retrieving her phone. A glance at the unfamiliar number and the last-ditch hope that maybe, just maybe, it was someone looking to book a trip rather than sell her a year's subscription to the jelly-of-the-month club had her accepting the call and pressing the phone to her ear.

"Hello?"

"Emma?"

She tried to place the voice, but other than putting the caller in the seventy-and-up bracket, she came up empty. "Yes, this is Emma. Who's calling?"

"This is Big Max."

Following Scout's gaze to a squirrel making its way down a nearby tree, she promptly grabbed hold of his collar. "I'm sorry, but I have a feeling you have the wrong number."

"If you're Emma Westlake, I don't have the wrong number. Dottie made me repeat it three times."

She closed her eyes. Swallowed. Opened them. "Did you say *Dottie*?"

"I sure did. You know her?"

"I just left her not more than three minutes ago. Tops."

"Dottie's a quick one."

"It definitely seems that way," she mused as Scout abandoned his view of the squirrel in favor of a little boy playing with a ball one yard over. "So, what can I do for you, Big Max?"

"Dottie says I can hire you."

This time when she closed her eyes, she added a mental prayer for a do-over on the day. *"For?"* she asked on the heels of a louder-than-intended sigh.

"To go with me to the dance at the senior center on Friday afternoon."

At her answering sigh, Scout looked up, his expression one of worry. "It's okay, boy," she said, patting his head.

"So you'll do it? You'll put on your dancing shoes and fawn all over me so them ladies will finally give me the time of day?"

She dropped down onto the curb and buried her face in Scout's fur. "Mr. Max, I—"

"Big Max" came the correction in her ear.

Pushing Scout and his overeager tongue away from her nose and chin, she straightened her back. "Big Max, I'm sure you're a fine dancer, and I'm sure, if you ask around, you can find someone who actually goes to the senior center to be your—"

"I'll pay you five hundred dollars!"

"Wait, what? Did—did you just say *five hundred* dollars?" she stammered between Scout's continued licks.

"For three hours!"

Scout's tongue followed her finger to her ear. "Five *hundred* dollars . . ." she repeated.

"That's right, and I'll even buy you one of them flower things for your wrist!"

"I-I don't know what to say. I—"

"Say you'll take the job."

Should she?

Could—

"You've got yourself a deal, Big Max."

Chapter Two

She was just dropping her keys onto the catchall table in the front entryway when her pocket buzzed again. A peek at the display screen revealed yet another number she didn't recognize.

"Hello?"

"Is this . . . um . . . Emma? Emma Westlake?"

Scout led the way into the kitchen, the thump of his tail against the wall, the refrigerator, the kitchen table, and, finally, his food bag making it difficult to place the woman's voice. "It is. How can I help you?"

A long, labored sigh filled her ear. "I know how this is going to sound. But sitting here, bemoaning the state of my life, isn't changing anything."

Not sure how to respond, Emma said nothing.

"I need a life. I need to go places and meet—"

"Oh! You're calling to book a trip!" She reversed course and made a beeline for her office on the other side of the hall. "Fantastic. Where are you looking to go?"

An awkward pause was followed by a cough and then

another pause. "I'm thinking the gym would be the best place to start."

"I'm sorry," Emma said, switching the phone to her other ear. "I'm not sure I caught that. Did you say the *gym*?"

"I kind of see it as the whole two-birds-with-one-stone thing."

Dropping onto her computer chair, Emma clicked her way into her master file even as her mind's eye began its mental search of the best locations. "You can find state-of-the-art gyms in many resorts across the country, but some of the ones on the West Coast are pretty spectacular if that's what—"

"I mean, why *can't* I get in shape and meet people all at the same time? Does sweat really have to be all that unappealing?"

Emma switched the phone back. "I'm sorry, I'm not sure I'm following."

"About that . . . Yeah . . . I tend to be all over the place at times. Works with my job at the VA, sure. But everywhere else? Not so much. But I'll try to keep it under wraps when we're together, I promise."

Defeated, Emma clicked back out of her master file and stood. "I have a feeling you have the wrong number and—wait. You knew my name . . ."

"My mom got it from her friend—something Adler."

Emma froze. "Do you mean *Dottie* Adler?"

"Yeah, that sounds right."

Once again, she found herself speechless. And, once again, the woman in her ear kept talking.

"I think my mom is tired of hearing me complain about my life. So while a part of me—a really big part, mind you—feels like the world's biggest loser calling you right now, there's another part hoping it actually does something. Times two."

She sat back down. "Times two?"

"Think about it. If we meet at the gym three mornings

a week, it gets me out of the house and around people. And by making the gym my so-called *friend time*, I'll also be doing something to counteract my stress eating."

Emma closed her eyes against the image of Dottie's smirk. "Can we start at the beginning? Maybe like with your name?"

"Why? So you can call the loony bin and file a report?"

"No, of course not."

"Something tells me if this was a video call, you'd be nodding."

Emma's answering laugh brought Scout into the room with his favorite ball clenched between his teeth. "I plead the Fifth."

"As well you should if you want the job."

"Wait. *Job?*"

"To go to the gym with me . . . three mornings a week . . . as my"—the woman sucked in a breath—"my gym buddy. This way I can have some semblance of a life when I'm not taking pulses and sticking my finger in places no finger should ever go."

"You're a doctor?"

"Nurse practitioner. At a VA. I'm there all day and into the evening. Five days a week. When I'm not there physically, I'm there mentally because I'm knee-deep in reports and charts and alerts and . . . yeah, my mother is right; I have no life. That's why I'm calling you."

At a loss for what to say, Emma remained silent.

"My mom said that this Dottie person told her I can hire you to . . ." The woman's words faded to a groan before returning in fits and starts. "That I can, um, hire you to, um, be like a *friend*. Someone to . . . um . . . give me a reason to . . . um . . . leave my house every once in a while."

"Surely you don't need to hire someone to hang out with you." The second the words were out, Emma wished she could pull them back. But just as she was searching for a way to lessen the sting, the woman reclaimed the verbal baton.

"Before I started at the VA, you'd have been right. But years of being *too busy* all the time has cost me my friends, my once in-shape body, and, according to my mother, my ability to carry on a conversation."

"I see."

"So? Will you do it? I'm figuring we can start with the gym first and see how it goes. But it will have to be early— at like 5:30 in the morning. Monday, Wednesday, and Friday. Roughly an hour or so on each of those days. Unless I'm late getting there. Which could happen, on occasion. I don't think I have an issue with lateness, but my mother and my boss think I do."

She felt Scout's ball land on her foot a split second before the voice returned in her ear. "Anyway, I'll pay for your membership to the gym on top of whatever your hourly rate is, of course."

"My *hourly rate*?"

"My mom said Dottie thought you might do it for a couple hundred a week?"

"A-a couple . . . hundred?"

"Plus the gym membership," Stephanie hastily reminded her. "Which you could use on more than just our three scheduled mornings together."

"I don't know what to say. This is all so . . . so . . . I don't know."

"I promise I'm not a psycho. Really."

"I'm sure you're not. It's just that . . ." Emma flipped open her notebook, looked at the blank lines where clients and upcoming trips should be listed, and slammed it closed. "I'm in."

"Really?"

She nodded.

"Emma?"

"Oh. Right. You're not here in the room . . . Yes, yes, I'm really in. One-fifty a week, with the membership, will be fine."

"Wow. Okay. My mother is going to be thrilled."

"I'm glad."

"Start Friday?"

She racked her brain for a conflict, but other than the afternoon dance with Big Max, there was nothing. "Friday it is."

"Cool. Main Street Gym?"

"Works for me."

"Okay, awesome. I'll see you there at five thirty."

"See you—wait!" Emma bolted upright in her chair. "Your name. You still haven't told me your name."

"Stephanie Porter."

"Stephanie Porter," she repeated. "And how will I know it's you?"

"Look for the forty-year-old who appears as if she's been held hostage in a windowless basement her entire life. You find *her*, you'll have found me."

E mma didn't need to open her eyes to know what time it was. Scout's wet nose, followed by his big, wet, slobbery tongue across her closed eyes could only mean one thing; it was seven o'clock and time to start the day.

"Ugh. Scout. Please." She wiped the dog drool off her face and rolled onto her opposite side, her eyes simply too heavy to open. "Did you not notice what time it was when I finally came to bed?"

In light of who she was talking to, it was a rhetorical question, of course. But still . . .

The wet nose and big, wet, slobbery tongue followed.

"C'mon, Scout. I was up until practically 3:00 a.m. Please!"

The nose and the tongue persisted.

Forcing her matted eyelashes apart, she yawned. And sighed. And yawned again. "You do realize that this crazy idea I spent all night naming and writing a mission statement for might be the only way I can keep food in your bowl, right?"

His answering bark, combined with the hearty tail wag that followed, alerted her to her mistake. "Did you not hear all of the other words *before* I said food?"

The corresponding, and even harder, tail wag had her lunging for her water glass before it fell off her nightstand. "Okay . . . Okay . . . I get it. You want your breakfast. Sheesh!"

She yawned once, twice, three times, threw back the covers, and slid her feet over the edge of her bed and into her—

Tilting her head, she nudged Scout's chin upward until his guilt-ridden eyes were on hers. "What did you do with my slippers?"

Seconds later, her slippers—albeit wet and more than a little misshapen—were in her hands and she was lunging for the teetering bottle of Tylenol next to where her water glass had been. "Okay. Okay. Bad boy for taking them, good boy for bringing them back. Now let's go get your breakfast."

With another bark and another tail wag, Scout led the way out of the bedroom, down the stairs, into the kitchen, and over to his food mat.

"You know, you really could stand to learn a thing—or ten—about subtlety, my friend," she said, digging the scoop into the dog food bag and dropping it into the same powder-blue bowl that had accompanied Scout home from the animal shelter on the day he'd become hers. "How about we work on one, okay? One would be an improvement."

She watched him for a few moments and then wandered across the hallway and into her office. Eyeing the pile of balled-up paper to the left of her computer, she pulled out her chair and sank onto its vinyl cushion. She'd tried so many names—written so many different ways—but, in the end, it seemed the most simple of them all fit best.

"A Friend for Hire," she read aloud. "For all those plus-one moments."

Even the font she'd chosen for the business cards she'd printed, separated, and stacked into a small pile before finally calling it a night looked good. Professional.

It was all still so . . . *weird*. So crazy. So—

With a click of her finger, her computer screen came to life. With another few clicks, she found herself staring at the virtual flyer she'd tacked to the Sweet Falls community bulletin board in the wee hours of the morning. It had been a whim to put it there, to take a chance that maybe, just maybe, Dottie's idea had legs beyond Big Max and Stephanie, but now, in the cold light of day, she couldn't help but wish she'd gotten into bed thirty minutes sooner.

Still, there was a delete button—a delete button she was subsequently distracted away from pushing by an incoming call. A quick check of the screen showed an unknown number.

"Hello?"

"Yes, hello." The man paused, inhaled. "Is this A Friend for Hire?"

She tried to catch her reflection in the computer monitor but stopped when she remembered it was a call, not a face-to-face meeting. "Yes—yes, it is. How can I help you?"

"My name is Brian Hill. I live and work here in Sweet Falls. I saw your post on the virtual bulletin board this morning and I'd like to hire you to accompany me to the Open Mic Night at Deeter's. You know the place?"

"I know the place, sure," she said, pulling her desk calendar into range. "When?"

"Tonight. I know it's short notice, but I'll be reading from my latest work and I want someone there who will clap for me when I'm done. Can you do that?"

She paused her pen before it hit the day's square. "You want to hire me so I can *clap* for you?"

"Yes."

"Mr. Hill, I'm sure, if it's an open mic night, the audience will clap for everyone who performs."

"Under normal circumstances, perhaps that would be true. But the people I've invited to the event will want to *kill me* when I'm done, not clap for me."

Her answering laugh met with a weighted silence in her ear that left her shifting in her seat. "Mr. Hill? Are you still there?"

"I am." He cleared his throat. "What's your rate for two hours?"

"I haven't really figured out a—"

"A hundred bucks. And I'll pick up the appetizers and one drink, as well."

"To clap . . ."

"Mainly, yes. But to sit with me before I go on, as well."

She pumped her hand in the air. "I can do that!"

"Tonight. Nine o'clock. Deeter's." A sudden flurry of tapping started and stopped in the background of the call. "I just emailed my picture to the address on your flyer so you'll know who to look for."

Her gaze flew to the email indicator on the right-hand side of her screen and, sure enough, there was a numeral one where, seconds earlier, there had been nothing. She opened her inbox to a message from a Brian Hill. "Got it."

"Good. I'll see you tonight."

"See you then." She ended the call, set the phone on the counter, and let out a squeal of delight that brought Scout running. "We did it, boy!" She returned his lick of her hand with a scratch of his neck. "An idea that seemed positively ridiculous yesterday afternoon has netted me three paying gigs already—one of them *ongoing*!"

Scout rolled onto his belly in a clear signal her hand

should oblige. "I guess I'm going to owe Dottie a straight-up *You were right*, huh, boy?"

She gave him one last scratch and then turned back to her inbox. With one click to open the email and a second click to view the attachment, she found herself looking at a face that felt vaguely familiar. Yet, at the same time, she knew it wasn't someone she'd ever met.

Intrigued, she minimized the picture, clicked out of the email, and entered her latest client's name in the search bar at the top of her screen. When the search parameter yielded too many entries to sift through, she added in *writer* and clicked again.

Sure enough, a list of links to news articles—all of which included the same image he himself had sent her—popped up on her screen. Story by story, she made her way down the page until the man she'd minimized on her screen was no longer just some guy with earnest eyes and a cowlick.

She didn't need to sit across a table eating appetizers and exchanging small talk with Brian Hill to know he was a local conspiracy theorist at best, an out-and-out troublemaker at worst. It was there in the articles written after the last mayoral race when the young underdog had won over the older, seasoned incumbent and Brian—a freelance journalist—had been repeatedly quoted as saying there was an age war brewing in Sweet Falls and the elderly might be wise to ready their walkers and canes for battle. It was there in the news accounts of a squabble inside the town's beautification committee that depicted him in a photograph with dirt on his head and a clearly seething committee member in the background. It was there in an article in which he referred to the sheriff's department as the donut patrol. And it was there in countless other stories—both big and small—and the fingers Brian continually pointed in one direction or the other.

"Great," she murmured. "I'm being hired to clap for a nutcase."

Scout peeked over the edge of the desk, released his rediscovered ball onto her keyboard, and licked her wrist.

"Think I should call him back?" she asked, moving the ball onto her desk. "Tell him I can't do it?"

Standing up against the desk, Scout grabbed hold of the first balled-up piece of paper he could reach and dropped it on her hand.

"I know. I know. You want to play. But you're supposed to be working on subtlety, remember? And I really should call this guy back before—"

His tail wacked against the leg of her chair. Hard.

"*What*, Scout?"

He looked from her to the balled-up piece of paper and back again.

"What's wrong? It's just a piece of paper, see? Nothing to . . ." She opened the paper ball, smoothed it across the top of the desk, and stared down at the final name she'd written—the same name now displayed on the business cards she'd printed just before calling it a night.

A FRIEND FOR HIRE.

Her last chance to be her own boss . . .

Closing out of her search, Emma turned and wrapped her arms around Scout's head. "You're right, boy. Beggars can't be choosy."

Chapter Three

⟨divider⟩

He was waiting outside the restaurant when she stepped around the corner, concern etched across his forehead like coast-to-coast interstates on a map. His gaze traveled down Main Street toward Sweet Falls Town Hall and then back up to the square and the handful of residents strolling around the gaslit grounds with an ice cream cone or a coffee in hand. The fact that he hadn't spotted her yet gave Emma the perfect opportunity to size up Brian Hill in a way a simple photograph didn't really allow.

Yes, the broad shoulders, wire-rimmed glasses, bushy eyebrows, and tousled hair were there, as expected, but it was the other stuff—the fidgeting hands, the constant licking of his lips, the way his feet seemed to move even while standing still—that she wouldn't have anticipated based solely on the man's picture. She watched his attention drop to his watch and followed suit with her own.

8:59.

"Brian? Hi. I'm Emma."

In lieu of the handshake she expected, he opted to push

his glasses higher on his nose, instead. "A punctual person. I like that."

Unsure of a proper response, she simply smiled and nodded.

"I'm up first," he said.

"You mean on the open mic schedule?"

"Yes."

"I imagine that's a little nerve-racking."

Shrugging, he swept his hand toward the restaurant's front door. "I procured a table in front of the makeshift stage. The appetizer I ordered should be there by now."

"Sounds great. Though my dog would be a little irked if he knew I was around food he couldn't pilfer." She followed him into the dark-paneled entryway, past the hostess quietly taking peeks at her phone while pretending to pore over a seating chart, and into the like-paneled dining room. "Or, as I learned just this week, pile it in a corner if he deems it unworthy of his royal tastebuds."

Brian stopped beside a table topped with two glasses of water and—she cringed—a plate of stuffed mushrooms. "You feed your dog from the table?" he asked, taking the seat with a view of the other diners, and motioning her to the one that faced the stage. At her half nod, half shrug, he pulled a face. "I don't like dogs."

"That's because you haven't met Scout." She pushed her fork and knife off to the side lest she stab her first official client. "*Everyone* likes Scout."

"I would be an exception."

Willing her breath to remain steady and her smile present, Emma took in the stage and its single stool and microphone stand. "So what will you be reading?"

"A poem."

She coughed to hide her answering groan. "That's wonderful."

"Mushroom?" he asked, scooting the plate in her direction.

Scooting it back, she did her best to breathe her way
through the answering flip-flop of her stomach. "No. No,
thank you."

"Suit yourself, but they're the best around." Brian
snatched a stuffed mushroom from the plate, crammed it into
his mouth, and nudged his chin toward a manila folder not
far from her water glass. "That's for you. To keep."

"What is it?"

"Open it."

She took a sip of her water and then pulled the folder
into the spot where her silverware had been. Inside it, she
found a single piece of paper adorned with four pictures—
two faces she knew outright, and two that looked vaguely
familiar.

"And why are you giving me this?" she asked.

"Do you know who they are?"

Again, she looked at the paper, her index finger leading
the way for her lips. "I know this is Sheriff Borlin, and I
know this is Nancy Davis, of Davis Farm and Greenhouse.
But these two? I'm not entirely sure who they are."

"Rita Gerard."

Emma abandoned the image of the young woman she
guessed to be about her age to glance up at the man seated
opposite her at the table. "The new mayor's wife?"

"Yep."

"I thought she looked familiar, but I couldn't place where
I'd seen her."

"If you've picked up a newspaper in the last six months
or so, you've either seen her or her name. She's made sure
of that."

"I don't really read the news section all that much," Emma
admitted. "The Lifestyle and Leisure section is more my
thing, I guess."

"Lifestyle and Leisure?" he repeated, his voice flat.

"It fit more with my career as a travel . . ." She let the rest
of the needless statement trail away in favor of a sip of

water and a glance back down at the paper. "And who is this other one?"

"Robert McEnerny."

She studied the male depicted just below the sheriff and found that, yes, she recognized him, after all. "Of McEnerny Homes, right?"

"One and the same."

When his confirmation failed to lead to anything resembling an explanation for the paper's existence, she closed the folder and slid it back across the table.

He slid it back to her. "I printed this for you. In case you need it."

"In case I need it? For what?"

"They're all here," he said, leaning back in his chair. "Right now. In this room."

Shifting her gaze from the paper to the tables around them, she spotted Nancy . . . the sheriff . . . the home builder . . .

She looked back at Brian, only to be directed to look over her left shoulder at a table near the back of the restaurant— a table that held a trio of women, laughing and talking over a carafe of wine. A second, closer look revealed the mayor's wife was one of them.

"Okay," Emma said, returning her attention to her tablemate. "That's an interesting coincidence."

"It's not a coincidence at all. I appealed to their curiosity, or, perhaps *their fear*, and they came. As I knew they would."

"Then why did you need *me* if you knew your friends would be here?"

A wry smile slipped across his lips. "They're not my friends."

"Then I don't understand. You just said you invited them, right?"

"I did."

"Okay . . ."

"They want me dead. Each and every one of them."

She felt her eyes beginning to roll of their own volition. *"Dead?"*

"Yep."

When his face showed nothing to indicate he was kidding, she nibbled back the urge to groan. "I'm sure that's not true."

"Oh, it's true. My poem will just seal the deal, more or less. Trust—"

A smattering of applause brought an end to his answer and sent their collective attention toward the stage and the beloved fiftysomething restaurant owner. "Welcome to Open Mic Night at Deeter's. When I decided to try this out, I never imagined I'd get this kind of turnout on the first try. So to those of you who will be up here tonight, don't mess it up, okay?" Then, turning his attention in their direction, he said, "Brian, take it away."

"Good luck," she whispered.

If he heard her, he didn't react. Instead, he wiped at a droplet of sweat on his forehead, chased another stuffed mushroom down with a gulp of water, and picked up his phone. With a single tap on the handheld screen, he lifted his eyes to Emma's, muttered the words "Just in case," and then made a beeline for the microphone and its accompanying stool. There, with little fanfare or posturing, he began to read . . .

"Look around, look around, here sit those you laud, but soon you, too, will know their fraud."

Chairs creaked around the room as others matched her own uncomfortable shifting. Throats cleared to her left, voices murmured to her right, but still, Brian kept reading. And sweating.

"I say it often, I say it now, unmasking truth, this is my vow. For far too long you've turned a blind eye, their misdeeds hidden by a wink and a smile."

The clang of a glass against a plate echoed in the suddenly silent room. A glance to Emma's right revealed the sheriff's wife scooting back in her chair to minimize the spill of her husband's drink across her cream-colored pants. Beyond them, she spotted Nancy Davis downing her own drink with record speed, and—

"But it's in seeking the truth that you learn the true why; the laws sidestepped, the roles . . ." Brian's words dissolved into a strange gurgling sound only to disappear completely as he fell forward off his stool and onto the ground.

Pushing back her chair, Emma started for the stage, only to have her efforts thwarted by the owner's yells for everyone to stay back. As she and everyone around her watched, he rolled Brian onto his back, checked his wrist and his neck, and finally stared out at the crowd, stunned. "He's . . . *dead*!"

She fell back onto her seat as utter pandemonium took over. All she could hear were gasps and shrieks from the crowd while the owner barked orders to every member of his staff within yelling range.

"This can't be happening. This can't be happening. This. Can't. Be. Happening," she murmured, gulping water between each denial. "He—he was just here . . . two minutes ago . . . being all weird and—"

Opening the folder, she stared down at the piece of paper he'd wanted her to have before he stepped onto the stage. A piece of paper containing the pictures of four people he'd said wanted him dead.

Four people who were all present in the room at that very moment. With Brian's dead body no more than a few feet away . . .

Stuffing the paper inside her purse, Emma headed for the door.

Chapter Four

Emma dropped onto the overstuffed couch and immediately dispensed with the notion of sitting like a civilized human being. She simply didn't have the energy to remain upright.

She'd tried to sleep, she really had. She just hadn't been able to close her eyes, shut off her ears, or quiet her thoughts well enough to keep from revisiting the moment Brian fell off his stool and onto the stage. It was surreal . . . It was unfathomable . . .

"And I just left," she said, in the wake of a moan. "I grabbed that stupid folder and I left . . . I should've stayed. I should've left that folder exactly where it was on the table. I should've—"

Undraping her arm from its spot atop her face, she looked down at her stomach and the red ball that had been discarded onto it by the tail-wagging golden retriever staring back at her with a mixture of hope and worry. In a world where thought-bubbles really existed, his would say, *Play with me—please, please, play with me.*

"Hey, sweet boy. Thanks for the ball, but I'm not really in a ball-throwing mood." She flung out her hand and, when he moved into range, gave him a quick scratch behind the ear. "Maybe later, okay?"

Hope traded places with worry, earning him a second scratch and, when he leaned in to lick her chin, a kiss between his eyes. "Why don't you get in your doggie bed for a little while, okay? Maybe take a nap? I need to think. To process."

He held her gaze as if trying to read her mind. When the movement in his tail lessened, she hooked her arm back over her eyes. "That's a good boy," she murmured as, once again, her every sense dropped her right back in the middle of Deeter's.

She could smell the hot wings as they passed by her shoulder en route to the table to her right . . .

She could smell the lemon that had clung to the side of her water glass . . .

"I just met him . . . Why would I stay, right? Others in that room knew him far better than I did. Could answer questions about him and his health that I couldn't or wouldn't know . . ."

Again, she undraped her arm and, again, she looked down at her stomach to find an all-too-familiar chew toy side by side with the red ball. And beside them both, the same tail-wagging dog sporting the same thought-bubble.

"Still not a good time, Scout." She pointed at the elaborate yet barely used dog bed wedged between the recliner and the bookcase and watched as, once again, his unrealized hope made its way from his eyes to his tail. "Later. I promise."

Returning her chin to center, she stared up at the ceiling.

She could smell someone's perfume—something with lavender . . .

She could smell the repugnant odor of the fried mushrooms that had been on the table when she sat down . . .

And the sounds? They, too, were still so clear, so—

Emma lowered her gaze back to her stomach and the growing menagerie of items it sported, including the latest addition—an unopened snack-sized bag of her favorite cookies.

"Scouuuut . . ."

Guilt took its rightful spot next to hope, thwarting any irritation she might've felt in favor of a tug on her heart. Yep, it was official. If and when she had children, they'd get away with murder . . .

Then again, with not so much as a boyfriend, let alone a husband, on the horizon, it was a moot point.

"You're incorrigible, do you know that?" At the increased pace of his wag, she tried to pull a serious face, but they both knew it was futile. "Can you at least *pretend* we have rules? Like the one about keeping your face out of the pantry?"

She watched him slink off in the general direction of his dog bed, the click of his nails against the wood-planked floor slowly fading to the hushed voices, occasional coughs, and the sound of the manila file folder sliding across the table in her direction.

It was all so bizarre . . . so strange . . .

"So what if everyone on that piece of paper was there in the audience? It's a small town. Everyone is everywhere. He was simply a pot stirrer doing what he did best at the exact time he had a heart attack, that's all. Case closed."

The thump of something hard against her abdomen stole her attention back to the ball, and the chew toy, and the bag of cookies, and, now, her phone.

"I don't need that, Scout. I'm just here, trying to rest." She waved him closer, closed her eyes briefly against the face bath that followed, and then cupped her hand under his chin and made full eye contact. "Besides, you don't like the phone, remember? It steals my attention from you. Which you *will* get, later."

Again she pointed him to the bed. "Rest now; play later."

This time, the click-clack of his departure was accompanied by a whimper so soft, yet so heartbreaking, she held her hands to her ears in an attempt to stave off its power. She needed to rest, to clear her head, to—

"*The remote* now?" she said, dropping her hands back to the couch and her gaze from her stomach to Scout. "*Really?*"

Picking it back up off her stomach, he inched his way closer until the part of the remote that was overhanging the right side of his mouth grazed her hand.

She took it out of his mouth, wiped it free of his drool, and scooted upward until her back was flush with the arm-rest and there was room on the cushion for her tail-wagging cohort. "Okay, okay, you win. I can't keep going over this. It's driving me batty. So c'mon up here, next to me, and we'll see what's on for a little while. But *if*, by the grace of God, I actually drift off to sleep, be a good boy and do the same, okay?"

The gentle pressure of his snout on her leg, paired with an exhalation of pure contentment, was as good an answer as any verbal agreement could ever be. Resting her cheek against the back of the couch, she aimed the remote toward the TV, pressed the power button, and happily surrendered herself to the sights and sounds her channel surfing afforded.

She channel surfed her way past a game show, a sports show, an old movie she hadn't liked the first time she saw it, a fitness show, and a sitcom before stopping on the opening montage for the local Sweet Falls noon newscast. The camera zoomed in on the afternoon anchor, Doug Sherman, and his head of perfectly coiffed hair.

"Good afternoon. What should have been an opportunity for writers and musicians to share their talents turned into something quite different last night when local freelance writer Brian Hill died during Open Mic Night at

Deeter's Grill and Pub on Main Street. Hill, believed to be a conspiracy theorist of sorts, had just started reciting a poem he'd written when he collapsed and died shortly after 9:30 p.m."

The same picture Brian himself had sent her by way of email just twenty-four hours earlier appeared on the screen, while the news anchor turned the story over to a female beat reporter standing outside Deeter's.

"Good afternoon, Doug. Fifteen hours after Brian Hill's death in this popular Sweet Falls eatery"—the stone-faced blonde motioned over her shoulder—"staff are still reeling from the untimely death of the local writer. An avid marathon runner, Mr. Hill was just forty years old at the time of his death—a death many will not soon forget."

Emma stared at the screen as the reporter's face was replaced by a twentysomething clad in a Deeter's shirt.

"I was putting an order on a table near the back of the room when I heard everyone gasping around me, and that's when I looked up. The victim—Mr. Hill—just fell off his stool, onto the stage. Next thing I knew, my boss was saying the guy was dead. After that, everything was"—the young woman widened her eyes at the memory—"just chaos. I mean, people that age don't just up and die like that, you know?"

The beat reporter took command of the camera again. "An autopsy by the county medical examiner is expected to take place today. We will of course be there to cover the M.E.'s findings when they are released. For now, though, we wait to find out whether Mr. Hill succumbed to natural causes or something entirely different. Back to you in the studio, Doug."

She saw the anchor's mouth moving as he continued on to the next story, but really, in that moment, all she knew with absolute certainty was that her head was starting to spin. Yes, she'd heard what Brian had said about the people depicted in the folder he'd insisted on her keeping. And yes, his words—followed closely thereafter by his unexpected demise—had made it so sleep had been impossible once she was finally back home and in bed. But surely he was being his usual conspiracy theorist self, right? Surely he'd had a heart attack or a seizure or . . .

"An avid marathon runner, Mr. Hill was just forty years old at the time of his death . . ."

An avid marathon runner . . .

Forty years old . . .

"I mean, people that age don't just up and die like that, you know?"

She closed her eyes. Swallowed. Made herself breathe.

No one had gone near him . . .

No one had touched him . . .

No one had fired a gun . . .

He'd just been sitting there, on the stool, with his glass of water in his hand . . .

And he'd been sweating. Profusely. Like someone who was either nervous about being in front of people or wasn't feeling particularly well.

Pulling her legs out from under Scout, Emma swung them onto the floor, her thoughts running a mile a minute. People didn't have allergies to water. They had allergies to things like medications and food . . .

"The *fried mushrooms*?" she said, standing, remembering, and quickly discarding the thought. "No. He said Deeter's made the best around, and he said that before he'd even taken the first bite."

Shaking off the idea of an allergy once and for all, Emma looked back at the screen, her mind's eye replacing the news anchor's face with that of Brian's. On the sidewalk, before he'd seen her, he'd been fidgety, nervous. But once she'd identified herself, any nervousness had disappeared, replaced by an attitude that could best be described as unexpectedly confident, a bit judgmental (he had, after all, taken issue with Scout's eating habits), and more than a little paranoid.

Then again, Brian was dead. And the people he'd claimed wanted him that way had all been there when he fell over, watching from their respective tables just like Emma. If one of them *had* actually killed him, she would have seen it happen.

Her mind made up, she scooped the remote back off the couch, aimed it at the television, and turned the screen black. "The possibility of the impossible: a veritable ratings bonanza. And for a minute there, boy, I was as guilty of falling for it as the next guy. And *I was there*, I *know better* . . . Well done, Channel Two. Well done."

Stretching her arms above her head, she allowed herself a big, noisy yawn before turning back to the couch and an at-the-ready Scout. Before she could suggest the walk she knew he wanted, though, the phone that had fallen off her stomach along with the rest of Scout's offerings began to ring.

She plucked it off the cushion, wiped it on the sides of her striped pajama pants, and took the call. "Hello? This is Emma."

"What color dress are you wearing tomorrow?"

Too startled to speak, she pulled back the phone, noted the unknown number on the screen, and returned it to her ear in light of the vaguely familiar voice. "Excuse me?"

"I want your corsage to match your dress. That way I look more enticing to the ladies at the dance."

She staggered her way back onto the couch as the dots finally connected. "Big Max?"

"That's right. So? What color? The sooner I know, the sooner I can start figuring out which of my neighbors' porch gardens I need to visit before sunrise. I know Deidre has white and yellow flowers in her planters. And Hester has purple, I think. Maybe some pink."

The dance . . .

At the senior center . . .

For five hundred bucks she really needed . . .

Then again, when she'd agreed to the job, she hadn't been front row to someone's untimely death or bleary-eyed from the lack of sleep that had followed. Now that she had, she really just wanted to shut herself in for the upcoming weekend, drown her misery in anything resembling chocolate, and brainstorm more viable (read: less deadly) ways to earn a living.

"I really hope this helps Beatrice see me as someone she might want to make a nice dinner for or hold hands with on a walk around the town square." Clearing his throat of a growing yet unmistakable rasp, Big Max continued. "It'd be nice to have a special someone to pass the time with after all these years, don't you know? And I'd take real good care of her, too. I'd be sure to pick her flowers on occasion, for no particular reason. Or maybe I'd pick her some every morning while she's inside making me pancakes or French toast. Because that would be mighty special, Emma."

Guilt lodged a lump near the base of Emma's throat, and she did her best to try to swallow it away. But the knowing look from Scout as he set his chin atop her leg kept it firmly in place.

"Do you know the jitterbug? Or how to Lindy? Because if you don't, I can teach you. I ain't never done them with a date before, but I've been watching videos on the computer at the library and I think I'm ready." A sip in her ear let her know Big Max's sudden pause wouldn't last long, and she was right. "Did you know you can learn to do just about anything by watching a video on the computer these days? I figured out how to sew a button on my britches week before. last that way. But before you get to thinking I should just watch a video on how to make pancakes and French toast, I know how to make 'em just fine. But something tells me they'd taste a lot better if they were set in front of my spot at the table by someone special."

Closing her eyes, she took in a breath, held it to a silent count of five, and then released it along with the answer she knew he needed. "It's mint green—a pale mint green."

"A pale mint green," he repeated. "Hmmm . . . Not sure which of my neighbors is growing something that color, but I'll find something that'll look pretty on your wrist."

"You don't have to get me a corsage, Big Max. It's really not necessary."

"It is to me."

"Okay." She parted her lashes to find Scout's undivided attention waiting. "What time should I meet you outside the senior center?" she asked.

"Could we meet at the bus stop just down the street from there, instead? That way we could walk up together and have it be more official-like."

"Of course. Just name the time, and I'll be there."

"The dance starts at three, and since you can set a clock by Beatrice, let's meet at the bus stop at 2:45. That'll give me time to give you your corsage, and for you to make sure my bow tie is straight before we have to head over to the center. Maybe my own punctuality, combined with my spiffy appearance and your presence on my arm, will put me on her radar once and for all."

"I hope so." And it was true. Granted, her only exposure to Big Max thus far was via the phone, but there was something endearing about his uncomplicated image of what it meant to have and be a special someone.

After reconfirming the time and place for their meetup the next afternoon, Emma clicked off the call with a Scout-aimed sigh. "I wanted to cancel, boy. I really did. But I'd have felt like a complete heel bailing on him on such short notice, you know?"

Scout's warm tongue found the inside of her still-bent elbow and quickly expanded its lick zone while she yammered on, her thoughts as unsettled as her heart. "That stuff Brian said last night? And the fact he—well, *you know* . . . It was a coincidence, that's all. It has to be. I mean, the four people he showed me in the pictures—they were all there, sure . . . But none of them ever went near him when he was on that stage. *No one* did. He just died. That's it."

She pulled Scout's snout close and planted a kiss on the soft spot just above his eyes. "Still, maybe the universe is trying to tell us this whole Friend-for-Hire business idea isn't for us. Maybe, after this dance with Big Max tomorrow, we need to go back to the drawing board and come up with something else, okay, boy?"

The licking stopped.

So, too, did any and all tail-wagging.

"Don't worry, sweet boy, I'm not going to starve you or turn you out on the street. For better or worse, you're stuck with me." She gave him another kiss and a quick scratch behind his left ear. "Fortunately, we're both smart, so we'll figure something out, I'm sure."

When the wagging resumed, she stood and made her way into the hallway with Scout close on her heels. "C'mon. Let's get your leash. I think there are some squirrels who might need a little chasing right about now, and this lazy bod of mine could certainly use a little exercise and—"

Sucking in a breath, Emma rerouted them into her office and over to her desk. Pushing aside the stack of business cards she'd been so proud of twenty-four hours earlier, she flung open her desk calendar and thumbed her way to the present. Sure enough, just above the words *Big Max* and

senior center dance was another entry, another record of
yet another promise she wished she could take back.

   Stephanie Porter
   5:30 a.m.
   Main Street Gym
   40. Pale.

Chapter Five

⚊•⚊

Emma would have known that the woman headed in her direction was Stephanie Porter, even without the pasty-white pallor. Everything she'd gleaned from their telephone conversation on Tuesday afternoon was alive and well in its most tangible form.

The hurried steps of someone who was a good, solid fifteen minutes late for their five-thirty start-time . . .

The blown-out hair and fresh swath of lipstick on someone who got out so rarely she'd clearly forgotten the difference between a night out on the town and a workout . . .

The expensive, name-brand sports bag that looked fresh out of the shipping box in which it had just arrived . . .

And the fidgeting fingers that moved between the hair, the lips, the strap of the sports bag, and the phone on which she was clearly noting the time in genuine disbelief . . .

Hoisting her own misshapen (Scout!) duffel bag higher on her shoulder, Emma parted company with the red brick wall and stepped forward. "Stephanie Porter?" she asked.

At the woman's surprised yet emphatic nod, she held out her hand. "Hi. I'm Emma —Emma Westlake."

"Emma . . . Hi. I'm sorry I'm"—Stephanie's green eyes traveled down to her phone and then back to Emma, her earlier disbelief crossing into panic—"a few minutes late. The garbage truck showed up just as I was getting ready to pull out of my driveway and took forever to pull away."

She waved away the reason she suspected was real to a point and focused on her new client. Roughly the same height as Emma, Stephanie's five foot, five inch frame was a bit more hunched, a bit more worn down. Her hair, too, was brown, but whereas Emma's had an almost honey-colored hue, Stephanie's was more the color of cocoa powder into which a bottle of gray sprinkles had been dropped.

Up close, she could pick out the effects of fatigue and unhappiness in everything from the shadows beneath the woman's eyes to the deep lines etching the skin around them as they, too, did a little sizing up of their own.

Clearing her throat, Emma hooked her thumb in the direction of the glass door that served as the entry point for Main Street Gym. "So? Are you ready to get your sweat on?"

"Yes?"

"That sounds like a question rather than a statement."

"If I worded my answer in statement form, it wouldn't have been a yes." The left corner of Stephanie's lower lip disappeared momentarily, only to return paired with a shrug and a nervous laugh. "Let's just say any sweating I normally do is usually in conjunction with news of my boss being on the premises or the first sighting of my credit card bill after a particularly restless night, or day, or both."

"Your credit card bill?" Emma asked.

Nodding, Stephanie stepped through the door Emma held open and then stopped on the other side to tap her hand atop her navy blue gym bag. "I ordered the same one in black, cream, eggplant, yellow, and maroon."

Emma opened her mouth to speak, but let it close—

along with the door—as Stephanie continued. "While everyone else is living life, I shop. It gives me something to do, and the package guy assigned to my street isn't half bad to look at, either."

"Ahhhh."

She trailed Stephanie over to the bored-looking teenager manning the front desk. After a few papers were signed and ID photos taken, laminated, and attached to a Main Street Gym lanyard, they were directed toward the locker room, where they proceeded to dump their bags en route to the treadmills they mutually agreed upon as their first endeavor. They selected a pair of open machines flanked by another early-morning (and handsome!) riser on the left, and an equally early-morning (but far less handsome) riser on the right.

Like the paid employee she was, Emma guided Stephanie to the treadmill on the left and then took the machine on the right for herself, her fingers making short work of the control panel's various buttons. Five minutes in, it became apparent (via much huffing and puffing and even a little whimpering) that Stephanie hadn't been kidding about the sweating remark.

"I'm . . . seriously . . . gonna . . . die," Stephanie rasped across their respective handrails. "How . . . do . . . people"— she narrowed her green eyes on Emma—"how . . . do . . . *you* . . . do . . . this . . . every . . . day?"

Her answering laugh was an echo of Early Riser (the handsome edition) No. 1. Fortunately, when Stephanie peeked over at him, he had the class to make it appear as if there were something humorous on his machine's personal television screen.

Not taking a chance, Stephanie lowered her voice to a volume that could still be audible over the moving belt. "Better yet, *why* do you do this?"

"Actually, this is my first time here."

Stephanie stared at her. "Your first time?"

"Yep."

"Your *first time* . . ."

"Still yep."

"You're not even sweating."

"Trust me; stick with me another forty minutes or so and you'll see sweat. Big time."

"We've been on this for"—Stephanie glanced down at the treadmill's built-in tracker—"six and a half minutes and I'm going to die."

"No, you're not."

"Yes, I am."

"No. It just feels that way. Keep going."

"Are you a sadist or something?" Stephanie asked between gulps of air and Early Riser No. 1's quiet laugh.

"Nope."

"So you're kidding on the forty-minute thing?"

"Nope. We need to break you in easy."

"Meaning?"

"Forty is a good place to start for your first day."

"To *start*?"

"Yes. It's important to work up a little at a time."

"Said the person who claims this is her first time here."

"Here, yes. Walking long distances, no." Increasing her pace a little, Emma looked over at Stephanie. "I have a dog. A golden retriever, actually. I adopted him six months ago and he's taken me for a walk three times a day ever since."

"He takes *you* for a walk?"

"Pretty much, yeah."

"Puppy?"

"Nope. Fully grown dog."

"What's his name?"

"Scout."

She caught a glimpse of a smile between swipes of Stephanie's sweat towel. "Cute name. I thought about adopting a dog once. Went to the pound. Found one I adored. Signed the papers. Made my donation. But when it was time to pick him up, he wouldn't leave his cage. So they gave me back my donation."

At a loss for a reply, Emma said nothing. Early Riser No. 1 remained quiet, as well.

"Probably a good thing, in hindsight," Stephanie continued. "I killed the one carnival fish I had growing up in record time, and I might've killed my college roommate's cat, Cuddles."

She met Early Riser No. 1's eyes for the briefest of moments before turning her full attention on Stephanie. "Did you run it over or something?"

"No."

"Then how did you kill him?"

"We lived in a fourth-floor apartment overlooking a parking lot. We didn't have screens on our windows. I was hot, I wasn't thinking, and I opened the window. Cuddles fell out."

Her answering gasp served as the soundtrack to Early Riser No. 1's wince. "Oh. Wow. I'm sorry."

"What can I say?" Stephanie said, shrugging. "Story of my life. Run while you still can."

They walked for another minute in silence save for Stephanie's continued huffing and puffing, but at least she was still going, still trying.

"I've got a story for you," Emma said, increasing her speed.

"Lay it on me."

"You catch the news at all yesterday? About that writer who died during Open Mic Night at Deeter's on Wednesday?"

"If I hadn't, my mother would've told me about it." Stephanie wiped at her face again. "She lives for that kind of stuff."

"I was there when it happened."

Lowering her towel to the control panel, Stephanie slanted a look at Emma. "Seriously?"

"Yep. In fact, I was there *with* him."

With the press of a finger, Stephanie's belt slowed to a stop. "Was he your boyfriend?"

"Uh . . . *no*."

"Friend?"

"Not that, either. I actually met him for the first time about twenty minutes before it happened."

"First date?"

"No. He hired me to be there. To clap for him, actually."

"To *clap* for him?"

"That's what he said."

Stephanie retrieved her towel from the control panel and mopped her face. "Wow. I didn't think it was possible, but maybe I'm not the most pathetic person on the planet. Or at least I wasn't up until Wednesday night."

"You're not pathetic, Stephanie." Emma, too, shut down her machine. "Really, you're not."

And it was true. In fact, there was something very endearing about the woman staring back at her across the top of a once new, yet now-sopping-wet towel.

"So what you're saying is we should wrap it up early today? On account of any trauma you may have incurred the other night?"

Emma felt her lip inch upward in a smile she knew was inappropriate yet couldn't seem to stop. "I didn't say that . . ."

"You inferred it."

"I'm pretty sure I didn't," she countered.

"Well, I think you should take the rest of the day off. For your well-being."

"*My* well-being? Are you sure about that?"

"Did you not see me on this thing?" Stephanie nudged her chin toward the dark control panel and then wiped her face yet again. "I can barely *walk*, let alone *run*. So let me bow out gracefully and I'll just see you back here on Monday morning."

"Are you sure?"

"Oh, I'm *very* sure—very, very sure." Stephanie stepped down off the machine and headed toward the locker room, Emma in tow. "But this was good. *Fun*, even. Though, if asked, I will categorically deny having said that word in relation to the torture I just endured."

"Word? What word?" Emma teased.

Stephanie's laugh echoed through the room. "Maybe this whole thing"—Stephanie motioned between them—"really is going to work out okay, after all."

Twenty minutes later, Emma stepped out of the locker room, freshly showered and surprisingly more chipper than she'd imagined she'd be. It had felt good to get out, to clear her head, to have a conversation with someone who didn't lick her face after every word. And while she'd had some concerns after their phone call and far bigger ones after her first Friend for Hire experience ended in death, Stephanie had been fine. Enjoyable, even.

"Excuse me? Miss?"

Pausing her hand on the outer door, she turned to find Early Riser No. 1 striding across the gym's entryway, his near-piercing eye contact ruling out any possibility he was talking to anyone but Emma. Still, she took the time to chronicle a few details like his hair (dark blond, cut close on the sides while still being finger-groomable on top), his eyes (blue, like the ocean off the Bahamas), his nose (possibly broken at some point), and the tiniest hole in his left cheek that hinted at a possible dimple, had he been smiling (which he wasn't).

"I saw your friend leave and was hoping you were still here." He stopped, thrust out his hand. "I'm Jack."

She retrieved her hand back from him and tucked it around the shoulder strap of her bag. "I'm Emma."

"Emma *what*?"

"Hmmm, you're direct."

"I'm paid to be." His hand led Emma's eyes to the pocket of his black pants and the silver badge he pulled out. "Deputy Riordan with the Sweet Falls Sheriff's Department."

"Getting in a little morning PT, I see?"

He nodded, his eyes never leaving hers. "I'd like to ask you about a conversation I overheard between you and your friend a little while ago."

"Overheard or eavesdropped on?" she countered with a grin. "Then again, if I'd been you and heard the story about her roommate's cat, I'd have been hard-pressed not to listen, too."

"I was actually talking about the conversation that came on the heels of that one."

She pushed a strand of damp hair from her forehead and returned her hand to her bag's strap. "Well, at least you're honest about your eavesdropping."

"You said you were with Brian Hill the other night at Deeter's?"

She drew back. "I did . . ."

"Can I ask what the nature of your relationship with Mr. Hill was?"

"We'd just met." Shifting her gaze from his to the badge in his hand and back again, she felt her lightness beginning to fade. Rapidly. "That evening, in fact. Why?"

"Was it some sort of online dating thing?"

"Is there a reason why you're asking me these things?" When he said nothing, she willed her thoughts back to his question. "He was a client of mine."

"What kind of business are you in?"

"I . . ." She stopped, swallowed, took a breath. "It's called A Friend for Hire."

"A Friend for Hire?" he repeated. "You do realize those kinds of businesses are illegal in Sweet Falls, right?"

"Those kinds of—wait!" Abandoning the strap of her

bag once again, she waved her hand in an effort to remove his insinuation from the air. "It's not an escort business, if that's what you're thinking. Or a—a . . . *you know*. It's exactly what the name says—a friend for hire."

"Who has to *hire* a friend?"

"Surprisingly, more people than you—or even I— might expect, that's for sure. Even today, that woman I was . . ." Again, she waved her hand, only this time it was at the words she chose not to share out of loyalty to Stephanie. "Anyway, Mr. Hill wanted a friendly face in the audience for him during Open Mic Night. I was that friendly face."

"Why would he need a friendly face?"

"I don't think he was a terribly popular person in this town," Emma said.

"I don't remember seeing you at the scene."

"That's because I left."

He pulled a face. "You left . . ."

"He fell over dead in front of me. My head was reeling. I just wanted to get out of there."

"But you didn't give a statement."

"No one was there to give a statement *to*," she managed to say, past the growing lump in her throat. "There was just screaming and chaos and I . . . panicked, I guess."

"You panicked," he repeated. "And so you just left . . ."

"That's what I said." She stared at the deputy. "Why are you asking these questions?"

"It's my job."

Something about the deputy's tone, combined with the way he was studying her, sent a shiver down her spine. "Does this mean that what that news anchor said yesterday is . . . *true*? That there may have been more to his death?"

"I'm not at liberty to discuss that at the moment."

"But you're asking me questions about my relationship with Brian."

"Just doing a little fact gathering. That's all."

"*Fact gathering* . . ." she repeated. "But the sheriff was there in the audience when Brian fell over, too. He wasn't asking questions."

"He was when *I* arrived on scene," Jack said.

"Okay, fine . . . But the sheriff was there when Brian died. He can tell you that *no one* touched Brian, right?"

"There is more than one way to skin a cat. Figuratively speaking, of course."

She drew back, his not-so-cryptic words igniting a roar inside her head that made it difficult to think, let alone respond.

"I can see this comes as a surprise," he mused.

"No—I mean, yes . . . I mean, I don't know . . ."

He folded his arms. "Which is it? Yes or no?"

"I don't know. I . . ." She shook her head, glanced over at the clock behind the front desk, and returned her hand to the door. "Look, I've gotta get home to my dog."

"Golden retriever. Scout."

His recall skills were impressive, yet also unsettling. "That's right."

"Okay. But if I need to ask you more questions, where can I find you, Emma—I'm sorry, I didn't catch your last name."

"Westlake. My name is Emma Westlake." Tugging her bag off her arm, she unzipped the exterior compartment, reached inside, and handed him a card. "That has my address and phone number on it. You can reach me there if you need to."

He looked down at the card and then back up at Emma, his blue eyes wary. "This says you're a travel agent."

"Because I was." She returned her bag to her arm and pushed open the door. "And right now, I'd give anything to still be one."

Chapter Six

It wasn't until Emma reached their prearranged meeting spot two short blocks from the Sweet Falls Senior Center that she realized she'd never asked Big Max for a description of himself. She knew he was a senior citizen, that his voice was fairly deep, and that he wanted someone to make him French toast for breakfast, but other than that, she was at a loss.

Sweeping her gaze in the direction of the center, she spotted a trio of women, all clad in simple but tasteful spring dresses, making their way toward the door. Behind them, and moving a little more slowly, was a trio of men clad in khaki pants and short-sleeved golf shirts.

She knew, based on the way the two groups interacted with one another, that they were likely together, either as husbands and wives or good friends. A half block beyond them was a couple dressed similarly, walking hand in hand, stopping every few steps to point out a tree or a flower or a house in much the same way Dottie and Alfred had been doing when she'd met them outside her own house five years earlier.

"So *that's* what mint green looks like?"

Startled, Emma turned to find a tall, lanky, late-seventysomething proudly holding a bouquet of flowers in front of his wrinkled and far too short tuxedo. "Big Max?"

"At your service, m'lady." He spread wide his flower-holding hand and bowed.

Returning her lower jaw back into its full and upright position, she took advantage of a long, hard swallow to chronicle a few more details. Like the jagged flower stems that suggested her bouquet had come straight from the ground . . . Like the paper towel, folded into a misshapen triangle, that was doing double duty as a peek-a-boo hand-kerchief in the front pocket of his tuxedo coat . . . Like the—

She stared at his shoes, shifted a step to the right to get a better angle, and stared at them again. Yep, one black, one brown . . .

"Let's see how these'll look on your wrist." Before she could speak, or even process what was happening, he stepped forward, took her wrist, held the bouquet to her skin, and slipped a rubber band over her hand. A few seconds (and a few beheaded flowers) later, her "corsage" was in place and Big Max was grinning from ear to ear. "Pretty as a picture, if I do say so myself."

"Big Max, I . . ." A second look at her wrist, followed by a second glance at his still-wide smile, had her shrugging away the rest of a sentence that didn't need saying. Instead, she slipped her hand through the gap made by his bent elbow and gave herself over to the moment, bizarre as it was. "Thank you, Big Max, they're lovely."

Together, they turned and walked toward the senior center, Big Max's freshly polished black shoe glistening in the sun. Along the way, he pointed out a house that had *once housed a spy*, a nasty crack in the sidewalk *the town could never seem to fix*, and finally, the town gazebo he'd *helped build back in the day*.

They were little stories, tossed out every few steps, yet they were fun in a way that had her wishing they had longer to walk.

"There she is," he said, stopping suddenly.

"She?"

"Beatrice."

She followed the path forged by his words to a white-haired woman, walking hastily toward the senior center's front door. Dressed to the nines, as Emma's own grandmother had been fond of saying, the object of Big Max's attention reeked of money in everything from the way she walked (sa-shayed, really), to the designer dress and the clearly expensive brooch she wore. And while Emma wasn't big on knee-jerk impressions of people, something about Beatrice's aura made her want to wrap Big Max's tuxedo-wearing, flower-picking, rubber-band-tying heart in bubble wrap.

"She looks . . . nice."

"Beatrice is as pretty as a picture, if you ask me. Real smart, too." Big Max brushed his free hand down his wrinkled jacket. "I heard her once, talking about a party she'd been to and how she loves a man in a nice tuxedo. So when I heard about this dance and you said you'd go with me, I took a bus to Cloverton and found me these fancy duds for just fifteen dollars—can you believe it?"

Oh, she could believe it alright. But still, somehow, even with the too wide (and too short!) legs, and the mismatched suit coat buttons, his chosen outfit just made him all the more endearing.

"Fifteen dollars," he repeated, proudly.

She patted his arm. "You look spiffy, that's for sure."

"Spiffy enough Beatrice will dance with me when you go off to the restroom or something?"

"Uh . . . sure." Making a mental note to refrain from drinking anything, she slowed their steps just long enough to give Beatrice time to enter the building. "So tell me about some of the other ladies you know from the center. Surely there are *lots* of nice ones, right?"

His bushy white eyebrows dipped down at the center as he considered her words. "Ethel is nice enough, though not much of a looker."

"Looks aren't everything, Big Max."

"They're not nothing." He guided her over to the door and held it open for her to walk through. "Beatrice and her late husband were good friends with Mayor Dalton and his wife, Theresa. She still goes to their house for those fancy dinner parties, only now she goes alone."

Lowering his voice to what was clearly meant to be a whisper even if it fell horribly short, he let the door swing closed behind them. "I'm betting they have those mini hot dogs at those parties. I love those, don't you? I like to swirl them around in a cup of mustard and eat them in one bite. But I don't use those little brown sticks people stick into 'em to do that. That's wasteful. I just use my fingers."

She nibbled back a giggle and, instead, swept her hand toward the community room decked out in balloons and streamers. Inside, she could see a band getting ready to start playing, spring-colored centerpieces on the handful of tables arranged around the roughly ten-by-ten temporary dance floor, and a buffet table against the side wall that was already yielding a line. "Ooooh, maybe they'll have your little cocktail wieners here," she mused.

"Nah, I think it's just desserts today. But maybe, after Beatrice sees me looking like this, she'll invite me to Mayor Dalton's house for a party one day. Unless, now that he's not mayor anymore, he can't afford to serve those."

Desperate to throw the heat off herself and the laugh she hadn't meant to release, she directed his questioning eyes back into the room as the band struck up its first song. "I could use a cookie or a brownie, couldn't you?"

"I wonder if she'll go to parties at the new one's house."

"New one?" she echoed, abandoning her view of what

looked to be chocolate chip cookies and returning her full attention to Big Max.

"The young one who beat him."

She started to ask for clarification but stopped as Big Max continued. "If Beatrice *does* go, I'll stop using jam just to make sure I don't drop any on her pretty face. Or maybe I'll just cut out her picture so I can save it. If I do, I can prop it against the sugar bowl so it's like she's sitting there having breakfast with me *every* morning, not just on a newspaper morning."

His gaze led hers around the room, only to stop and widen as they landed on the face he so clearly sought. "Oh yes, if that happened, I'd quit my grumbling once and for all." Big Max's brown eyes scrunched as he paused to consider his words. "Most of it, anyway."

She'd been so close to following along, but somewhere between mention of the old and new mayors and something about jam, he'd lost her. "I thought you were talking about the new guy who beat out Dalton for mayor."

"Sebastian Gerard," Big Max said. "And I was."

"You were . . ." At his nod, she continued. "And the whole picture-cutting, sugar-bowl-propping thing—that was what again?"

"If Beatrice goes to one of the new mayor's parties, I'd get to see her in the paper every time I opened it. Because the new mayor's wife likes to be seen. Though, in my opinion, Beatrice's brooch is much prettier."

"Ahhh, okay. I'm with you now." She thought back to the rolled-up paper Scout had happily retrieved from the bottom of the front steps shortly after Emma had returned home from the gym. The paper, of course, had been covered in drool by the time he'd relinquished it in exchange for a scratch behind his ear, but she'd been so rattled by the deputy's questions she hadn't really paid it much mind.

"You ever count them?" Big Max asked.

She shook herself back into the moment. "Count what?"

"How many pictures of them are in the paper each time." He puffed out his narrow chest. "Because I do. Every time. At first, it was just about him winning—shaking hands with the old mayor, giving a speech, sitting at his desk in Sweet Falls Town Hall, that sort of thing. But they're still coming. The other day, it was him in the park, him at the ice cream stand, him at church, and him petting someone's puppy. So if they have a party like Mayor Dalton had, there is sure to be pictures. Though, if Beatrice is gonna be in one, she might want to make sure she does a lot of standing next to the mayor when his wife is around."

"Why is that?"

"Because if his wife isn't *in* the pictures, she's the one taking them."

"How do you know she's taking them?" Emma asked.

"You ever look at the name under all those pictures I mentioned? Every one of 'em is taken by Rita Gerard— Sebastian's wife."

And just like that, she was back at Deeter's, sitting across the table from a still-alive Brian Hill, looking down at the printed image of a woman about her own age—a woman who'd struck her as familiar even though she'd needed Brian to supply the elusive name.

Rita Gerard, he'd said . . .

One of four people he'd invited to the open mic that night that wanted him dead, he'd said . . .

And then, sure enough, he'd up and died. Right there on the stage.

Closing her eyes against the images that followed, Emma drew in a steadying breath.

"Emma?"

Slowly, she parted her lashes to find Big Max, in his fifteen-dollar tuxedo, eyeing her with a mixture of curiosity and concern that anchored her back to the present. "I'm okay, Big Max. Really."

"You sure? 'Cause you looked like you saw a ghost there for a minute."

She swallowed. Hard. "Nope, no ghost."

"You're wishing you were here with your own fella, aren't you?"

"Nope."

"Why? You have a fight or something?"

"Nope. Don't have a fella."

Big Max stuck his finger in his ear, wiggled it around for a moment. "Did you say you don't *have* a fella?"

"Yes."

"*You* don't have *a fella* . . ."

"That's right."

"No fella . . ." he repeated, yet again.

"Still, no."

He narrowed his eyes. "You *want* a fella?"

"One day, sure. If he's a good one. But until that day comes, Scout and I are doing just fine on our own."

"Who is Scout?"

"My dog." Emma followed Big Max's eyes back to Beatrice and the tall, well-dressed man who'd claimed her attention.

"*He's* not wearing a tuxedo," Big Max said.

Resting her hand atop Big Max's arm, she waited until his eyes were back on hers so she could lead them to the opposite side of the room and the dessert table, with its rapidly decreasing selections. "How about we grab a cookie or something, and you can tell me whether or not you have a pet."

"I don't."

"Then I could tell you about Scout."

Again, he looked back at Beatrice and the non-tuxedo-wearing object of her attention and—

"No, I think it's time I show off my skills." Grabbing Emma by the hand, Big Max tugged her into the center of the room. "Let's dance."

Chapter Seven

Lifting her hand as a shield against the afternoon sun, Emma watched Scout bound down the hill and across the sun-dappled grass in pursuit of the same misshapen tennis ball she'd thrown at least a dozen times over the past thirty minutes. On any other day, she'd have snapped his leash back in place by now, ready for the next stop on their weekly trek around Sweet Falls Park. But it wasn't any other day and for that she had no one to blame but herself.

She should've taken Scout for his walk when she got back from the dance, made a sandwich for supper, and then lost herself in the pages of a book before calling it a night. She had several novels she'd been wanting to read and all of them had been sitting on her nightstand, waiting.

But nooo . . . Instead, after Scout's walk, she'd been propelled by a desire to forgo the ease of a sandwich and instead whip up a batch of tacos she then proceeded to eat in front of the television. One sitcom had led to another, and another, and another; right up to the opening montage of the eleven o'clock news. She'd yawned . . . She'd slid her hand between the cushions in her nightly hunt for wherever Scout's nose had pushed the remote . . . And—wham! The anchor's lead story had left her reeling.

Brian Hill's death had officially been ruled a homicide.

And just like that, all thoughts of donning her favorite pajamas and spooning with Scout until morning had been gone, replaced instead by a less-than-pleasant reunion with her evening meal, and what appeared to be an actual door-to-window-length path worn into her bedroom carpet from hours of mindless pacing. At first, the need to be moving had been all about trying to slow her breathing. Once she'd accomplished that, her aimless trek was merely a backdrop to a string of self placations (*You saw nothing*), shocked murmurings (*Murdered . . . really? No . . .*), and the occasional attempt to soothe Scout's concern (*I'm okay, boy*).

She'd probably still be there, doing the same thing, if not for Scout's tail having knocked her open purse off the bed he'd finally jumped into when it became apparent their nightly spooning session wasn't going to happen.

Out came her wallet . . .

Her keys . . .

The travel pack of tissues she always had but never used . . .

The napkin-wrapped cookie half Big Max had managed to procure for her a mere second before the volunteers tasked with post-dance cleanup had descended on the picked-over dessert table. . . .

And the impossibly crinkled paper she wished she'd never *seen* in the first place, let alone taken from what was now, according to the perky news anchor, a murder scene.

Yet she had.

She, Emma Westlake, had left the scene of a crime. With what was very likely a significant—if not the only—piece of evidence.

It hadn't been intentional, of course. She'd truly chalked the piece of paper up to the ramblings of a man who loved creating chaos, and his death to natural causes.

But it wasn't natural causes.

And, because of that, a case could be made by the police that she'd stolen—

"Will he fetch sticks, too?"

Startled back into the moment, Emma dropped her hand onto her bent knees, only to reclaim it as the sun shield she needed in order to see anything other than a tall shadow approaching her from the left. When her efforts failed to bring enough clarity to make an identification, she added her other hand and a tilt of her . . .

Uh-oh.

"Or just a bouncing ball?" Early Riser No. 1 (aka the sheriff's deputy with the name she was suddenly too flabbergasted to remember) closed the remaining gap between them with two long strides and a deliberate repositioning of his ball cap to show more of his face. "Jack. Jack Riordan. We met yesterday at the gym."

Nodding, she straightened her legs back down to the grass and took advantage of the moment it gave her to find her breath. "He likes tennis balls best, but he'll chase and bring back anything I throw."

"My kid would love a dog like that."

Grateful his chosen words weren't the *You're under arrest* her overactive imagination anticipated, Emma looked back up at Jack and managed a half smile. "You could get one . . . The shelter just outside of town has lots of good dogs looking for homes."

"Is that where you got him?" he asked, his blue eyes tracking a rapidly approaching Scout. "The shelter?"

"It is."

"Any regrets?"

"Not a one."

Like the horrible guard dog he was, Scout made a bee-line for the tall (and maybe not hulking, exactly, but impressively built), cap-wearing stranger, dropped his misshapen tennis ball on Jack's shoes, and sent his always wagging tail into overdrive.

"His name is Scout, right?" Jack asked as he squatted down (thereby blasting her face with sunlight again) to Scout's eye (and tongue) level.

"That's right."

"Well, hello, Scout." Jack's blue eyes disappeared momentarily as Scout's tongue found its way from the deputy's chin to his forehead, unearthing the suspected left cheek dimple in the process. "He's a friendly one."

"That he is."

"Any protective instincts at all?" he asked, reclaiming his face from licking territory.

"Not really, no."

"Retriever, right?"

"Mostly. The vet thinks there might be a little lab in there, too."

Scout dropped into the grass and rolled onto his back, his tongue lolling to the side as Jack's hand took the bait. "You didn't get him as a puppy?"

"Nope. He was four."

"Why'd the previous owner give him up?"

"New baby, I think. Maybe a move. Might've been both. I didn't really ask for too many details. I just knew, the second I saw him, that I wouldn't be leaving without him." Pulling her knees back up to her chest, she wrapped her arms around them and gave in to the smile Scout's utter joy in that moment demanded. "If you're wanting to find reasons not to get your kid a dog, Scout and I can't help you."

He gave Scout's stomach one last rub, and then lowered himself all the way to the ground. "No worries. I've got the only one I need, unfortunately."

"Oh?"

"A dog like this needs time —something I don't always have. Not the way I'd want to, anyway."

"How old is your kid?" she prodded. "Caring for a dog is a good way to learn responsibility."

"Tommy *is* responsible—probably more than he should have to be at eight years old. But that's par for the course with kids of divorce, I guess." He pulled up a piece of grass from the hillside beneath him, and turned it around and around between his fingers. "I'd actually want to get him a dog so he could be more of a kid, but my ex isn't a dog person."

"You could have a dog at your place for when Tommy is with you."

"Yeah, but it's all that time when he's *not* with me that makes it so I can't."

Sensing he'd gotten all the belly rubs he was going to get from Jack, Scout flipped over and nosed his way over to Emma. "I know you're a deputy and all that, but lots of working people have dogs," she countered. "You could hire someone to walk it in the middle of the day or just do it yourself at lunchtime. It's not like Sweet Falls is all that big."

"True. But it's not just about the workday. It's about driving out to Hartville to see Tommy one or two nights a week, it's about needing to catch up on sleep when I'm moving between shifts, and it's about spreading myself a little too thin the rest of the time."

"Maybe one day, then." She snapped her fingers and Scout's attention back to his ball and, when he brought it over to her, threw it back down the hill. Like a flash, Scout was gone, his boundless energy on full display once again. "In the meantime, if you're ever at the park with your son on any given Saturday, we're either in this exact spot doing this exact thing, or over by the pond scaring as many ducks as we can before heading home. Scout will play fetch with anyone, anytime. Especially an eight-year-old boy who just so happens to love dogs as much as Scout loves making new friends."

"Thank you."

"You're welcome." She watched Scout pick up the ball, drop it, smell the ground a few times, and then return to the ball for his trot back up the hill. Grabbing his leash from its resting spot atop the grass, she waved him over, clicked it into place on his collar, and stood. "Well, we should probably move on to the ducks or I'll be here until dark."

Jack, too, stood, his lean yet muscular body blocking her intended path. "How come I've never seen you at the gym before yesterday?"

"Because I've never gone. Before Scout, I was too busy with work. And since Scout, *he* has become all the exercise I could ever need."

"So why the gym yesterday, then?"

"Oh. That." She waved at the air. "I was there for work."

"For work . . ."

"Yes."

"Your new work or your old work?" he asked.

The uneasiness was back. "My new work."

"You mean your Friend for Hire business?"

She swallowed. "Yes."

"So the cat killer hired you to be *her friend*?"

"More like an accountability partner, I guess." Emma tightened her hold on the leash. "Anyway, Scout and I should really be going. We spent way more time playing fetch than we should have."

Jack fell into step with them. "You seemed really distracted before I finally came over just now."

"Finally?" she echoed. "Does that mean you were watching us?"

"I was."

Thrown, she stopped. "Um . . . *why*?"

"You looked more troubled than a person should when they're playing fetch with a dog."

She urged Scout to walk a little faster, only to find that Jack was more than happy to match their pace. "I'm just tired, that's all. I didn't sleep all that much—or, really, at all—last night."

"Oh?"

More than anything, she wanted to take off in a run. But considering the fact he was a deputy and he was already watching her, it probably wouldn't bode well for her. Instead, she stopped, pulled Scout alongside her legs, and lifted her gaze to find Jack's waiting. "The woman on the news last night said it's a done deal—Brian was murdered."

"That's right."

"But that doesn't make sense. I was right there."

"We'll know more when the toxicology reports come back."

"Toxicology?" she parroted.

"That's right."

Her thoughts scattered as Scout began to sniff the grass around her feet. "But if he was into drugs, that wouldn't be murder, right?" she asked.

"If they were taken willingly, no. But if they weren't, or if it was some sort of poison . . ."

She knew his mouth was still moving, sensed she should probably be paying attention, but really, in that moment, the only thing she could think about—could truly see—was Brian and the plate of mushrooms that had been waiting on the table when he'd accompanied her into the restaurant.

Was it possible?

Could someone have—

"Emma?"

Tightening her hold on Scout's collar once again, she abandoned her crazy thoughts in favor of Jack's inquisitive eyes.

"Is there something you'd like to tell me?" Jack asked. "Something—"

She thought back on the four faces depicted on the paper

Brian had insisted she keep and did her best to hide the growing tremble in her hands. Part of her wanted to come clean in that moment—to tell him about the paper and beg for mercy. But another part of her was afraid.

Afraid of being arrested . . .

Afraid of leaving Scout to fend for himself while she was remanded to prison for obstruction or hampering or whatever the charge for holding back evidence would be . . .

Afraid of retaliation from—

"I know, from the research I did on Mr. Hill before meeting him that night, that he had a reputation for being difficult," Emma managed to blurt out.

"You researched him?"

She shrugged. "Of course. I was meeting a man I didn't know."

He looked at her with such intensity she had to fight off an answering shiver. "Do you research all of your clients?"

"He was the first one who didn't come via a friend's recommendation."

Jack rubbed at his freshly shaved jawline as if pondering her words. "How *did* he come to find you, then?"

"By way of a flyer I pinned to the town's virtual community board."

"And since you didn't know him, you looked him up before taking him on?"

She gave a half nod, half shrug. "I guess I'd unknowingly read a column or two of his over the last few years. But it wasn't until I looked him up on the Internet that I realized just how truly prolific he was in relation to the goings-on in this town. With many, many of those stories being rather unflattering to Sweet Falls and the powers that be."

"Unflattering. That's one word for it." Jack palmed his mouth, held it there for a moment, and then let it drop back down to his side. "Brian Hill was a pot stirrer, no doubt."

"A pot stirrer," she repeated, letting the words linger in

the air. "Does that mean he stirred *yours* on occasion? Or, maybe, your *boss's*?"

His gaze lit on hers. "Excuse me?"

The little voice in her head that told her when to speak and when to stay silent was screaming. Loudly. But, for whatever reason, the notion of him surreptitiously watching her while she played with her dog bothered her—stirred her pot, to borrow his phrase. "It seems to me, if Brian was truly murdered, a good place to start in figuring out who did it would be to look at all of those people whose pots he stirred."

"That's obvious."

"Is it?" she prodded. "Because you seem pretty focused on me."

"You were the person he was with when he was murdered."

"Me and a roomful of about thirty other people."

He crossed his arms in front of his chest. "All of whom stayed afterward, except you."

"Did you question everyone?"

He cocked his head. "Meaning everyone other than you?"

"I'm answering your questions now, aren't I?"

"You're not giving me anything."

Oh how she wanted to—wanted to hand over Brian's paper and be done with it once and for all. But then again, if she did, would he be so focused on the fact she'd withheld evidence that he'd let the real culprit go?

"I want the person who did this to Brian to be held responsible," Emma finally said.

"As do I."

"Regardless of who it might be?"

He stepped forward, lessening the gap between them. "Is there something you want to tell me, Miss Westlake?"

Something about the sudden use of her last name, along with an unmistakable icing of his tone, served as an internal warning to tread lightly. "No. I-I guess I'm just thinking how hard it must be for you to lead this investigation."

"I'm not the lead. The sheriff is."

"The sheriff?" she echoed in shock. "He can't do that!"

Jack's answering laugh increased the speed of Scout's tail. "Oh? And why is that?"

"He was in the audience when Brian died," she said. "Surely that's a conflict of interest, yes?"

"You can't be serious . . ."

"Have they had any run-ins that you know of?"

"Who?" Jack asked.

"Sheriff Borlin and Brian." There was no doubt about it, her words punched him back a full step. The sudden draining of anything resembling color in his cheeks was simply the icing on the cake. "Clearly, I struck a nerve just now, no?"

"No, I . . ." He stopped, dropped his gaze to the ground, lifted it to the sky, and then, slowly, returned it to Emma. "There was some bad blood there, sure. But that was a year ago. In the immediate aftermath of his reelection."

"Whose reelection? The sheriff's?"

His nod was quick, the silence that followed much longer. When he finally did speak, his tone was tired, even strained. "I should probably let the two of you get to those ducks."

"Thank you."

He walked a few steps in the direction from which he'd come and then stopped. "Emma?" he said, turning back to her and to Scout, his expression difficult to read. "Make sure you don't leave town."

Chapter Eight

⋙•⋘

They were barely a mile down the road when she felt the
angst of the past week drift away through the open
driver's side window. Something about the combination of
the air on her cheek and Scout's pure joy over going for a
car ride just felt good—*really* good. The fact that their excursion, born on a post-breakfast whim, would culminate
in the kind of hours-long distraction she needed at the moment made her positively giddy with excitement.

"Are you going to help me dig today, Scout?"

Ducking his windblown face back into the car, Scout
wagged his tail and barked, a sure sign, at least to Emma,
that her pooch was the smartest in the land.

"I figured as much. But Scout?" Again, he looked at her,
but his urge to stick his face back into the wind was palpable. "When I tell you it's time to stop digging, I really
need you to stop, okay? It won't do us any good if you go
back and dig up all of the plants we put in the ground. That,
boy, is what we call *counterproductive*.

"And *this*"—she swept her hand at the vacant spot where

Scout's face had been at the beginning of her diatribe—"is what's called *losing a room*."

Turning her full attention back to the country road that wound past the sporadic smattering of some of Sweet Falls' older homes, Emma found herself thinking ahead to the flowers and plants she wished she could get, and the flowers and plants that might actually be possible with the limited discretionary funds she currently had. Granted, the *wish-she-coulds* and the *actually coulds* were light-years apart at the moment, but she refused to count herself out. At least for now.

After all, in less than a week, she'd worked twice—three times, if you counted Open Mic Night with—

"Nope . . . Nope . . . We're not going there today, are we, boy? Today is about digging in the dirt and having fun. No traumatic moments allowed."

Scout, of course, wagged his tail at *boy*, and wagged it even harder at *digging*, but his head remained outside the window the whole time, the joy of the wind on his face simply too hard to resist. And that was okay. She got it, she really did.

Stepping her foot more firmly on the gas, Emma lifted her own chin to the wind as she drove the remaining few miles to Davis Farm and Greenhouse. Located on the outskirts of Sweet Falls on Rural Route 50, the nursery and its adjacent orchards had been in the Davis family for generations, with its most recent owner—Nancy—the last of the original clan. Born with a green thumb, Nancy fancied herself a distant relative of Mother Earth, determined to get Sweet Falls on the map as the prettiest, greenest, landscape-iest (if that wasn't a word, it should be) town in North America. A lofty goal, no doubt. But if there was even a remote chance of it happening, Nancy was the woman to do it.

"And to let you know it at the same time," Emma murmured, earning herself an obligatory wag from the passenger seat in the process. "Ever the male, aren't you, Scout? Finding a way to look as if you're listening even when you're not. Well done."

Just north of the road's fourth substantial bend, Emma decreased her speed in advance of the nursery's entrance that was now less than a hundred yards away. A hand-painted sign, bearing the Davis name, pointed from Scout's side of the road to Emma's and reminded her to put on her turn signal. Scout, sensing the change in wind velocity, popped his upper body back into the car in order to visually inspect the shift in direction. When they were safely on the dirt lane that would deliver them to the parking lot, he continued his stint at the window with increasingly vigorous wagging.

Slowly, they bumped and lurched their way between towering oaks with their stunning canopy of green. At the end of the lane, where it widened out into a large, sparsely graveled parking lot, Emma turned left and headed toward a smallish white SUV with the Davis Farm and Greenhouse logo on the side. Beyond the lot were the gardens, the greenhouse, the main building, and the orchard fields.

"Wow, this place is dead," she said as she pulled to a stop beside Nancy's van and cut the engine.

At the cessation of all movement (and thus wind), Scout popped back into the car, and crossed into the back seat via the armrest between their seats. He scoped out the view the new vantage point afforded, and then returned to the passenger seat for a quick lick of Emma's face and a wag of excitement over the beckoning aromas of dirt, plants, and trees, and the many possibilities they birthed.

"No peeing in places you shouldn't pee, okay?" Scout turned his lolling tongue in her direction, licked his lips, and panted his excitement, if not his agreement. "C'mon, boy. Let's go. It looks like we've got the run of the place today."

She pushed open her door, stepped onto the lot, and, as

Scout took his place at her feet, closed the door and headed in the direction of the barn-turned-storefront. Along the way, she slowed here and there to check the name (and price) of a few flowering plants. Scout, in turn, took advantage of the change in pace to sniff a little dirt . . . a few plants . . . an abandoned pacifier . . . a child-sized footprint . . . and a wooden flower bed with an array of plastic flowers that lazily spun in the afternoon breeze.

"You like those?" she asked as she, too, stopped to admire a yellow one that would look awfully cute in the flower bed at the base of her front steps. A peek at the price had her moving on with a dejected Scout in tow.

At the entrance to the barn, she attached Scout's leash to his collar and stepped inside, the natural light streaming in rendering the overhead fluorescent lights virtually unnecessary. To her right were aisles of gardening implements (hand trowels, rakes, and fold-and-go-style shovels), interspersed with clever gadgets to make the task easier (kneepads, compact folding chairs, and cutesy gloves for those who liked to keep their hands clean). To her immediate left were dozens of seed packets displayed in little hand-woven pockets that hung from a paneled wall. Those who had visions of growing their own vegetables gravitated toward the dark-brown pockets. Those intent on growing flowers from seed sought the light-brown pockets. And straight in front of her was the counter at which questions were asked, purchases were made, and self-proclaimed experts imparted their advice to novices while waiting on line.

If she turned right, she could find a replacement hand trowel for the one that not-so-mysteriously disappeared the last time she and Scout took a stab at sprucing up the flower bed next to the front steps . . .

If she turned left, she could go in search of a flower that might complement the blue of her window shutters every spring and summer . . .

If she headed straight for the counter, she could ask the

kind of questions that might make her limited resources
(read: money) go as far as possible . . .

After Emma spent a few moments hemming, and an
equal number of moments hawing, Scout smartly took
point all the way to the counter. There, between a glass of
water to its right and a gardening magazine to its left, was
a bell. In lieu of ringing it, she jangled her keys en route to
their temporary resting spot inside the front pocket of her
jeans, cleared her throat of nothing, and followed both up
with a fake cough.

Sure enough, Nancy's voice emerged from behind the
accordion screen tasked with distinguishing the employees-
only area from the rest of the gardening shop. "I'll be right
with you!"

Pulling her gaze from the bell she'd intentionally re-
sisted but secretly wanted to ring, Emma took advantage of
the momentary wait to really absorb the framed pictures on
the wall behind the register—pictures she'd seen in bits and
pieces while waiting in line over the years. The first few
were in black and white, with the subjects wearing attire
that spoke to a different time.

To the right of those were a pair of pictures clearly taken
when Nancy had been given the reins of the family business. In the first one, an older version of one of the men
from the black-and-white photographs was handing her an
apron with the Davis Farm and Greenhouse logo emblazoned across the front. In the second picture, Nancy was
wearing the apron and ringing up a customer at the very
counter where Emma stood now, the woman's pride on full
display in everything from her confident stature to the face-
splitting grin she wore.

A glance farther down the wall yielded yet another picture; this one of current-day Nancy, smiling ear to ear
while holding a certificate in one hand and a ribbon-strewn
watering can in the other. Next to her stood Steve—

"I'm so sorry to make you wait. I'd just finished my

lunch when I heard you out here and I wanted to make sure I took a moment to wash my hands." Nancy breezed around the edge of the screen, her hands making short work of the apron she secured into place around her burgeoning mid-section. When her gaze fell on Emma, she stopped and smiled. "Emma! How lovely to see you, as always. How did those petunias work for you the last time?"

"You remember my last purchase? Wow. That had to have been"—she searched her memory for the last time she'd had a little extra cash—"months ago."

"It was. But you know as well as anyone that's the Davis Farm and Greenhouse difference: *customer service*." Nancy stepped up to the counter like the force she was. "Did you hear about Maime Rogers?"

"Maime Rogers? I don't think I know—wait! She was Great-Aunt Annabelle's biggest nemesis at bingo!"

Nancy laughed. "She was indeed."

"Okay, so what about her?"

"She's taken up with a man in the room next to her at the nursing home. Says they're getting married."

"Interesting . . ."

Nancy leaned across the top edge of the counter. "I know one of the orderlies at that home. He says the poor old fella has taken up with *all* of the ladies in the home. Including Maime's roommate."

Emma laughed. "Uh-oh."

"Uh-oh is right. Maime doesn't like to lose." Her lips twitching, Nancy pushed away from the counter. "Anyway, you didn't come to hear me gossip, so tell me . . . How's the yard coming? Any new pictures for me?"

"Maybe. Let me check." Emma plucked her phone from her back pocket, pressed her way into her album, and froze as her gaze fell on the picture she'd felt an inexplicable need to take after returning from the park with Scout the previous day. Why, she still didn't know, but there it was . . .

"Did you find something?" Nancy asked.

She stared down at the thumbnail of the paper Brian had foisted on her in the moments before his death and shivered at the sight of the one person she knew couldn't be involved—the same person now watching her, waiting.

"Emma?"

Shaking the ludicrous notion from her head, Emma slid her phone back into her pocket and forced her smile back into place. "Nope. Nothing new."

"Next time, then?"

"Sure." She sucked in a breath and released it slowly. "How are you doing after the other night?"

"Other night?" Nancy asked.

"At Deeter's. For Open Mic Night."

A cloud not unlike a summer storm's made its way across Nancy's face as she checked and rechecked her apron for wrinkles that simply weren't there. "Deeter's?"

"Yes. You were seated about three tables over from where I was."

"Was I?" Nancy asked. "I don't recall."

"That's okay. It's hard to remember much of anything besides what happened to Brian up on that stage, isn't it?" Emma drew in a breath, released it with a shake of her head. "For me, if I'm not replaying the *thud* over and over, I'm hearing the gasps and the screams that followed."

Nancy stopped fussing with her apron. "Thud?"

"When his body hit the stage."

"Of course." Nancy turned her continued restlessness toward the counter and the cup of pens she swapped with a stack of scrap paper. "I guess I've chosen to focus on the silence that came between them, instead. It's a much more pleasant sound to remember compared to the alternative."

Emma drew back. "I don't remember any silence."

"Oh, it was there. Trust me. And if that doesn't work, lose yourself in something that makes you happy. Like flowers and plants, or that wonderful dog of yours."

Peeking down at Scout, Emma smiled. "He *is* pretty wonderful."

"He is indeed."

Emma brought her gaze back to the wall and the picture of a smiling Nancy standing next to Sweet Falls' former mayor, Steve Dalton. "You sure look happy there."

Nancy's brows dipped in confusion only to reset—with a smile to boot—when she followed the path indicated by Emma's pointed finger. "How could I not be? Leading the Sweet Falls Beautification Committee to its first-ever state award was a dream come true."

"I can see that." Emma shifted her finger to the right and the series of pictures showing the town square at its finest. "It really did look incredible. Like something you'd see in some fancy magazine—where the town is just too pretty to actually be a real place. Only it was."

Nancy retrieved a stool from beneath the eave on her side of the counter and lowered herself onto its well-worn seat cushion. "People are quick to forget, aren't they? Not that you can blame them when it"—Nancy hooked her thumb back toward the picture—"was all so ridiculously short-lived. But that's what happens when folks fall for the old bait-and-switch trick."

"Bait and switch?" Emma repeated, glancing down at Scout.

"Meaning what you see is entirely different than what you get."

"I know what bait and switch means." She loosened her hold on the leash and leaned against the counter's edge, her desire to talk plants momentarily sidelined by the need to follow a conversational sidebar to its full conclusion. "I was more wondering about it in the context you gave. Or, rather, in relation to the award you got."

Nancy studied her for a moment and then reached into a drawer at her back and fished out her phone. A few taps of her finger later, she handed the device to Emma. "You see that shot right there?"

Emma took in the struggling plants and wilting flowers depicted on the handheld screen. "Yes."

"Do you recognize it?"

"Should I?" Emma asked, searching the picture closely.

"That section right there"—Nancy pointed at the phone screen and then again toward the calendar-worthy picture on the wall—"is *this* section less than twelve months later."

She tried to recover her wince lest it seem unkind, but she was a beat too late. "Oh. Wow."

"That's what you get when someone who doesn't care a hoot about plants vows to take care of them."

"Wow," Emma said again, earning her a raised eyebrow from Nancy in return.

"Surely you've seen the difference with your own two eyes while walking around the square this year, yes?" Nancy prodded.

Had she? She wasn't sure. Still, Nancy was clearly waiting for her answer.

"I think it's safe to say, I've been a little distracted this year. But looking at these pictures now? It's clear there's a big difference."

"A *huge* difference," Nancy corrected. "Monumental, in fact."

Emma nodded her agreement. "Did some sort of bug do that? Because if it did, I don't want it anywhere near my plants."

"No, a *green-eyed monster* did that . . . *Neglect* did that . . . *Inexperience* did that . . . An *inflated sense of self-importance* did that . . . Take your pick." Nancy shot up her hands in disgust. "They all point to the same place—the *same person*, anyway."

"Oh?"

"Some people crave the limelight. Some need it so badly they can't handle someone else having it even for a little while. And when people don't recognize jealousy for what it is, you get"—again, Nancy moved her finger between the framed photograph and the one on the rapidly dimming phone screen—"*this*."

Emma looked back at the framed photograph long enough to pick out the same exact corner of the town's gazebo that was shown on the phone. Same angle, same section of landscape, yet everything else was different. "Wait. Did someone have a problem with you getting all the attention for last year's award?" she asked.

"If by someone you mean the mayor's wife, yes."

"*Mayor Dalton's* wife?"

Nancy's hand practically flew to her chest in shock. "Theresa? Good heavens, no. Theresa was grace personified. Twenty-four/seven. She gave her time to groups she truly cared about, regardless of her husband's political career."

Emma nodded at the information that matched with what she knew but stopped as her thoughts circled back around to Nancy's words. "So, then, I take it you must be referring to the new mayor's wife, Rita?"

"What was your clue? The green-eyed monster part or the inflated self-importance?"

"Um . . ." She sensed Scout getting cozy at her feet. A glance down served as confirmation. "Actually, you said 'the mayor's wife' and since you weren't referencing the former mayor I figured it must be the new one."

"Voting that woman into office was a huge mistake for this town, you mark my words," Nancy said, her finger pointed as if to admonish. "*Huge.* She doesn't care about this town."

"You mean voting her husband into office . . ."

"No. I mean her—Rita. People in this town wanted change and they got it, alright."

"Not a fan, I take it," Emma mused.

"Of the mayor himself? I can't really say. It's too early

to know. But his wife? Positively not. That woman fancies herself living in the Whitc House one day and Sweet Falls is merely a stepping-stone on her path to get there."

She let Nancy's words marinate for a moment and then did her best to bring the conversation back to the picture on Nancy's phone. "So what did Rita do to make the square go from the way it looked last year to *this*?"

"She only joined our committee in the months leading up to the election. For show, clearly. But everyone knew her husband was running and the thought of cozying up to someone like that—just in case—was appealing to a handful of our members. As a result, when she started whispering things in those same members' ears, they listened."

"What kind of things?" Emma asked.

"Like, why was *I* getting all the press? Why was *I* getting the accolades from the town council? She said it was a committee effort and I was but one member. It was ridiculous, of course, because"—Nancy spread her arms wide to indicate the gardening shop and the grounds outside its walls—"this is what I do for a living. But the damage was done. Suddenly, at the meetings, conversations stopped when I arrived. Eyes rolled when I spoke. Suggestions I made for things we could do in the future were stepped on or ignored completely."

"Oh, Nancy, I'm so sorry. I had no idea. I guess I'm even more out of the loop on the inner workings of this town than I thought."

"Be glad you are because it was awful, it was hurtful, and it was completely uncalled for." Nancy slid off the stool, pushed it back into its spot beneath the counter, and began to pace from the register to the accordion screen and back again. "So I quit, and I wished them the best of luck in trying to bring home another award for the town. And, as you can see, based on this picture"—Nancy tapped her phone screen back to life in Emma's hand—"there was absolutely zero chance of that happening."

"Why would they let it get to that, though?" Emma asked.

"Because the woman who set all the ugliness in motion doesn't care about plants. She never did. She only joined the group when her husband set his sights on running for mayor—so it would look like she was involved in our community. And pushing me out made it so she could get any residual press from the award."

Emma looked again at the phone. "But this looks awful."

"You're right. It does. Which is why the letters to the editor started pouring in."

"Letters to the editor?" Emma echoed.

"You don't read the paper much, do you?"

She felt her face flush with embarrassment. "Not really, no. And when I do, it's the frivolous stuff."

"I guess that explains why you're here, then."

"Excuse me?"

Nancy waved aside Emma's question. "To answer your original question, the letters were all versions of the same thing. *Why does the square look so bad? What happened to the way it looked last year? Surely the tax dollars this town pilfers from its residents each year can pay for some decent flowers.* And on and on it went until someone with a brain in their head put two and two together."

"Meaning, you were the missing link between last year and this year?"

Nancy beamed. "Exactly."

"That had to feel good."

"It should have. And it did for a little while. Right up until that awful—well, there's no need to discuss any of that unpleasantness now. What's done is done."

"My great-aunt Annabelle used to say that same thing—what's done is done," Emma said. "I remind myself of those words whenever I need to let something go in order to move forward."

"Sometimes that's all you can do."

With one last look at the sorry state of the town square's once-prized flower beds, Emma handed the phone back to Nancy and then reached inside the back pocket of her jeans for the notes she'd made before loading Scout into the car. "So . . . what would you suggest for a flower bed at the base of my front steps? Something that will give a little splash of color and not lose it too soon?"

"Full sun for the majority of the day?"

She weighed the woman's question in relation to the appropriate answer. "Late morning to early afternoon . . ."

"Late morning to early afternoon," Nancy repeated. "Well, let's look at the possibilities, shall we?"

With well-honed efficiency, Nancy swapped the phone for a navy-blue binder while Emma glanced back at the door and its view of the still-empty parking lot. "I can't believe how empty this place is. It's *always* packed when I come." The second the words were out Emma wished she could recall them. Not because they weren't true, but because of the way they made Nancy visibly stiffen and step back.

"I-I didn't mean that to be a bad thing," Emma rushed to clarify in an attempt to lessen any unintended sting caused by her observation. "In fact, it's a *good* thing, actually. For me, anyway. Lord knows I need all the time and all the hand-holding I can get with this kind of—"

"It's like I said earlier; people are quick to forget." Reclaiming her spot, Nancy turned the binder around to Emma and yanked open the cover. "Which means we'll be back to lines here again soon. Now let's find you some new plants, shall we?"

Chapter Nine

Emma was waiting outside the gym at five thirty Monday morning when Stephanie came around the corner, wincing and moaning.

"You okay?" Parting company with the brick wall on which she'd been leaning, Emma retrieved her bag from the sidewalk and slung it over her shoulder. "You're moving a little slow."

"At least I'm *moving*. Which is more than I was doing most of the weekend." Stephanie stopped, released a long, labored sigh, and nudged her chin and Emma's attention toward the gym. "There should be a warning on that door. Something like *Inability to move may occur* or, even better, *Working out is bad for your health*."

Emma's answering laugh filled the otherwise quiet dawn. "Oh, come on, you're really *that* sore after Friday's workout?"

"You're not?" Stephanie asked, staring.

"No, of course not. It was just the treadmill."

Stephanie's mouth gaped. *"Just the treadmill?* Seriously? I walked six miles!"

Her laugh led to a snort and, thanks to Stephanie's rapidly widening eyes, another laugh. "Stephanie, you walked *point* 6 miles. As in just a scooch over *one half* of *one mile.*"

"I saw a six . . ."

"You did. You just missed the decimal point in front of it, apparently." At Stephanie's silent display of horror, Emma laughed and tugged her toward the door. "But *today,* we're going to put an actual number in front of that decimal point."

"Meaning?"

"Meaning, you are going to walk a whole mile."

"I can't!"

"Yes, you can."

"I won't be able to move for days!"

Emma opened the door and gently pushed Stephanie inside. "Of course you will. The more you do, the more used to it your legs will get. And then, before you know it, you *will* be walking six miles."

"Bite your tongue!"

She guided Stephanie over to the front desk, showed the attendant her ID, waited for Stephanie to locate hers in her bag, and then led the way to the locker room. "So how was your weekend? Do anything fun?"

Stephanie looked at Emma as if she had sprouted three heads. "I wasn't able to move, remember?"

"Oh. Right." She found two empty lockers next to each other, pulled her hair into a ponytail, and shoved her bag through the first of the two doors. "So what *did* you do?"

"I watched a few movies, ate my way through a bag of potato chips, and, after about the hundredth disgusted sigh from my mother, started perusing the meager rental house market."

Emma took a spot on a nearby bench and watched as

Stephanie riffled through her bag for a brush and a hair tie, only to put the brush back, unused. Seconds later, when the woman had the hair tie in her hands and began looking around the floor, and in the open locker, and on the bench beside Emma, Emma pointed her back to the bag and the brush with a grin.

Stephanie was, in a word, a disaster. But in a sweet, scatterbrained, endearing sort of way. "You're looking for a place?"

"I've been looking for years. Mostly in spurts born of my mother's conviction that I'll never find a man living at home with her." Stephanie finished with her brush, popped it back inside her open bag, and sank down onto the bench a few feet from Emma. "But seeing as how I'm forty, still living at home, and"—she swept a hand toward herself—"look like I'm ten years older than I am, I think that ship has long since passed."

"Whoa, now. This is a no-trashing-yourself zone."

"Just stating facts."

Emma pushed off the bench and stood, arms crossed, in front of Stephanie. "First up, you don't look ten years older than you really are. You just look tired."

"Because I am. Always."

"Next, forty is not too old to find love. Two of my aunts found their soul mates in their *fifties*."

"Were they living at home with their mother?"

"Well . . . no. But you just said you're looking to move out."

"Looking and doing are two very different things. At least that's what my mother says."

"And she's right. It is. But you wanted to start getting fit and here you are, right?" Emma countered. "That's *doing*."

Wincing, Stephanie stood. "Is it really? Because it feels more like I'm dying a slow, painful death, quite frankly."

"You're not. It just feels that way. For now." Emma plucked Stephanie's bag off the bench, stuffed it in the empty locker next to her own, and beckoned toward the door. "Come on, let's do this."

"Why?"

"Because you'll be glad you did when we're done."

"Somehow I doubt that."

"Okay, then come because you're paying me to work out with you, remember?"

Rolling her eyes, Stephanie followed Emma out the door and into the workout room. "I could always just fire you."

Emma froze en route to the treadmills. "You're going to fire me because you don't want to walk on a treadmill?"

"Part of me wants to say yes." Stephanie glanced down at herself and then up at the handful of women scattered about the room in their workout gear. "But another part of me knows I need to do this."

"Why?"

"Why what?"

"Why do you *need* to do this?"

"Because dropping dead of a heart attack on a treadmill will look better than dropping dead of a heart attack while stuffing potato chips down my face."

More than a few heads turned in their direction as Emma laughed. "Has anyone ever told you you're pretty funny?"

"I don't know. Maybe." Stephanie's gaze moved beyond Emma to the bank of treadmills. "We could always move this to the coffee house down the street. Less distractions."

"Nah. We can talk *here*. *While* we're getting fit."

"We can talk here while we're getting fit," Stephanie repeated, mimicking her. "Man, has anyone ever told you that you're a real buzzkill, Emma Westlake?"

Emma grinned. "Maybe. But that's okay. I can handle it." She motioned Stephanie over and onto Friday's treadmill and then nudged her chin at the control panel. "You remember what to push?"

"I remember what to push *to stop* . . ."

"Then I'll show you again." And she did. Button by button, Emma painstakingly walked Stephanie through the start-up process. They argued about the program (Flat. No, hills!), and the speed (A casual stroll. No, a trot!), but eventually, they were moving. "What kind of house are you wanting?"

"I . . . can't . . . talk . . . and . . . do . . . this," Stephanie said, huffing. "Not . . . if . . . you . . . want . . . me . . . alive . . . to . . . pay . . . you."

"Fine. *I'll* talk. My weekend was—"

"Wait . . . Friday evening news . . . Dead guy . . . They say it was . . ."

Emma ratcheted up her speed to a slow run. "Murder. I know. I saw the same report."

"Are . . . you . . . freaked out? They . . . could . . . have . . . gotten . . . you . . . too . . ."

She considered Stephanie's words, discarding them immediately. "No. Whoever it was wanted *Brian* dead. Just like he said."

"Just . . . like . . . he . . . *said*?" Stephanie slanted a glance in Emma's direction. "Explain . . . that."

Emma looked to the empty treadmills beyond Stephanie, and then turned and looked at the empty treadmills to her right. When she was satisfied no one was lurking within listening range, she decreased her speed a notch. "That night? Before he went onstage? Brian gave me a piece of paper with pictures of four people he said wanted him dead."

"Talk about a . . . strange dating technique . . ."

"It wasn't a date, remember?" Emma said. "He hired me to be there in the audience for him during Open Mic Night."

"Oh. Right. I guess I just . . . have a hard time . . . imagining there are others as desperate as me. I thought I was one of a . . . kind."

Emma looked from Stephanie to the empty handrails and back again. "Don't look now, but you're actually pump-

ing your arms and you're not huffing and puffing nearly as
much as you were a few minutes ago."

Stephanie looked down at her machine, the shock on her
face unmistakable. "Huh . . . Would you look at that."

"See? I *told* you you'd get used to it." It was fast, and it
was fleeting, but still, Emma caught Stephanie's quiet grin.
"And soon, you'll get used to the stair machine, and the
rowing machine, and the weights, too."

"Hmmm. Perhaps the wrong person was murdered at
Deeter's," Stephanie quipped.

"Ha. Ha."

Turning her finger in a *let's move it along* circle, Stephanie took command of the conversation. "Getting back to
the other night . . . at Deeter's . . . this paper you mentioned.
Do you think any of them were actually there that night?"

"They were all there that night," Emma said. "In the
audience."

Stephanie grabbed hold of the emergency-stop cord and
pulled, bringing the treadmill to an immediate stop. "Whoa."

"Um, we're still working out here," Emma said.

"*Um*, no, we're *not*. Do you know what I watch on TV
every weekend when the rest of the world is going to bar-
becues, or hiking, or hanging out with friends, or playing
with babies, or whatever else it is normal people do?"

Emma pulled a face. "You're normal, Stephanie, you
just—"

"I watch crime shows."

"O-kay, so . . ."

"That means I sit on the couch and, between potato
chips, I play armchair detective. And you know what? I'm
pretty darn good at it." Stephanie paused, her brow furrowed. "I figure out the bad guy at least fifty percent of the
time."

"Which means what?"

"Let's do it. You and me. Let's figure out who killed
your date."

"Once again, he wasn't my date. He was my client."

Stephanie rolled her eyes. "Semantics."

"No. Not semantics. Facts."

"Then you have an even bigger vested interest in his murder being solved."

Emma pulled her own emergency-stop cord, the sudden cessation of movement necessitating a quick grab for the treadmill's handrails. "How do you figure that?"

"Hello? Your client died on your watch?" Stephanie leaned against her own handrail. "I can't imagine that would be good for business."

She opened her mouth to protest, only to close it as the validity of Stephanie's words took root. "It's not like anyone in the room that night knew why I was there with him."

"It'll come out. *Everything* comes out in an investigation—trust me." Tapping her chin, Stephanie lifted her gaze back to the ceiling in thought. "Soon, the cops will want to know about your history with the victim. Then, some"—she made air quotes with her fingers—"*anonymous source* on the inside of the sheriff's department will leak some information and, bam! Your Friend for Hire business is the talk of the town."

Stephanie pinned Emma with a warning look. "Oh, and FYI? You can't give me up as a client, okay? It's bad enough *you* know how pathetic my life is. I don't need all of Sweet Falls—or, at least, the part my mother doesn't play bridge with—to know it, too."

"I wish I could."

"Wish you could what?" Stephanie echoed.

"Not give you up as a client."

"Meaning?"

Emma sat down on the edge of her treadmill, her head beginning to pound. "I had to tell the sheriff's department. Or, at least, one of the deputies, anyway."

Stephanie pulled a face. "Excuse me?"

"He was here on Friday. On the treadmill next to yours,

in fact. He heard me say I'd been with Brian at Deeter's on Wednesday night. And that's why he was waiting for me when I came out of the locker room after my shower."

"Oh, man." Stephanie's moan was long and drawn out. "*Why, oh why* did I leave when I did?"

"You said—"

"Rhetorical question," Stephanie said, stopping Emma with a raised hand. "So you told this deputy that Brian hired you to be there with him?"

"I did."

"And the paper Brian gave you with the suspects on it? What did he say about—"

Emma held up her own hand. "We don't know they're suspects, Stephanie. They're just faces of people Brian copy and pasted onto a piece of paper."

"People he said wanted to kill him," Stephanie countered. "People who were all there when—guess what?—he was *murdered*. That makes them suspects in my book."

It was Emma's turn to moan, and moan she did.

"Did you at least take a picture of it before you gave it to the cop so we can work it?" Stephanie asked.

Emma glanced up. "Work it?"

"Investigate it. Ourselves."

"You do realize Brian Hill was a conspiracy theorist, right? Meaning he always thought someone was up to something . . ."

"I'm pretty sure this wouldn't qualify as a conspiracy theory, seeing as how, *A*, he said all four"—she slanted a glance Emma's way—"it *was* four, right?"

At Emma's nod, Stephanie kept going. "All four wanted him dead. *B*, all four were there the night he—*C*—did, in fact, die."

It wasn't anything she hadn't thought about. In fact, everything coming out of Stephanie's mouth was the same stuff that had made sleeping difficult, if not downright impossible, since Brian's death had been ruled a homicide.

Still, hearing the thoughts she'd done her best to ignore coming out of another person's mouth was disquieting, to say the least.

She moaned again.

"So?" Stephanie prodded, sitting down across from Emma. "I ask again; did you snap a picture of the paper before you gave it to the cop?"

Emma squeezed her eyes closed. "I took a picture of it, yes."

"Okay, good. Smart."

"You might want to hold up on that word," Emma murmured.

"Which one? Good, or smart?"

"Maybe both." Slowly, Emma parted her lashes to find Stephanie staring at her, waiting. "I still have the actual paper, too."

"Come again?"

"I didn't give it to him or anyone else."

"*What? Are you serious?*" Glancing over her shoulder at the heads turning in their direction from every corner of the gym, Stephanie lowered her voice to a near-whisper. "Why?"

Emma swallowed again. "I don't know. At—at first, I think, I managed to convince myself, in the immediate aftermath of it all, that Brian had some sort of health issue that killed him and that the paper he gave me was just par for his conspiracy theorist lifestyle. Same old, same old, you know?"

"No, but go on," Stephanie said.

"Then, when it became official, it dawned on me that I'd taken evidence from the scene of a crime and I guess I sort of shut down, or freaked out, or a whole lot of both. And then yesterday, when the deputy started grilling me at the park, I—"

Stephanie leaned so far forward, she had to grab the edges of the treadmill to keep from falling into Emma's lap. "You saw the same cop the very next day?"

"Yes."

"At the park?"

"Yes."

"So he's *following* you now?"

Emma swallowed. "I'm not sure. Maybe?"

"They probably see you as a suspect." Pushing off the treadmill, Stephanie stood. "Which isn't a bad thing."

She stared up at the woman. "It's not a bad thing I might be a suspect in a murder?" Emma echoed. "How on earth do you figure that?"

"You didn't do it, right?"

"No! Of course not!"

"Then they'll be distracted enough by you that they won't be looking in the same places that we'll be looking." Stephanie traveled the distance of three treadmills before turning and making her way back to Emma, her face unable to contain her excitement. "Which means we can really do this."

"Do what?"

"Investigate a real, live murder." Stephanie took another lap. "Though that might be a bit of an oxymoron, come to think of it . . . But, either way, it'll give me something to do after work that doesn't include listening to my mother bemoan the grandchildren I've yet to give her."

Emma looked down at the ground. Swallowed. "I *couldn't* give it to him."

"What, the paper? To the cop? Why not?"

"Because then he'd have to show it to others in his department." When it became clear Stephanie was waiting for more, Emma drew her knees up to her chin and covered her head with her hands. "Which could be an issue—a big one. At least insofar as *one* of the four is concerned."

"What are you saying?" Stephanie asked as she returned to her treadmill. "Is someone on the paper connected with the sheriff's department?"

This time, when she nodded, she did it while looking straight at Stephanie. "Tell me I'm being paranoid. Tell me I should just give him the paper instead of nudging him toward Sheriff Borlin."

"*Sheriff Borlin?*" Stephanie echoed, her voice shrill.

Emma looked over Stephanie's head at the faces turning in their direction once again. "Shhhh . . ." she hissed back. "Keep your voice down!"

"*Sheriff Borlin* was on that paper?" Stephanie repeated more quietly. "Are you serious?"

"Yes."

"Oh. Wow." Stephanie ran her fingers through her hair, dislodging her ponytail in the process. "So what do we do with that?"

"*We?*"

"Yes, we. I'm paying you to be my buddy, remember?"

"Your *gym buddy*, yes." Powered by the breath she hadn't realized she was holding, Emma stood. Half a second later, Stephanie did, as well. "But this is different."

"I'll double your pay!"

"*Double my pay?*" Emma echoed.

"Yes!"

"Are you nuts?"

Stephanie shrugged. "Maybe. But c'mon, this'll be a blast! And it'll make my mother happy because I'll be participating in life instead of just watching everyone else live theirs."

A steady ringing in her ears was making her head ache. Or maybe it was just the conversation—one she had better control over when it was happening solely in her brain. At least then she could chalk it up to sleep deprivation.

"Someone killed him, Emma," Stephanie insisted. "That's not okay."

"I realize that."

"More than that, he clearly felt someone was out to get him, *and* he clearly wanted you to know who and why."

"He didn't tell me any whys."

"That's okay," Stephanie said, shrugging. "That's what an investigation is for: to find out that kind of stuff. Once we do, we can see who the most likely suspect is."

"Maybe I should just turn it over to Jack."

"Is Jack the cop?"

"Deputy, yes."

"His boss is on that sheet, Emma."

She sighed. "I know."

"Which means there's no way he'll do anything with it."

She thought back to the park, to Jack's face as he revisited whatever conflict Brian had had with the sheriff. The worry she'd seen there had been real. "I don't believe that," she said.

"Seems to me you're putting a lot of faith in a guy you just met three days ago."

"Maybe."

Stephanie watched her for a long moment—waiting, Emma imagined, for any sign of internal second-guessing. Emma gave her nothing.

"Okay. Fine. We'll give him a little time. In the meantime, we can focus on the other three for now."

More than anything, she wanted to point Stephanie back onto the treadmill so they could finish their walk and get on with their respective days. But she couldn't. Brian Hill was dead—*murdered*. And as much as she hated to admit it, Stephanie was right. He'd been murdered on Emma's watch. In fact, she'd watched him take his last breath while her elbow had been resting atop a folder containing four suspects—suspects he himself had named.

She didn't want to be involved, she really didn't. But Brian had made it so she didn't have any real choice in the matter.

"Okay," she finally murmured. "We'll investigate. *A little*."

Chapter Ten

At precisely three o'clock, Emma held the Limoges teapot above Dottie's cup and tried her best to keep the fatigue she felt clear down to her toes from manifesting itself in her voice. "Your tea, Dottie."

At the single nod she earned in return, she filled the matching cup atop the matching saucer to within exactly a quarter inch of its gold-trimmed lip and followed it up with a single splash of cream and two pinches of sugar.

She waited the standard three beats for the *Lovely, dear* that always followed, but it never came. Instead, Dottie peered up at her from behind stylish bifocals, tsking not so softly beneath her breath. "You look awful, dear. Truly awful."

At a loss for a response to the unexpected script change, Emma made her way around the linen-topped table to her own seat and her own cup as she had every Tuesday for the past eighteen months. "Biscuit?"

"No."

She paused, her hand atop the basket, and stared at the octogenarian. "That's not what you're supposed to say."

"Then let me rephrase," Dottie said in what could only be described as a bored drawl. "Why, yes, Emma, I think I will *not*."

"Will not what?"

"Have a biscuit."

"But you have to. It's what you do." She held the basket still closer to Dottie. "I ask you if you want a biscuit . . . You answer with, *Why yes, I will* . . . Then I hold it out for you like I am right now and you hem and haw to my silent count of three Mississippis before you actually take one . . . And, finally, I hold it a little tighter while you reach back in for the *I really shouldn't* second biscuit."

Dottie's eyes widened on Emma. "You make it sound as if you've been following a script."

"Not in the written sense of the word, no, but we certainly have a routine." Retrieving her napkin from the table, Emma unfolded it across her lap and tried her best to hold back a sigh. "It's what I promised Alfred I would do, what he told me you wanted."

"The time—yes. The tea—yes. The china—yes. But now that we've shared our mutual dislike for those dreaded biscuits, I think we can dispense with them, don't you?"

Hit by a loss of words, Emma merely nodded.

"I almost said something to you when you put them on the table, but it's more fun watching your expression as it is at this moment." Disengaging her wheel brake, Dottie rolled her chair back a foot to afford a view of their silent companion positioned beneath the table. "What do you say, Scout? Would you like a biscuit?"

At the lack of anything resembling an answering thump, Emma laughed. "I'm afraid he knows that word as well as we do."

Dottie's eyebrows dipped below the top edge of her bifocals, only to return to normal as the meaning behind

Emma's words grew clear. "They really are dreadful, aren't they . . ."

As it was a statement, rather than a question, Emma remained silent as Dottie's attention returned to their tea-party stowaway. "Would you like a *cookie*?"

Lurching forward, Emma held fast to both of their tea-cups, the liquid inside them sloshing with each answering wag of Scout's tail. "Whoa . . . Whoa . . ."

"I take it that was a *yes*?" Dottie asked, momentarily abandoning her view of Scout.

"That was a yes." When the threat of a veritable tea-sunami was over, Emma stood, grabbed the basket of un-eaten biscuits, and ventured her way back around the table to the hallway beyond. "I'll get the—" She stopped, glanced back at the table and its unprotected teacups, and pointed a warning at the golden retriever parked beneath it all, his eyes sparkling, his tail poised in anticipation of her next word. "Oh no . . . don't even *think* about it, mister."

Less than three minutes later, she was back in her chair, the biscuits replaced by a half dozen (minus one eaten en route back to the living room) shortbread cookies. Hovering the basket above the table, she hurried to get their weekly ritual back on track. "Dottie? A *you-know-what*?"

"Why, yes, I think I will."

Grinning, Emma held the basket firm as Dottie helped herself to a cookie, hemmed and hawed for the right amount of time, and then reached inside for the *I really shouldn't* second helping.

"Thank you, Emma."

"Thank *you*, Dottie. For reminding me that things can be tweaked without changing everything." Retrieving her napkin from the table once again, Emma unfolded it across her lap, set two cookies on her own plate, and then held the last one below the edge of the tablecloth. "This is one treat your housekeeper won't be finding in the corner of Alfred's study, that's for sure."

Dottie's laugh segued into a comfortable silence as they sipped their tea as per the Tuesday tradition. Halfway through her second cookie, though, Dottie veered off script again by leaning back in her wheelchair and lifting a knowing brow at Emma. "I'm waiting."

Emma glanced across her own cookie to the empty basket. "You want *more* cookies?"

The second the words were out, she realized her mistake as cups rattled atop their saucers. "Sorry . . . his tail gets a little boisterous at times."

"I see that." Dottie wiped her lips with her cloth napkin and then lowered it back to her lap. "And no, I don't want more."

Emma leaned forward far enough to see the sip or two of tea that still remained in Dottie's teacup. "What am I missing?"

Dottie crossed her arms in front of her chest. "You tell me."

"I would if I could."

"Then perhaps I should help you."

"Perhaps you should."

Clearing her throat, Dottie returned her hands to the armrests of her wheelchair and sat up tall. "*Why, Dottie, you were right after all. Thank you—thank you so much.*"

"Right about what?" Emma prodded as her eyes returned to the empty basket.

"My idea. For your livelihood."

"Your idea for my—" She stopped. Pushed back her chair. Stood. "You want to talk about your idea? Fine. We'll talk about it. In terms of the two people you sent my way, yes, I got two jobs out of those calls—a one-off to accompany someone to a dance at the senior center, and—"

"Big Max."

Emma retrieved the serving tray from the buffet table under the front window and placed the empty basket and their dirty plates in the center. "Sidebar: he's completely adorable."

"And the other?"

"One ongoing client who wants a gym buddy."

"MaryAnn's daughter."

"If MaryAnn's daughter is Stephanie, then yes." She pointed at the last of Dottie's tea and, at the elderly woman's nod, placed the cup and saucer onto the tray along with her own.

"So I was right." Dottie handed Emma her napkin to add to the tray, smiling triumphantly. "Doing what you do for me *is* a viable employment option."

"I can't make a living on a one-off and a three-mornings-a-week gym visit, Dottie."

"You could if you solicited more business in the Sweet Falls paper or with a mass mailing to the town." Dottie pointed at a few crumbs on the tablecloth. "After all, you can't expect me to find *all* of your business, dear. You need to put in a little effort yourself."

She didn't mean to laugh. She really didn't. But, in all fairness, it wasn't a *ha-ha* kind of laugh. Rather, it was one steeped in disbelief with a little fatigue-based sarcasm thrown in for good measure. "I actually put in a little effort, as you say. In fact, that same day you posed this whole notion, I stayed up almost all night long working on a name, designing and printing some really cute business cards, and pinning a notice to the town's virtual bulletin board— which, by the way, is far better for the environment than printing up flyers people are just going to throw away, anyway."

"Can I see your card?" Dottie asked.

"Now?"

"Yes."

Shrugging, she set the tray down on the table, crossed to the hallway and the spot where she always left her purse on tea day, and returned with the fruits of her labor. "Here."

Dottie's silent perusal of the business card sagged Emma back onto her chair. Scout, sensing teatime was over, ventured out from his spot beneath the table to set his head atop Emma's leg. Like the dutiful dog mom she was, she rubbed the area behind his ears, willing the feel of his fur beneath her fingers to work their calming magic on her soul.

"A Friend for Hire," Dottie mused. "Clever. Creative. To the point. Inviting."

"You sound surprised."

"I am."

"About which part? That I'm clever or that I'm creative?"

Dottie took one last look at the card and then placed it on her spot at the table. "That you did it all so fast."

"I've been self-employed since college, Dottie."

"I realize that." Dottie lifted her sage-green eyes back to Emma. "Did your efforts net anything?"

She paused her hand atop Scout's head long enough to laugh. "Oh, they netted something, alright."

"Very good."

"Actually, no, it wasn't very good. It was disastrous." Again, she stood, only this time she bypassed the serving tray in favor of the front window and its view of the sprawling lawn and flowering hedges Alfred had loved so much.

"Disastrous?"

"As in, it couldn't have gone any worse."

"Tell me."

"I'm not sure you want to hear this."

"Try me."

She shifted her field of vision to include the bird sanctuary Alfred had added next to the rosebushes just before his death and drew in a slow, resigned breath. "I really didn't think anyone would call when I posted the virtual flyer. I really didn't. Sure, I was excited about the name I'd settled on and the cards I'd made, but by the time I woke up the next morning, some of the wind had left my sails, so to speak.

"So, with that said, you can imagine my surprise when I got a call from someone wanting to hire me."

"*I'm* not surprised."

Emma watched a pair of finches fight over the last of the thistle Dottie's gardener would need to replace and gave into another mirthless laugh. "Oh, just wait. I'm not done. So the guy on the other end of the phone is doing a reading at Deeter's open mic that night and he wants someone— which, in this case, would be *me*—there to support him."

"Open Mic Night?" Dottie echoed on the heels of a quiet gasp. "At Deeter's?"

Pressing her forehead against the window, Emma nodded.

"Does that mean you were *there* when that young man was killed?"

"Oh, I was there, alright. Front and center to the whole thing, in fact." She closed her eyes against the memory of Brian pitching forward on his stool a split second before hitting the stage. "As Brian Hill's friend—his *friend for hire*, that is."

This time, Dottie's gasp wasn't the slightest bit quiet. "You can't be serious, dear."

"Oh, I can be. And I am," she murmured. Seconds turned to minutes as the silence in the room grew deafening. Slowly, Emma turned around and made her way back to the table. Scout, sensing a change in mood, was waiting beside her chair to offer a lick and a quick wag of his tail. "I keep thinking it's all some weird repetitive nightmare I'm having night after night, but that would mean I was sleeping long enough each night to *have* a nightmare, and I'm not."

"This is a very unfortunate turn of events, dear. One you might not want to mention in your literature."

She stared at Dottie. "My literature?"

"Yes, for your business. Though I imagine most of that is done via a website these days, yes?"

At the feel of Scout's chin on her leg, Emma rested her hand atop his head by feel rather than by sight as her eyes were still trained on the elderly woman seated opposite her at the table. "You did hear what I just said, right? That my first client dropped dead while I was with him—*murdered*, according to the news. And"—her thoughts traveled to the park and Jack—"the cops."

"I am not deaf. Of course I heard you. But," Dottie said, wagging her finger at Emma, "Mr. Hill was not your first client, dear. Big Max was. And MaryAnn's daughter was your second."

"They may have retained me before Brian did, but he was the first one I actually worked with," she countered.

Dottie pulled a face, only to release it along with a sweep of her hand. "I wouldn't recommend mentioning that to future clients, either, dear. It might scare them off."

She saw her elderly friend's mouth moving but instead of Dottie's voice, it was Brian's that suddenly filled her head.

"Look around, look around, here sit those you laud, but soon you, too, will know their fraud."

His words had been designed to stir intrigue in some, and discomfort in others. And, based on the throat clearing and nervous coughs she remembered in their wake, he'd succeeded.

"You know something?" Emma said aloud as much for herself as for Dottie. "Maybe I was meant to be with Brian that night. So I could see to it that justice is served in the wake of his murder.

"I mean, Stephanie is right. We—*I*—need to stop pretending this has nothing to do with me and figure out who did this to him and why. So they can be held responsible." The click of Dottie's hand brake cut through Emma's thoughts and returned her gaze to her friend. "Dottie, where are you going?"

"Not me, *both* of us." Quickly, Dottie backed her chair from the table, spun it around, and made a beeline for the hallway beyond. "Come, dear. There's something I must show you."

Scout's ears perked up and his tail wagged.

"Sorry, boy, I'll be right back."

Scout's ears drooped, his tail stilled.

"He can come," Dottie tossed across her shoulder before disappearing from sight.

Shrugging, Emma gave Scout a quick scratch and then stood. "You heard Dottie. You're invited, too."

Together, they trailed the wheelchair-bound woman down the hall, through the master suite at the back of the house, and into the kind of personal library guaranteed to make a diehard reader swoon. There, with a speed that defied the normal drag of carpet against wheels, Dottie made her way to the bookshelves and the hundreds of colorful mass-market paperbacks they housed.

"Wait." Emma looped her way around Dottie for a closer look of the collection she'd long envied. "Are you finally going to let me borrow one of your books?"

Dottie waved her question off as if it were a pesky gnat or a bothersome child. "No, of course not. Books loaned are rarely returned and then I'm left with an incomplete series. We've been over this, dear."

"I know, but you told me to follow and—"

"Do you know what these are, dear?" Dottie asked, pointing at the books.

Again, she took in the paperbacks with their punny titles, the answer to Dottie's question coming easily. "They're those cozy mysteries you love so much."

"They are."

She waited for more. Dottie, of course, didn't disappoint.

"I've learned a lot in my years of reading these books."
Dottie ran her fingers along the spines of the books positioned within reach of her wheelchair. "Things that could
be a real asset in your endeavor, dear."

"*My endeavor?*" Emma echoed.

"To see justice served in that young man's murder."

She dropped her gaze from the shelves to Dottie. "I don't
understand . . ."

"A person doesn't spend the kind of time I've spent
sleuthing alongside so many wonderful characters and not
learn a thing or two about murder. And, frankly, I've gotten
quite good at guessing the who and the why before the
book's sleuth."

At the risk of sounding like a broken record, Emma
tried again. "I still don't understand what you're trying
to say."

Muttering something about youth and their inability to
follow along, Dottie rolled her eyes. "Are you *trying* to be
addle-headed right now, dear?"

"No, I'm not trying to be addle . . ." She sighed the
rest of her protest away. "Okay, so I'm *tired*, sure. *Exhausted*, actually. But I think that's probably par for the
course when you watch someone drop dead in front of you
and then find out, a few days later, that he was actually
murdered."

"Okay, good. We're back on track."

She stared at the elderly woman. "Back on track? Back
on track for what?"

"You said that you think you were meant to be at
Deeter's with Mr. Hill when he was murdered. So you can
seek justice for him, yes?"

Emma nodded.

"Likewise, dear, *I* think you were meant to voice that
feeling in front *of me*."

"I'm not following . . ."

Dottie led Emma's gaze to the shelves of books. "Because I believe I have the experience you need to get to the bottom of Mr. Hill's murder."

"Oh no . . . not you, too . . ." She scrubbed her face with the palms of her hands in a desperate attempt to make it all go away—Brian's death, the folder, the craziness spewing from Dottie's mouth—but to no avail. "What is it with everyone wanting to play detective?"

"Everyone?"

"You . . . Stephanie . . ."

"Stephanie?"

Sighing, Emma wandered over to the library's single (but oh so gloriously comfortable) reading chair and slumped down onto its thick cushion. "Stephanie Porter— your friend's daughter."

"What about her?"

"She apparently binges crime shows on TV on the weekends."

"And . . ." Dottie prodded, her voice frosty.

"And so she wants to help me figure out who murdered Brian and why." Emma folded herself over in the chair and cradled her head in her hands. "Which is so strange because *I* was the one there, and I'd rather do anything other than be involved in this whole mess."

"She's too close in age."

Thrown off by the odd statement, she peeked up at Dottie. "Too close in age to whom?"

"You." Dottie perused her bookshelves, narrowed her attention on the top shelf, and, with the help of her grabbing stick, plucked off a book and lowered it to her lap with unmistakable reverence. "The most enduring duos contrast one another in some way, dear. Sometimes it comes down to personality differences, sometimes it's about size, sometimes other things—like Mel and Angie in the Cupcake Bakery Mysteries. Mel is the brains; Angie is the muscle.

"And sometimes, as will be the case with us, it comes down to age. Meaning, the naive, wet-behind-the-ears early-thirtysomething such as yourself, and the far more endearing elderly neighbor or friend."

Amusement arched Emma's brow. "And you're the latter, I take it?"

"Of course. I'll be the Margaret Louise Davis—minus the eight grandchildren, of course—to your Tori Sinclair in"—Dottie lifted the clearly treasured book from her lap and shook it at Emma—"the Southern Sewing Circle Mysteries. Although, truth be told, Margaret Louise Davis was only in her sixties and, thus, shouldn't have been labeled *elderly* the way she was. Which, I imagine, earned the author an email or two from readers, but I digress."

Emma scrubbed her face again. Harder. When she was done, Dottie was still there and still talking.

"At least, in *our* case, dear, I *am* elderly. I'm also wealthy, wheelchair-bound, attractive, and well-connected in our little town. Which makes me the far better choice to be your sidekick than MaryAnn's daughter."

"Wait. *You* want to be *my* sidekick? I thought you said, just last week, that I'm *your* sidekick."

"In this home, you are. In the incredibly creative business I dropped in your lap that you've managed to mess up right out of the chute, yes. But—"

Emma unfurled her body in a show of protest. "Managed to mess up? Are you kidding me? I didn't ask Brian to hire me! In fact, if it wasn't for you and—and your *creative business* idea, I'd be watching all of this unfold on the eleven o'clock news every night with a bowl of hot buttered popcorn on my lap!"

At the mention of popcorn, Scout gave up sniffing his way around the bookshelves and came over to Emma, tail wagging. "Wouldn't we, boy?" she added for good measure.

"That's neither here nor there," Dottie said with an audible huff. "The time for being overwhelmed and scratching your head over this has come and gone. It's time to pick up the pace and get to work solving this—with *me* as your sidekick in this one very particular instance."

"Sorry. Too late. I already promised Stephanie she could help."

Dottie's eyes darkened behind her bifocals. "And what has she brought to the table so far?"

"Well, nothing yet." Emma stilled her ear-scratching hand. "Stephanie works crazy hours during the week. We'll probably talk about it a little tomorrow morning at the gym and then really get into it over the weekend at some point."

Dottie stared at Emma. "Proper and successful sleuthing isn't a weekends-only activity, dear. Tell me you realize that."

"Maybe. I-I don't know. It's not like we're really going to solve this, anyway."

"With *that* attitude and *Stephanie* as your sidekick, you're right, you're not. But with a little"—again, Dottie retrieved the paperback novel from her lap and shook it at Emma—"*experience* and *know-how*, along with *me* as your sidekick, we'll deliver the culprit to Sheriff Borlin by week's end."

"Week's end?" Emma echoed.

"Most likely, yes. *If* we work hard, and *if* we work smart. But in the event we fall short, we'll definitely have the culprit behind bars by the end of *next* week at the latest." Dottie lowered the book back to her lap, took a moment to finger the details on the eye-catching cover, and then slowly lifted her gaze back to Emma's. "Let me help you with this, Emma. Please."

"And what am I supposed to do about Stephanie? She's got nothing going on in her life except work. Cutting her out of this will crush her." And it was true. It would.

Dottie moved her head as if weighing Emma's question. "I suppose we could be more of an ensemble team, if we must. After all, Margaret Louise's sister, Leona, *did* help on occasion."

"Margaret Louise? Leona? Who *are* these people? And why do you keep saying their names?"

Rolling her eyes along with her wheels, Dottie closed the gap between them to hand her beloved book to Emma. "Read this. But if you crack the spine or fail to return it— leaving me with a gap in the series—there will be a second murder in Sweet Falls, dear. And it will be *yours*."

Chapter Eleven

S he'd just hiked her gym bag higher up on her shoulder when she felt the quick yet unmistakable vibration of an incoming text. Releasing a not-so-quiet moan, Emma slipped the bag back off her arm, unzipped its side compartment, and fished out her phone. A glance at the screen showed Dottie's name rather than her still MIA gym buddy.

She opened the text.

I made a few lists after you left yesterday.

She traveled her tired eyes the whole length of the block. But still, there was no sign of Stephanie. Quickly, she typed her reply.

You do realize it's 5:40 in the morning, right?

The trio of dots indicating a forthcoming reply were immediate.

I do. I also realize Mr. Hill is still dead.

"Touché," Emma murmured before returning her thumbs
to the keypad.

So what are these lists?

The dots danced and danced and danced.
"I don't need a novel, Dottie . . ."

A list of motives. A list of ways he might have died. A list
of things we need to do/ask/find out in our investigation.

Before she could reply, another, follow-up text came in.

We can discuss at 8. Sharp. Glenda is making scones.

She started to type her regrets but stopped as a glance
down the street yielded a very different familiar face. Clos-
ing her way out of the text conversation, Emma pushed off
the brick wall at her back and drew in a fortifying breath.
"Hello, Emma."
"Hello, Deputy Riordan."
"Are you waiting or procrastinating?"
Glancing down at her phone as it vibrated inside her hand,
she noted Dottie's name on the screen and then stuffed it
back inside her bag. Unread. "Must they be mutually exclu-
sive at this time of the morning?"
"I guess not."
"I'm waiting for my friend from the other day."
"The one who killed Cuddles?" He closed the gap be-
tween them with several long strides. "Think she's off help-
ing another cat to its premature death?"
Her answering laugh echoed in the early-morning air.
"Let's hope not."
"Yeah, let's hope not. I've got enough on my plate."

Something about the change in tone stole her attention from the corner it had returned to and placed it firmly on the handsome deputy. Sure enough, the smile she'd heard in his voice just moments earlier was nowhere to be seen on his face. And his eyes? They still looked like the ocean in the Bahamas, but with a little stirred-up sand making it difficult to see beneath the surface.

"Long night?" she asked.

"You could say that."

She studied him studying her, only to stop as her phone—set to vibrate on texts and ring on calls—rang. Reaching back into her bag, she fished out the device once again, fully expecting to see Dottie's name. But she was wrong.

"I'm sorry, I have to take this."

"Of course. Go ahead."

When it was clear he wasn't going to head inside the gym, Emma stepped away, holding the phone to her ear as she did. "I'm here. Outside. Where are you?"

"Home."

She glanced back over her shoulder to find Jack watching her. "Uh, why? It's Wednesday. Five thirty . . . Or at least it was when I got here."

"I'm sorry, Emma. I was buried in patient charts last night. By the time I finally got into bed, I was so exhausted it's really no surprise I slept through my alarm."

"I can wait if you want to come over now. It's only"—she pulled the phone away long enough to check the time—"five fifty."

"I'm actually still in bed," Stephanie admitted.

"Oh."

"I know. I'm pathetic. Tell me something I don't already know."

"You're not pathetic, Stephanie."

"If I wasn't, I wouldn't have been doing work until three in the morning. Instead, I'd have spent the evening with some dashingly handsome man, sipping wine over whatever dinner he'd whipped up for me after giving closing arguments on his big case, or bringing some poor schlep back to life on the operating table, or . . ." Stephanie sighed in her ear. "You get my point."

"You overslept. It's no big deal."

"Yeah, but when I realized what time it was, I reached for the phone instead of getting up and getting dressed."

"We all have days like that," Emma said.

"Maybe. But some of us live our life on a daily basis that way. Which is why I have no friends, no social life."

"You have me."

"Because I hired you."

"True. But if I hadn't liked you, I wouldn't be standing here on the sidewalk, in gym clothes, with a certain sheriff's deputy watching me while I talk to you."

Any and all signs of sleepiness disappeared from Stephanie's voice. "You mean the guy from last week?"

"Yep."

"What's he want?"

She wandered to the edge of the sidewalk, pretended to look at something on the street, and slowly slid a peek over her shoulder. "He's dressed to work out, but he seems to be waiting for me to get off the phone."

"You didn't give him the paper our vic gave you, right?"

"Our vic?"

"It's cop-speak for victim. You really need to learn these things, Emma."

"No, I don't. And no, I didn't. I don't have it on me."

"And you don't want to go to jail for suppressing evidence, remember?"

Emma felt her stomach lurch. "Would you please stop with that?"

"Why? It's the truth," Stephanie said. "Don't. Give. It. Up."

"Give it up?" Emma echoed.

"Tell him about it . . . turn it over . . ." Stephanie drew in a breath. "I am so making you a cheat sheet of lingo."

Emma groaned. "Please don't."

"Anyway, are you going to go inside and work out?"

"I guess. For a little while, anyway."

She could tell, by the sudden shift in Stephanie's voice, that the woman was no longer in bed. "I don't have to be at work today until ten. I'm going to shower and get caught up on a few more charts, and then let's meet at Mrs. Bean's at eight."

"Or you could come here now, and *then* shower and do your charts . . ."

"Mrs. Bean's is better."

She rolled her eyes. "Better? Or less painful?"

"I plead the Fifth."

"Fine. But we're getting the coffee to go and sitting in the square so Scout can come, too."

"Cool. I can't wait to meet him." Stephanie's smile was audible over the phone. "Eight o'clock, then?"

"Yes. But you're back on that treadmill on Friday morning—no excuses, okay?" She grinned at the sudden, yet clearly fake static in her ear. "I mean it, Stephanie."

"Yeah, yeah . . ."

Chuckling, Emma ended the call, stuffed the phone back in her bag, and made her way back toward the gym and . . . Jack. "No cats were harmed in the making of her excuse."

He tried for a smile but gave up when it stopped short of the midway point. "So you're on your own, then?" he asked.

"I am." She paused a beat. "You look wiped out."

"I've got a lot on my mind."

She tightened her hold on the strap of her gym bag in an effort to keep her hands from trembling and willed herself to do what she knew was right. "I-I made a mistake. A big one. And I-I think I need to come clean."

All signs of fatigue faded as he stepped forward. "I'm listening."

"Brian gave me something the other night. Just before

he stepped onstage." She stopped. Shook her head. Made herself continue despite the pounding of her heart inside her chest. "But you have to understand that I really thought it was all a coincidence. That he was just stirring pots, as you say."

Jack's eyes remained glued to her face, his expression not much different than the proverbial cat waiting for the mouse to emerge from its hole.

"Then it turned out to be murder and I hadn't turned it over and I was afraid for just myself, at first. And then Brian. And now . . ." She willed her breathing and the pace of her words to slow as he looked down at her, but it was hard. "I don't know, I guess I want to trust that you'll do the right thing, regardless."

She started to reach into her bag but stopped, her eyes finding his once again. "May I reach into my bag for my phone so I can show you?"

His nod was short, clipped.

Unable to keep her fingers from trembling, Emma reached into her bag, pulled out her phone, and opened her album. "He gave me this before he stepped on the stage that night."

Jack took the device from her hand and looked down at the picture she'd pulled up on the screen.

"He said they all wanted him dead."

She followed his eyes as they bounced from face to face and then, finally, looked back at Emma. "He sent this to you?"

"No. He gave it to me. In paper form. I just took a picture of it."

"Why?"

"Why did I take a picture?" She threw up her hands. "I don't know. Maybe because Scout has a tendency to mess with paper . . . I can't really say."

He stared at her for a long moment and then returned his

attention to the image. "No, I mean, why did he say they wanted him dead?"

"That's the thing. He didn't. He just pushed this folder across the table at me and told me to open it. When I did, this paper was inside it. He asked me if I knew who they were."

"And did you?" Jack asked without looking up.

"I knew Nancy Davis, and I knew Sheriff Borlin. The other two seemed familiar, but I needed Brian to tell me who they were."

"Go on . . ."

"Then he told me to look around the room. That all four of them were there. I made a comment about it being a coincidence. Only it wasn't. He told me he invited them."

Jack's head whipped up but he remained silent.

"I asked him why he needed to hire me to be there in the audience if he already had friends there."

"What did he say to that?"

She shrugged. "He said they weren't his friends. That they all wanted him dead."

"What did you say?" Jack asked.

"I tried not to groan, honestly. Figured I was seeing, firsthand, what my research on him had turned up. But since he had hired me, I felt the need to assure him that wasn't true."

Jack looked back at the picture. "Anything else?"

"He told me it was true and that his poem would seal the deal."

Again, his eyes shot back to hers. "His poem?"

"The one he was just starting to recite when he fell off the stool." She closed her eyes, drew in a breath, and then opened them to find Jack watching, waiting. "I was so thrown by all of it—by seeing this man I'd just met keel over in front of me—that I left. With the paper. Like the idiot you surely think I am, but I'm really not. I swear."

Seconds turned to minutes as Jack said nothing and she braced herself to be handcuffed. Finally, just as she was on the brink of tears, he looked from Emma to the phone and back again. "Just before you showed me this, you said you were afraid for Brian. How so?"

"Your boss is on that list."

The same fatigue that had been so evident in his face when he arrived was back, and he palmed his mouth. "You're right. He is."

"And—and I worry that might mean Brian won't get the justice he deserves," she said, her voice barely more than a whisper.

He broke eye contact long enough to survey the empty sidewalk to their left and right. "I did a little digging. Not a ton, but some."

"On your boss?"

His answering nod was hesitant at best. "They were like oil and vinegar," he said, raking his fingers across the top of his head. "I mean, I always knew the sheriff despised that guy and rightfully so. Hill tried really hard to cast doubt on Borlin's reelection."

"In what way?" Emma asked.

"Every way he could. Accuracy of poll numbers . . . insinuating Borlin greased a palm or two to fudge results . . . You name it."

Something about the deputy's words knocked at a discarded memory. "Now that you're saying this, I sort of remember a few stories about it in the week or so after the election. But I don't remember it going anywhere."

"Because it didn't. Brian Hill was a pot stirrer, like I said the other day. He lived to create drama, to question everything and everyone, to argue for the sake of arguing, and to be contrary about everything, no matter how big or how small. It was his thing, like being a cop and a dad is my thing." Jack blew out a long breath. "I remember one time I was patrolling the town square and came across him sitting on a park bench. As I do with just about everyone I see sitting alone, I said hello and commented on the weather—which was beautiful. He, in turn, went on to cite how low the water table was and how rain would be so much better."

"Okay . . ."

"Not a big thing, sure. But, since you say you'd just met him right before he died, it gives you an idea of what I mean by the contrary part."

She found her way back to the wall and leaned against it again. "Actually, I saw a little of that myself in the brief time we had before he got onstage to read his poem."

"Oh?"

"Like your example, it wasn't a big thing, but it still bothered me."

"Go on . . ."

"I said something to him about my dog—"

"Scout," Jack interjected.

Impressed by his continuing memory skills, she nodded. "Right. Anyway, I said something about how he likes scraps from the table, and Brian went into what could best be described as judgment mode. And when it should've been clear that I loved dogs, he made sure to let me know he didn't. Which seemed unnecessary in the moment."

"For anyone else, sure. For Brian Hill, not so much." Again, Jack let his frustration loose on his hair. "But my example and your example are minor in the grand scheme of things. Brian enjoyed messing with everyone—the bigger, the better."

She waited for more, but it was clear the deputy was conflicted. "Like questioning Sheriff Borlin's reelection last year?" she prodded.

"That, yes, and now . . ." He took in another breath and let it out, slowly. "It seems Mr. Hill—Brian—had started poking around about Borlin again just before his death."

Like Scout when the words *food*, *treat*, *walk*, or *cookie* were uttered, her ears perked up. "How did you find *that* out?"

"By accident, really. I was at a town meeting last night and one of the councilmembers pulled me aside afterward to ask about Brian's death and to let me know that, prior to it, Brian had been sniffing around about his kid's full-ride military scholarship."

"Why?"

"I'm guessing because I arrested this guy's kid three different times for drug possession—well, technically twice. The first time we graced him with the assumption his dad would straighten him out."

"Oh. Wow," she said, drawing back. "I didn't know the military overlooks stuff like that in terms of putting a kid through college."

He leaned against the wall next to her and looked up at the sky. "They don't."

"But you just said this councilman's kid got a full ride."

"You're right, I did."

"But—"

"His record is *gone*."

"Gone?" she echoed. "What do you mean, *gone*?"

"The kid's name isn't anywhere in the Sweet Falls system."

"But you just said you caught him three times and arrested him twice."

"Because I did."

"So, then, how can his record be gone?"

Once again, Jack took in the empty sidewalk to their left and right before offering a sort of shrug. "Someone made the kid's arrests disappear."

It was a lot to take in, a lot to digest, but the unspoken message driving the worry she saw in Jack's face wasn't all that hard to pinpoint. "You think Sheriff Borlin had a hand in that?"

"Considering this same councilman went on to squeeze

my shoulder and tell me he appreciated my cooperation and decorum, yeah . . . I do."

She stared at him. "Wait. *Your* cooperation?"

"A *cooperation* that, on the surface, would've had to come from me as the arresting officer. But since I knew nothing of this until last night, it couldn't have."

"So—"

"Wait. It gets better." He blew out a breath, looked back at the sky. "This guy then goes on to tell me it was money well spent, in his opinion, because his kid is doing great now."

"Money?"

"Yep."

"Money?" she echoed again.

Slowly, he lowered his gaze back to hers and held it there for a silent beat. "He appreciated my cooperation and decorum, and it was money well spent," he repeated.

"I heard that, but . . ." She sucked in her breath as the meaning behind the replay became crystal clear. "You think Sheriff Borlin took a bribe?"

Jack pushed away from the wall, walked a few feet, and then returned, his angst tangible. "I don't *want* to think that. But how can I not? The kid has no record. His father thanked me for my cooperation and mentioned money . . . And—"

"And Brian was asking questions about it before his death," she finished as she, too, began to pace. "Assuming the sheriff was involved, he could get in a lot of trouble for taking a bribe like that, couldn't he?"

Linking his hands behind his head, Jack blew out a troubled breath. "Oh yeah. *Huge.*"

"So now what?"

"I dig deeper." He dropped his hands to his sides. "And I shouldn't have said any of that to you just now."

She stopped in front of the troubled deputy. "I want justice for Brian, too, Jack. Pot stirrer or not, he didn't deserve to be killed."

"I need that paper, Emma. The actual one he gave you."

"Of course." She looked up at the sky, mustered every ounce of courage she could find, and then returned her gaze to his. "Am I going to go to jail for taking that paper?"

"No."

Relief sagged her shoulders. "Thank you. And I'm sorry. Truly."

"I know. That's obvious. But—"

"Don't worry, Jack. I've got no intention of leaving. Sweet Falls is my home."

Chapter Twelve

Elongating Scout's leash, Emma let him lead her past Alfred's prized rosebushes, around the flowering bird sanctuary, and across the flagstone walkway that bordered the eastern side of Dottie's sprawling Mediterranean-style home. He, like Emma, was singularly focused on reaching the back patio, though his reason was likely the aromas his nose had seemed to hit on from nearly a block away, while hers was all about the voices peppering the morning air.

"I'm here . . . I'm here . . ." She caught up to Scout at the wrought iron fence separating the grounds from the patio area and reached through the iron bars to unlatch the gate. "Sorry I'm a few minutes late."

Dottie waved her over to the table on which a platter of scones sat between a china butter dish and a matching sugar bowl and creamer. "While tardiness will not bode well for your business, dear, in this particular case it has given Stephanie and me a chance to get to know one another a little bit."

She held back on the urge to point out her on-time record

for all of their Tuesday afternoon teas over the past eighteen months and instead shifted her full attention onto the fortysomething making googly eyes at Scout. "Stephanie, this is Scout. Scout, this is Stephanie."

"Oh, Emma, he's precious." Stephanie pushed back her chair, patted her knee, and, when Scout rewarded her efforts with his front paw, let out a happy squeal.

"Thanks, Stephanie. We'll keep each other, right, boy?" At Scout's emphatic wag of affirmation, Emma shifted her focus to their wheelchair-bound host. "Is he free to roam back here, or should I keep him at my feet?"

Dottie looked toward the back door of her home and, when she failed to see whatever she was looking for, rang the bell at her elbow. "You can let him wander. I had Glenda put the wire screen around Alfred's lily of the valley before you came, so he'll be fine."

"I don't think I've ever seen this many flowers outside of a floral shop in my entire life," Stephanie mused.

"Dottie's late husband, Alfred, was quite the plant whisperer, for sure." Breathing in the potpourri of floral aromas floating in the air around them, Emma looked back at the woman still fawning over her dog. "I'm sorry I changed our meeting spot on you at the last minute, Stephanie, but—"

"It wouldn't have *been* last minute if you'd acknowledged my text when I first sent it," Dottie said, helping herself to what looked to be a blueberry scone. "*Had* you, you would have had a solid two hours' notice."

She pulled out the empty chair Dottie directed her toward and lowered herself onto its cushioned seat while Glenda, Dottie's morning housekeeper, made her way around the table, pouring coffee into everyone's cups. "I figured it was better to give the deputy my full attention in the moment."

Widening her eyes behind her bifocals, Dottie waved Glenda back inside the house and then lowered her scone back to her plate. "Deputy?"

"That's right."

"I don't know, Emma . . . Three times in the span of a single week?" Stephanie, too, took a scone. Broke off a piece. Stuck it in her mouth and chewed. "That says you're being *followed*, in my book."

Dottie's eyes narrowed on Emma. "You're being followed by a member of the sheriff's department? Why am I just now hearing about this?"

"Because he hasn't been following me. Or, if he was, he's not anymore." Emma pulled her napkin out from its sterling silver holder and unfurled it across her lap. When she, too, had secured what Dottie confirmed as a gingerbread scone, she took a bite, savored the sudden pop of flavor, and then chased it down with a sip of coffee.

Stephanie bolted upright, rattling her own cup of coffee. "Does this mean he found something?"

"*Found* might not be the best word choice, but yeah." Emma took another bite of scone, another sip of coffee. "In fact, I think there's a very real possibility we won't have to play sleuth at all."

Dottie's shoulders slumped in tandem with Stephanie's but recovered faster. "I take it you haven't started reading yet?"

"You mean the book you sent me home with yesterday?" At Dottie's nod, Emma took yet another bite of scone. "I did, actually. It's more entertaining than I expected it to be."

"You have *no* idea." Dottie pushed her own plate off to the side in favor of the notebook and pen her housekeeper magically produced on some silent cue. "You've surely read enough to know that identifying the true culprit isn't always as easy as it may seem at first."

Emma stared down at the rest of her scone, her appetite suddenly gone. "Even if the evidence against one particular person seems pretty damning?"

"Even if."

A glance at Stephanie yielded a nod of agreement.

"Ugh!" Emma slumped back against her chair, defeated. "I so wanted to be done with all of this."

"*We* don't," Stephanie said, earning an emphatic nod from Dottie. "So, what did your own personal shadow get on the sheriff? Anything?"

"*The sheriff?*" Dottie echoed.

It was Stephanie's turn to nod. "That's right. He was one of the four people pictured on the paper Brian gave to Emma right before he got onstage that night."

Dottie's eyes shot back to Emma. "Mr. Hill gave you a piece of paper with pictures on it before he died?"

"Emma didn't tell you this?" Stephanie asked, leaning forward in excitement. "Oh, Dottie, you've so got to hear this . . . The faces on the paper? They're of people Brian was convinced wanted him dead. And then"—Stephanie hit her hand on the table, rattling spoons and cups in the process—"Bam! Less than ten minutes later he was dead . . . with all four of the people on that paper sitting right there in the room!"

Slowly, and oh so deliberately, Dottie once again slid her attention off Stephanie and onto Emma. Only this time, Emma could swear she smelled her own flesh starting to burn. "Is this true, dear?"

"I . . . uh . . ."

"You betcha it's true." Stephanie pushed her own scone plate to the side and planted her hands on top of the table in anticipation. "So, let's see it, Emma!"

Afraid to break eye contact with Dottie lest she burst into flames, Emma settled, instead, for a swallow. "See what?"

"The paper!"

"I don't have it anymore."

Stephanie's mouth gaped open. "Why?"

"I gave it to him before I came here."

"Why?"

"Because it's evidence. Because he's a cop. Because I should've given it to him the moment I realized Brian hadn't just died for some random reason."

"And he didn't arrest you?" Stephanie asked, wide-eyed.

"No."

"Was he angry?"

Emma ran her finger along the edge of the patio table. "He wasn't happy . . ."

"Well, I have to give it to you. You've got guts." Stephanie shifted toward Emma. "But you still have the picture you took of it, right?"

Emma nodded.

"So . . ." Stephanie shot out her hand. "Let's see the picture."

"Fine." The scrape of her chair against the patio ended Scout's fascination with a small koi pond and brought him back to her side. "We're not leaving yet, boy. Just need something from my bag."

Pulling her bag up and onto her lap, Emma reached inside and procured her phone from its depths. A well-played lick on her hand as she started to lower the bag back to its spot beneath the table had her retrieving a dog treat, as well. "Here you go, Mr. Subtle."

"You mean Mr. Adorable," Stephanie said, eyeing Scout before slumping back against her chair. "Yet another reason I really need to get off my duff and find a place to live. Then again, even if I do, I can't get a dog. I'm not home enough."

Aware of Dottie's gaze, Emma opened the picture in question on her phone, set it atop the table, spun it around so it was easier for everyone to see, and waited.

"Whoa," Stephanie said, sitting upright for a closer look. "That's it? That's what he gave you?"

Emma nodded.

"I know them! I mean, I don't *know them*—know them, but I know who they are!" With her finger as a guide for her words, Stephanie moved her way around the paper. "Sheriff Borlin, the farmer lady—"

"Nancy Davis," Dottie supplied as she followed along with Stephanie's finger. "And Mayor Gerard's wife, Rita, and—"

"That guy from the McEnerny brochures!"

Dottie nodded along with Stephanie's identification and then took one more lap around the faces before lifting her gaze back to Emma's. "They were all there that night?"

"Yes."

"And what did he say about each of them when he gave this to you, Emma?"

"Nothing, really. He just asked if I knew who they were. I knew the sheriff and Nancy Davis, of course. But I only knew the other two by face. He filled in the blanks on them and—"

"Filled them in *how*, exactly?" Dottie picked the pen up off her notepad and held it at the ready.

"Well, for the mayor's wife, he said he wasn't surprised I recognized her because she likes to see herself in the newspaper. Which is something Big Max mentioned the other day, and Nancy confirmed on Sunday when I saw her out at her nursery."

Dottie's eyes narrowed on Emma yet again. "You've already started investigating? On your own?"

"Investigating? No."

"But you've talked to Nancy Davis . . ."

"I just went out to her place to talk through my ongoing vision for my front landscaping." She considered her scone, decided against another bite. "Why would that make you think I was . . ." The words trailed off as her answer came via a glance at Nancy Davis's picture alongside Sheriff Borlin's and the rest of the suspects Brian had fingered in his own death. "Oh. Right."

Dottie exchanged a brief eye roll with Stephanie before

focusing, again, on Emma. "What did he say about the last picture?"

Again Emma looked at the picture on her phone, and shrugged. "He just said his name—Robert McEnerny—and then confirmed, when I asked, that he is the McEnerny in McEnerny Homes."

"And?"

"That's it. There are just four people."

"What did he say next?" Dottie said, modulating her voice to a level more befitting a conversation with a pre-schooler. "After you knew who everyone was?"

"Ahhh. Right." Emma finally gave into the continued pull of the scone and popped the last bite—which really should've been two bites if she were more refined—into her mouth. "Well, I tried to give him back the paper, but he wouldn't take it. When I asked why, he said all four of them were there, in the room with us, at that very moment."

Stephanie took a gulp of her coffee, wiped her mouth. "If I were you, I wouldn't have been able to resist looking."

"Oh, I looked. And, he was right, they were all there."

"And then what?" Dottie prodded.

"He said, and I quote: *They want me dead. Each and every one of them.*"

Dottie wrote the sentence down, studied it, and then looked back up at Emma. "Did you challenge him?"

"I told him I was sure that wasn't true. And he said, and I quote again: *Oh, it's true.*"

Pausing her pen atop the notepad, Dottie stared at Emma. "Did he say anything else?"

"Did he say anything else . . ." Emma repeated as, once again, her thoughts returned to her final moments with Brian Hill. "Actually, he said something about his poem sealing the deal."

Dottie leaned forward. "Go on . . ."

"That was it. The owner at Deeter's came out on the

stage to announce the start of Open Mic Night and Brian just stopped talking. Less than ten minutes later, he was dead."

Stephanie shivered.

Dottie began to write at warp speed.

"What are you writing?" Emma asked, peeking around the coffeepot in the center of the table.

"A plan."

"For what?"

"Looking into Mr. Hill's affiliation with all four of these people." Dottie stopped, tapped her pen to her chin, and then began to write again, her spoken words explaining a list Emma wasn't close enough to read. "In order for him to believe these four people wanted him dead, he must have had some sort of dealings with them—something he knew made them mad."

Stephanie nodded her agreement.

"Do you remember the poem?" Dottie asked, looking up from her notepad.

"He was only into the second or third line when he fell over."

Dottie rolled her pen in the air, her impatience palpable.

"What?" Emma asked.

"Do you recall anything about the lines he *did* read?" Dottie asked.

"Recited, not read," Emma hastily corrected. "And yes, actually. They're seared into my brain, thank you very much."

Stephanie sat up tall. "Tell us . . ."

"Look around, look around, here sit those you laud, but soon you, too, will know their fraud. I say it often, I say it now, unmasking truth, this is my vow. For far too long you've turned a blind eye, their misdeeds hidden by a wink and a smile. But it's in seeking the truth that you learn the true why; the laws sidestepped, the roles . . ." Shrugging, Emma took another sip of her coffee. "And that's it. He fell over."

"Wow. Wild." Stephanie turned her attention back on Dottie. "Too bad he didn't get to finish. If he had, I suspect we'd have some motives to work off of."

Backing out of her phone's album, Emma opened her web browser. A few taps later, she began to read. "The top motives for murder include greed, revenge, and fear."

"There's also lust, self-defense, power, and fear," Stephanie added.

"I already said fear." Emma glanced up from her phone, first at Stephanie and then at Dottie. "And come to think of it, I'm pretty sure Sheriff Borlin would've had reason to be fearful where Brian was concerned."

Quickly, she filled them in on everything Jack had shared with her not more than two hours earlier, stopping every once in a while to accommodate Dottie's desire to write something down—on a page devoted solely to the sheriff—or to answer an occasional question lobbed in her direction. When she had nothing left to share, she let her focus gravitate back to her phone's screen. "So, maybe Sheriff Borlin is our guy."

Stephanie started to say something, glanced down at her watch, and, instead, released a Scout-summoning sigh. "Ugh. I have to head out or I'll be giving my boss—Mr Evil—an easy one in his ongoing quest to make my life as difficult as possible." Pushing back her chair, Stephanie pulled Scout's face close and kissed him on his snout. "I could soooo take you home with me, you know that?"

Scout wagged his tail.

"And he is soooo working you right now," Emma said, laughing.

"That's okay." Stephanie stood. "Dottie, thank you for letting me crash your breakfast. It was lovely. I can't think of the last time I've eaten in a seated position that didn't include the television being on."

Dottie didn't even bother to hide the disgust creeping across her lined face. "I don't know what to say to that."

"Neither would I, if I were you." Turning, Stephanie pointed at Emma's phone. "Don't go solving this without me, okay? I'll have some time over the weekend, if I'm lucky."

"Ahem. Friday comes before the weekend . . ." When Emma's words failed to register any sort of understanding on Stephanie's face, she cut straight to the chase. "Which means I will see you bright and early at the gym in just a little less than"—she looked at the time on her phone—"forty-five hours."

"No, you won't."

"Yes, I will."

"No. This Friday is my monthly sit-down with Mr. Evil." Stephanie pulled a face. "Which means, instead of sweating on a treadmill with you, I'll be sweating in a metal office chair."

Emma made a mental note to adjust her calendar. "I didn't realize."

"Yeah, sorry about that. I'd have remembered, eventually." Stephanie stopped, shook her head. "Who am I kidding? I wouldn't have remembered until you called me on Friday morning to find out why I wasn't at the gym."

"Then I'm glad I asked."

"Sorry," Stephanie said, again. "I wish I could tell you organization was my thing, but I can't. And now, I've really got to go."

When Stephanie was gone from view, Emma reached across to the now-vacant spot at the table and stacked the woman's empty plate atop her own.

"What are you doing, dear?"

She looked up from the napkin she'd just retrieved from Stephanie's chair to find Dottie watching her every move. "Cleaning up. So you don't have to do it."

"It's not Tuesday. You're not here as my employee."

"Oh. Right. Sorry."

Resting her pen atop the notepad, Dottie leveled a hard

look at Emma. "I'm not the least bit pleased about being left out of the loop on the evidence you were in possession of, but I'll let it go. This one time. What matters is that I'm aware of it now and I can work on our plan of attack.

"On the one hand, there may be some merit in divvying up the suspects in true divide-and-conquer fashion, but I have a good deal of concern regarding Stephanie's ability to give this investigation the full attention it requires."

"She works crazy hours, Dottie."

"That's neither here nor there, dear. We have four suspects we must investigate and interrogate."

"Whoa." Emma shot up her hands, crossing-guard style. "*Interrogate?*"

"Of course." Dottie tapped her finger atop her notepad. "How else are we going to get the answers we need in order to solve Mr. Hill's murder?"

Before Emma could formulate a response, coherent or otherwise, Dottie continued, "So, I think it's time I check in with Sheriff Borlin and see if there's anything his department might be in need of at the moment."

"Wait. You're going to try to *bribe* him?"

"Of course not, dear. I'm just going to touch base under the guise of my well-documented reputation for making generous donations and see what I can find out."

"Okay, and—" A lack of movement in her peripheral vision had her halting her sentence in favor of scanning the patio, the walkway, and the flowering bushes for any sign of Scout. When she found nothing, she furthered her search zone by standing. "Scout? Where are you?"

Dottie waved her back down. "He's fine. I supervised the placement of the screen myself. Anyway, in regard to the other three on your sheet, we need to find out what Mr. Hill's connection was to all of them."

"Like the way I told you he was asking the councilman questions about Sheriff Borlin?" At Dottie's nod, Emma again scanned the gated enclosure for any sign of Scout. "Do we even know how he died yet?"

"No. And that's likely something the police will hold back from the general public. But that doesn't mean you can't work your budding relationship with the deputy to get ahold of a little insider information."

"There is no *relationship*, Dottie. Budding or otherwise."

Dottie moved her head as if weighing Emma's response. "That doesn't mean you can't fake one until we get what we need."

"Dottie!"

"Stephanie *is* in the medical profession, dear. Which means she could read an official autopsy report should you be successful at luring it out of your deputy."

"*Budding relationship? My* deputy? Where is this coming from, Dottie?"

"Do you want to solve Mr. Hill's murder?"

"Not particularly, no. I'd rather the police do it since, you know, it *is* their job."

"Then let me rephrase, dear. Do you want to be able to keep your *house*? Your *car*? *Your dog?*"

She knew where this was going. And, like it or not, the elderly woman had a point . . .

"Fine. I'll see what I can find out from Jack."

Dottie's eyebrow shot up. "*Jack?*"

"That's his name."

"*The deputy?*"

"That's who we're talking about, isn't it?" At Dottie's answering—and oh-so-smug—grin, Emma retrieved her tote bag from the ground and stood. "Scout, come! We're leaving . . . *now!*"

Chapter Thirteen

"You weren't kidding on the whole pot-stirrer label, were you, Jack?" Emma mumbled as she scrolled through one page after another of stories written by or about Brian Hill in just the past twelve months alone.

The articles themselves all followed what she'd come to realize was a predictable pattern. Something happened in Sweet Falls—a complaint made by a resident, an award won by a committee or a high school student, a major renovation at the library . . . The story was depicted in a picture or an article of some sort . . . And—wham!—Brian either contributed a bylined article in opposition, or penned an op-ed piece as a Sweet Falls resident. But regardless of the form it took, it always sought to expose an ugly counterpoint.

And if a resident or official sought to challenge Brian's take on whatever the original topic had been, he'd come back again. Harder. No one and/or nothing had been safe from Brian Hill's accusations.

He was, as Emma's grandmother had been fond of saying, the type of person who'd argue with the devil if he could.

Relinquishing her hold on the mouse just long enough to help herself to the lone remaining potato chip on her plate, she moved her shoulders and her neck while she chewed. She hadn't meant to still be at the computer nearly forty minutes after turning it on, but what had started out as the proverbial itch that needed scratching had turned into a laundry list of people who'd been on the receiving end of Brian's need to cause trouble.

Granted, if it weren't for Brian's persistence where the various contractors and their bids were concerned, the library's renovation would have cost taxpayers significantly more money than necessary. Likewise, when Brian found an off-the-beaten-path supplier for a supposedly obsolete part the fire department was using as its reason for needing an all-new (and crazy-expensive) fire truck for its fleet, he had done the town and its residents a favor.

But it was when he unleashed his expose-and-punish mentality on a class of kindergartners who embarked on a project Brian insisted was not eco-friendly—or pointed to aesthetics in his successful quest to have a local church cited for housing a food collection trailer in their parking lot—that he found himself in the crosshairs of many a person's wrath. Including—

Rocketing upright, Emma stared at a headline halfway down the latest page of links visible on her laptop screen.

WIFE OF NEWLY ELECTED SWEET FALLS MAYOR ACCUSES BRIAN HILL OF BULLYING.

"Well, well, well. What do we have here?" Emma returned her hand to the mouse, hovered it over the link, and clicked. In little more than a blink of her eye, a letter to the editor at the *Sweet Falls Gazette* popped onto the screen alongside one of the four pictures Brian had foisted on her before his death.

Dear Editor,

I was raised to have good manners. I was raised to respect my elders. I was raised to be kind. I was raised to lose with grace and humility. And I was raised on the mantra, if you have nothing nice to say, don't say it at all. As the newly elected first lady of Sweet Falls, I'd hoped all residents would embrace and utilize the same rules of etiquette in their own lives. Sadly, I have learned that is not the case.

I realize there are people in this town who find comfort in what they know, even when what they know may no longer be what's best. That's why, when my husband won the mayoral election, I tried not to take it too much to heart when, in this very column, people acted as if Sweet Falls was doomed. I knew that, given time, my husband would prove the naysayers wrong, that they, too, would come to know what I—and clearly the majority of voters in this town—already know.

And they would come around to that, I'm certain, if not for the likes of the town bully, Brian Hill.

Brian Hill is the epitome of a sore loser. When something doesn't go his way, he has a fit—only instead of doing it behind closed doors, he does it here in your paper, and you allow it, time and time again.

Why? I ask.

Aren't we living in an age where bullies are seen for what they are? I thought so. Yet, still, you give him a pedestal on which to stand, allowing the more impressionable members of our community to be molded by his unfriendly and unwelcoming ways. And that is a shame. Because when the day comes that my husband has moved on to the next level of government, and then the level beyond that, and the level beyond that, people will look to the town in

*which he took flight and we should want Sweet Falls to be
reflected well.*

*It is my hope that you and your staff finally stop giving
this man space in which to blemish Sweet Falls and its
people.*

Sincerely,
Rita Gerard
The First Lady of Sweet Falls

"Huh . . ." Quickly, Emma speed-read the article a second time, her mind's eye filing away bits and pieces even as
she moved the cursor up to the printer icon and clicked.
While it printed, she took a peek at the responses garnered
by the so-called first lady's letter. Some, like Rita herself,
found Brian's seemingly ongoing efforts to place a cloud
over the town onerous. Others liked knowing residents had
a watchdog keeping the town's officials on their toes. In
fact, after reading through the first fifteen or so comments,
she was surprised to find a nearly fifty-fifty split between
those who liked and disliked Brian's whistleblowing ways.

Curious, she kept scrolling, the first sentence of every
comment a clear indicator of the camp in which the reader
fell. Those who appreciated Brian batted around words like
whistleblower and *townsman*. Those who were sick of him
and his ways preferred words like *troublemaker* and *use-
less*. Back and forth it went until it seemed the comments
were more focused on battling each other than weighing in
on the original letter.

She pulled her hand off the mouse, stretched her arms
above her head in conjunction with a satisfying yawn, and
smiled at the answering click of Scout's nails on the hallway floor as he found his way back to her side. "Hey, boy. I
was beginning to think you forgot about me."

Scout rested his head atop Emma's knee and gazed up at
her in a way that left little doubt she was his world.

"Yes, sweet boy, I'm done in here for now. What do you say we go outside and play a little fetch?" At his answering wag, she returned her hand to the mouse and her gaze to the comments she'd grown bored of reading and—

"Whoa . . ." Leaning forward in her chair, Emma stared at the name of the next commenter.

Brian Hill

A check of the date next to his name revealed the comment, which had come in a solid month after the posting of Rita's letter, was written less than a week before his murder.

The pot calling the kettle black. How very interesting . . .
Do you want to address that, Rita, or should I?

"Wow. That's awfully strong . . ."

She heard Scout's quick bark and knew it was a plea to get her back on track for the promised outdoor time, but really it was just white noise against the whir of thoughts racing through her head.

Had Brian caught Rita in something?

Was that last line the threat it sounded like?

Had Rita seen it?

Returning her finger to the mouse, Emma moved her way down the page, searching for Rita's name on any subsequent comments, but there was nothing. In fact, other than a handful of ads disguised as replies, Brian's late response was the last pertinent to the original post.

Scout barked again, then followed it up with a whimper.

"Shhh. I know, I know. But this could *be* something, boy—something for our investigation and . . ." She stopped and shook her head. "Wow. Would you listen to me? *Investigation*. Ha!"

Still, before she clicked off the page and set her computer to sleep mode, she grabbed a sticky note and wrote down Brian's comment. "Just because," she said to Scout as she pulled a tennis ball from her desk drawer and stood. "C'mon. Let's go have some fun."

Dropping her hand onto her lap, Emma leaned back against the slate step and reveled in the feel of the late-afternoon sun on her face. There were weeds that needed to be pulled, laundry that needed to be done, and bills waiting to be paid. But in that moment, she just didn't care. Those things would get done. They always did. This time with Scout, though? It was teaching her to slow down, to breathe, and to just be; and she was grateful.

Before Scout, she'd been all work and no play.

After Scout, she felt . . . *different*. Happier, calmer, and—

"Definitely wetter," she mused as, once again, Scout dropped his soggy tennis ball onto her sandal-clad foot. Retrieving the ball for what had to be the thirtieth time, at least, she cocked her arm back and waited as her beloved rescue prepared for his next chase. "Are you ready?"

Scout's tail wagged.

"Are you set?"

It wagged harder.

"Are you sure?"

It wagged harder still.

"Go!"

In a flash of fur and tongue and tail, Scout was off and running across the yard toward the oak tree that served as both his favorite shady spot to sit, and his favorite spot to mark at the end of every day. "Hurry . . . Hurry . . . Get it . . ." she shouted, only to transition into the wag-generating *Good job, Scout!* when he emerged from behind the massive trunk, victorious in his pursuit.

This time though, when he brought the ball back, she patted the empty spot on the step beside her and rewarded him with a chin and neck rub when he obliged. "I love you, Scout."

She didn't need words to know the feeling was mutual. It was there in Scout's eyes as he cocked first one, and then the other, at her. Sighing, she draped her arm around his neck and led his gaze back to the yard for a verbal tour of their current view.

The car pulling into their neighbor's driveway . . .

The teenager being paid to cut an elderly neighbor's yard . . .

The lawn flag across the street blowing ever so gently in the—

The ringing of her phone through the screen door brought Scout's eyes back to hers. "I know, don't worry. I don't intend to get trapped on the phone by anyone."

Rising, she trotted up the last two steps to her front door, plucked her phone off the catchall table just inside the front entryway, and took in the name on the screen as she carried it back to her spot beside Scout. "Big Max?" she said, pressing the phone to her ear.

"Emma? Is that you?"

"It is, Big Max. How are you?"

"I guess that depends on your response to the question I'm about to ask."

Her answering laugh earned her an adoring glance from Scout. "Are we going to another dance together?" Emma asked.

"Not this time, no." A beat of silence was quickly followed by a steady scraping sound. "This time I was hoping you'd be available to accompany me to a party—a *garden* party. And guess who's hosting it?"

"Who?"

"Beatrice." The scraping slowed. "Which means I'll have the opportunity to show her I'm not a one-trick pony."

She dug her hands into Scout's fur and slowly massaged the back of his neck. "A one-trick pony, eh?"

"That's right. Last week's dance at the senior center was all about showing her I've got moves. This garden party will be about demonstrating my ability to know a daffodil from a-a . . ." His words ceased in favor of what she'd bet good money was papers being shifted. "A dandelion!"

"Those are two very different things, Big Max. One is planted intentionally; the other is a weed."

"I read that, but that don't mean dandelions aren't pretty. Why, you come across a field of 'em, it's like looking at a sea of sunshine with all that yellow."

She moved on to Scout's head. "A sea of sunshine . . . I like that."

"Maybe Beatrice will, too." The scraping was back. "So? Can I hire you to go with me? I heard there will be food."

"When is this party?"

"Tomorrow."

"Tomorrow," she repeated as her thoughts narrowed in on her calendar and the empty square she knew she'd find.

"About noon."

"I—"

"I'll pay you the same as I did for the dance: five hundred dollars. And I'll even get you another corsage for your wrist."

She smiled. "I'm pretty sure corsages aren't needed for garden parties, Big Max."

"Just dances?"

"Just dances." Stilling her fingers atop Scout's head, Emma strained to make out something in the background of the call that could identify the source of the scraping, but there was nothing. "What's that scraping sound I'm hearing on your end?"

The sound stopped. "Scraping?"

"Yes."

"I don't hear any scraping."

"That's because it just stopped," she said.

"Sounds do that, sometimes," Big Max said. "They come and they go."

The scraping returned.

"There it is again, Big Max!"

The scraping stopped for a beat before starting up once again. "You mean *this* sound?"

"Yes. That sound."

"I'm refinishing a ukulele I found on top of someone's bulk trash pile." The scraping grew still louder and faster before ceasing completely. "*There.* Now all it needs is some fresh paint and some new strings and it'll be good as new."

"You know how to play the ukulele?" she asked, moving on to Scout's ears and chin.

"I don't, but I aim to learn. So? What do you say, Emma? Can I hire you to go with me tomorrow? Beatrice will be busy greeting everyone, I'm sure, but that don't mean she can't look over in my direction and catch me talking about flowers with you."

"You sure you don't want to ask one of those other ladies from the senior center? I mean, I know that one woman— Ethel, I think—seemed to have a real soft spot for you."

"No. I'm a one-woman man, Emma, and Beatrice is the woman I want to be eating French toast with each morning, God willing."

"What happens if Beatrice doesn't like cooking, let alone French toast?" she asked, only to find herself back-pedaling in the wake of his answering silence. "Actually, that was silly of me to say. I'm sure she loves French toast, Big Max. Who doesn't, right?"

"Right."

Her exhale of relief earned her a quizzical look from Scout. "Tomorrow at noon, you say?" she asked.

"That's right."

"Do you want to just give me the address and we'll meet there or—"

"Can you drive?" Big Max asked.

"I can."

"Good. Then I'll meet you at noon. Same spot as last time."

Chapter Fourteen

───•·•───

Emma was just a little over a block away from the senior center, heading south, when she caught sight of the shiny white top hat making haste down the sidewalk. Taking advantage of the four-way intersection between her car and her meeting spot with Big Max, she allowed herself a moment to take in the spectacle.

Shiny white top hat . . .

White dress shirt with black suspenders . . .

Red-and-white-striped knickerbockers . . .

White tube socks, trimmed in thick red . . .

Giggling, she waved another car through the intersection in an attempt to buy herself a little more stationary time and then looked back at the sidewalk and—

"Big Max?"

A horn behind her forced her hand off her mouth and back onto the steering wheel for the remaining half block to the bus stop. To her left on the opposite side of the street, a man walking his dog was so taken by the sight he nearly walked into a streetlamp, and a pair of schoolgirls fell against each other, laughing and pointing. On the road in front of her, in both directions, drivers were slowing—and in some cases stopping—to rubberneck.

And Big Max—the knickerbocker-wearing, top hat–sporting reason for it all—just kept right on walking, oblivious to everything except whatever tune his rounded lips were whistling. Breathing in the smile born from his clueless innocence, Emma pulled into the first open parking spot just beyond the bus stop and carefully exited her car onto the sidewalk.

"Big Max, I'm over here." She saw a passing driver slow still further, glance from Emma in her floral sundress to Big Max in his outfit, and then grab for his phone to immortalize the image for the world to see.

"So? What do you think?" Big Max asked, striding over to the car. "Do you think I'll catch Beatrice's eye at her garden party today?"

Nibbling back a laugh, Emma willed herself to keep any and all sarcasm from the reassurance he sought. But when she forgot the slowing cars at her back (and the peals of laughter from the other side of the street) and let herself truly see the hope emblazoned on her new friend's face, it wasn't hard at all.

"If Beatrice knows a good thing when she sees it, you will most definitely catch her eye, Big Max."

He paused beside the car just long enough to check his reflection in the passenger-side window, her words igniting a painfully sweet smile on his leathery face. "I sure hope you're right, Emma."

"I am; don't you worry." She reopened her door but held his eye contact above the roof of her car. "Shall we go?"

He answered by opening the passenger door, removing his hat, and carefully lowering himself onto the seat while she reclaimed her own spot behind the steering wheel. "So, do you know how to get where we're going, or do you have the invitation with you so I can plug the address into the car?" she asked.

"I don't have an invitation. But I know Beatrice lives out on Walloby Road. Heard her say it with my own two ears one day." He buckled himself into place and then pointed her back onto the road. "House is white. With black shutters."

"Got it." Shifting into drive, Emma maneuvered out of the parking spot and headed south, the car's movement welcoming a pleasant breeze into the car. "So, how's the ukulele coming along? Did you get any more work done on it after we spoke yesterday?"

Big Max extended his arm along the passenger-side windowsill and tapped his fingers in a steady pattern. "I went looking for some string, but the only string I could find was attached to a kite. So I settled on some rubber bands I found in the bottom of a drawer and they make a real nice sound."

She stopped at the end of the road and stole a glance in his direction. "Rubber bands?" she echoed. "They really work?"

"Like a champ. But you'll see for yourself when I have one of those lawn concerts. Everyone can bring blankets and food and it'll be a real nice time. You can sit with Beatrice while I'm playing the ukulele for everyone. When I'm done, you can keep right on sitting with Beatrice and me because we'll have plenty of food to share—chicken, and grapes, and wine. Although, truth be told"—he glanced across at Emma—"I'd prefer a soda pop over wine, but that's not the way it's done at picnics or lawn concerts."

A right turn put them on Main Street heading west. They passed the gym, the library, the coffee shop, the town hall, and Deeter's. At the crosswalk to the town's green, she slowed to allow a young mother and her two children to pass in front of the car before resuming the posted speed limit.

"It's nice to see the flowers looking the way they do, isn't it?" Big Max stopped tapping his fingers to point at the flowering bushes around the gazebo. "Don't matter to me none why it stopped looking the way it did. I'm just glad that it's back to being pretty again. It's like we *all* get a fancy award that way."

She looked across at him, his words tickling her thoughts in a most peculiar way. "Fancy award? What do you—"

Her phone's ringtone filled the cabin and drew her eyes to the dashboard screen.

DOTTIE ADLER

"I'm sorry, Big Max, but I probably should take this in case there's a problem." At his nod, she took her right hand off the steering wheel just long enough to press the green button. "Hey, Dottie, is everything okay?"

"He had a drug in his system his doctor didn't give him."

Confused, Emma turned up the volume on her speakers. "I'm sorry, Dottie, I'm not sure I caught that. Can you say it again?"

The answering sigh-to-end-all-sighs had her backing the volume down a notch before Dottie began speaking again. "I *said*, he had a drug in his system his doctor didn't give him."

"Who and what are we talking about?"

The sigh was back, only it was even louder and more put-out than the first one. "Our *victim*, dear. Who else?"

"You mean *Brian*?"

"Unless there's been another murder of which I'm un-aware, yes, I'm talking about Mr. Hill."

Nerves had her glancing in Big Max's direction. Intrigue had her looking back at Dottie's name. "How do you know this?"

"I have my ways, dear."

"Your *ways*?"

"Yes."

She slowed at yet another crosswalk and then, when the road was clear, continued west toward Walloby Road. "And you're sure this is accurate information?"

"The total in my checking account this morning assures me of that."

"*Dottie?* What did you do?"

"I sent a donation to the sheriff's department, dear. Just like I do every year. Only this time I called it into Rhonda, Sheriff Borlin's secretary—a dear, *dear* friend of mine I haven't spoken to nearly enough in the past year. I took advantage of my desire to donate to the new gym they're putting in for the officers to catch up on her family, her knitting club, and, of course, our shared horror over a murder in our beloved Sweet Falls."

"Of course." Emma pressed her head back against the seat rest and released her own sigh. "So what you're telling me is that you bribed the sheriff's secretary for details of the autopsy . . ."

"Not just details, dear. The whole report. And I bribed no one. I *donated*. To a worthy cause. There is a difference."

She didn't mean to laugh. Or, actually, maybe she did. Either way, she didn't try to call it back. Still, her mirth dissipated quickly as the crux of what Dottie had said took its rightful place in her thoughts. "So it really was drugs, huh? That surprises me a little. I mean, I realize I'd only met Brian that night, but I just can't picture him being involved in recreational drugs. It just doesn't fit."

"Because it wasn't a recreational drug. It was a medicinal drug."

"But you said his doctor didn't give it to him."

"According to Rhonda, he didn't," Dottie mused.

"Then—"

"Oh, I have to go, dear. It looks as if Stephanie is calling on the other line and Glenda needs to accompany me across the street before . . ." Dottie's voice trailed off momentarily, only to return just as quickly. "Is that *you*, dear?"

"Is what me?" Slowing at the first sign of cars lining both sides of Walloby Road, Emma nodded as Big Max pointed at a white Victorian with black shutters on their left.

"The whole creeping-up-the-street-like-a-veritable-stalker thing you're doing right now."

"What are you talking about?" She stopped talking as her gaze, which had been sweeping both sides of the street in search of a parking spot, landed on a wheelchair-bound woman seated next to a silver van with a phone in her hand and a look of utter shock on her face. "*Dottie?* What are you doing here?"

"I believe the more appropriate question is, What are *you* doing here?"

"I'm going to some sort of garden party at the house just across from where you're standing."

"Some *sort* of garden party?"

"Yes. Big Max said it's—"

"Maxwell is with you?" Dottie asked, lifting her hand to her salon-styled hair. "*Here?*"

"If by here you mean seated next to me, yes."

Wedging her phone between her face and her shoulder, Dottie backed herself behind the car and thus out of Emma's view. "I have to go, dear. Stephanie is trying again."

Chapter Fifteen

"Invitation, please."

Emma shifted her attention from the well-dressed gate attendant to Big Max and back again. "He left that behind. Fortunately for me, though, the right street name, coupled with the near-constant flow of people up the front sidewalk, was all we needed to know we'd found the right place."

The young woman's answering sigh hung in the still afternoon air even after her crystal-blue eyes dove down to the clipboard clutched firmly between manicured fingers. "Your name?"

"Sure. I'm Emma West—actually, no. My name isn't going to do any good as I'm just a guest." Stepping to the side, she waved Big Max into her spot. "She needs your name."

Tucking his thumbs underneath his suspenders, he expanded his chest with pride. "Big Max, at your service."

"Oh, you're part of the serving . . ." The rest of the question died on the twentysomething's lips as she finally looked up, her mouth gaping and then tightening as she took in Big Max's top hat . . . suspenders . . . knickerbockers . . . and, finally, his knee-high sports socks. "I asked for a *strolling magician*," she hissed through clenched teeth. "Not a *clown*."

Like Scout at the mention of a treat (or a walk, or a squirrel), Big Max whirled around, his eyes wide with hope. "Clown? Here? Where?"

A flash of anger zipped Emma's own gaze back to the attendant. "He is here as a *guest* of Beatrice, and *I* am a guest of *his*."

The woman looked from Emma to Big Max and back again, her irritation slowly morphing into amusement. "A guest?"

"That's right."

"Without an invitation . . ."

Emma pointed to the flipped-over page on the woman's clipboard. "His name, as he already told you, is Max."

Again, the attendant's gaze moved from Emma to Big Max, who was still searching for a clown, and back again, her voice fairly dripping with condescension. "Does *Max* have a last name?"

"Of course." Yet even as her mouth closed over her own snippy retort, Emma realized she didn't know the answer. And, based on the ever-growing glint in the attendant's eye, that was becoming more and more apparent with each passing—

"His last name is *Grayben*. G-r-a-y-b-e-n." Emma's eyes snapped toward the now-open gate to find Dottie shooting her own visual daggers at the attendant. "But as they are *my* guests, there is no need to delay their entry with any more of this unnecessary nonsense."

The young woman's swallow was audible as she stole another look at Big Max, her shock palpable. "Of—of course. I—"

"We're going inside now." Dottie backed her wheelchair through the gate and motioned for Emma to follow. "Come along, dear."

Reaching back, Emma grabbed Big Max by the arm and tugged him through the gate, stopping once he was safely inside to lob a final—and oh-so-triumphant—glare at the still-stunned, clipboard-wielding woman.

"She was just doing her job," Dottie murmured as Emma stepped away from the now-closed gate.

"What? Being nasty to—" She swallowed back the rest of her sentence as their surroundings came into focus. To their left, positioned around a waterfall feature flanked by flowering shrubs, was a smattering of quaint tables and chairs housing well-dressed pairs and trios. To their right, along a lavishly landscaped walkway that came and went through an archway of morning glories, were even more groups of people, some holding wineglasses, some munching on finger foods being passed around by a uniformed serving staff, and some enjoying both as they periodically glanced toward an empty podium clearly set up for some sort of talk. "Whoa!"

"And thus the reason for the list, dear."

"I thought this was just some sort of small backyard party."

"It's the Sweet Falls Garden Club and Beautification Committee's annual gathering, Emma. It's one of the biggest and most lavish private parties of the year, which means its guest list is quite exclusive, to say the least."

Emma glanced at Big Max, who was walking from server to server peeking at the various trays of hors d'oeuvres. "And Big Max made the cut?"

Dottie's lips quivered with the faintest hint of a smile. "No."

"Then how did he score an invite?"

Dottie's gaze traveled across the backyard to yet another contingent of servers that had drawn the interest of Big Max. "I'm quite certain he didn't, dear."

"Then how did he—"

I don't have an invitation. But I know Beatrice lives out on Walloby Road. Heard her say it with my own two ears one day.

"He just overheard someone talking about it, didn't he?" Emma mumbled, raking her fingers through her hair. "Oh, Dottie . . . I-I had no idea . . . We shouldn't be here . . ."

"It's fine. My invitation said I could bring up to three guests." Dottie chinned Emma's gaze to their left and their right. "Besides, he helps offset a little of the pretentiousness, don't you think?"

Again, Emma took in the top hat . . . the suspenders . . . the knickerbockers . . . the athletic socks. "He has a crush on the woman hosting this," she murmured.

"I know."

Emma dropped her attention to her friend. "He doesn't stand a chance, Dottie."

"I know."

"It breaks my heart."

"Mine, too."

She sat with that for a moment while Big Max checked one last tray and then, shoulders slumped, began the trek back across the yard in their direction. "That was really nice of you to vouch for us out there the way you did." She nudged her own chin toward the spectacle that was Big Max at a garden party for the elite. "So, how do you know him?"

"Maxwell?" Dottie countered Emma's nod with a shrug. "He was a friend of Alfred's."

Disbelief pushed Emma back a step. "A friend of *Alfred's*? Really?"

"You sound surprised."

"Because I am. I mean, Alfred was so refined, so—" And then she knew. "So *bighearted*."

Dottie nodded, cleared her throat of the same emotion that glistened her eyes, and then wheeled her way toward an empty table with enough space for her wheelchair and seats for Emma and Big Max. "I spoke with Stephanie briefly. She'll take a look at the autopsy report with us on Saturday, over breakfast."

"How very appetizing," Emma said, trailing behind the woman. "Are you sure about this? I mean, I would imagine this contact of yours could get in big trouble for sharing *anything* about the case, let alone the actual preliminary autopsy report."

"My donation was more than generous, dear. And no one will know."

"I'll know . . . Stephanie will know . . ."

"As we should if we're going to solve this case." Dottie engaged her chair's brake and pointed Emma onto a neighboring seat. "In the meantime, we need a game plan."

"For?"

"For striking while the iron is hot. Or, in laymen's terms pertinent to this specific opportunity, taking advantage of an opportunity when wine is flowing and people are hiding behind their party faces."

She tried to connect the nonsensical dots without asking for help, but it was no use. Somehow, someway, she'd missed a significant shift in conversational topics. "You lost me, Dottie . . . Wine? Party faces? What am I missing?"

"People tend to let down their inhibitions when liquor is involved." Dottie accepted a glass of water from a passing server and took a sip. "Which means we could get lucky."

Emma's left eyebrow rose of its own volition. "Oh?"

"The fact that Alfred was a founding member of this group would make it stand to reason that the new mayor's wife will approach at some point. When she does, we need to be ready with our—"

"Wait. Rita Gerard is coming here? To this party?"

"She's already here, dear. See?"

Emma followed Dottie's pointed finger to the flowered archway and the slender blonde she recognized from the newspaper, the fateful night at Deeter's, and the picture currently immortalized on her phone. "Oh. Wow. Did you know she would be here like this?"

"It's why I came, Emma."

"Wow. Okay, so yeah . . . Interesting."

"And then there's *her*." This time, Dottie's finger led her attention toward a woman seated by herself at the table closest to the water feature, her back to Emma. "Whom, truth be told, I'm rather surprised to see here, all things considered."

Emma bobbed her head to the left and right in an attempt to make out the woman's identity, but to no avail. Still, there was something familiar about the stocky build, the sprinkling of gray in an otherwise dark head of hair, the—

"I looked on every tray and on every plate I could find, but there's not a single cocktail wiener anywhere." Big Max dropped onto the vacant seat across from Emma, his top hat swaying as he shook his head slowly in disbelief. "And the clown? I didn't find him, either."

It was on the tip of her tongue to tell him there would be no clown and no cocktail wieners but, before she could, he broke out in a grin. "But I think you and me going places together is working like a real charm, Emma."

"Oh?" Abandoning her efforts to put a name to the lone figure she still couldn't fully see, Emma willed her focus back to her own table. "Why is that, Big Max?"

"I saw Beatrice looking at me as I was talking to a few of the servers and she couldn't take her eyes off me."

She exchanged glances with Dottie, the sadness she saw in the octogenarian's eyes surely a reflection of her own. Still, it wasn't in her nature to knowingly burst someone's bubble, and so she went with the closest thing to a smile she could muster while sending up a silent prayer of gratitude for the new server with the all-new tray of hors d'oeuvres that stole Big Max from the table.

"I feel like a heel staying silent about something that's

never, ever going to happen," Emma murmured as she tracked Big Max and the server toward the group gathering on the podium side of the archway. "But I think I'd feel even worse if I told him. Like I was somehow crushing a dream, you know?"

An odd sound sent her attention skittering back to Dottie in time to see the woman close her eyes with a slow, pained nod. Reaching across the table between them, Emma covered the elderly woman's hand with her own and squeezed. "It must be both hard and also satisfying to see a group Alfred started being this successful and this well-supported."

"It is. On both accounts. But he wouldn't have wanted to see what has happened to the group—the gossiping, the boasting, the pettiness. He was drawn to flowers for their quiet beauty. The ugliness that has sprung up around them in his absence would pain him. Deeply. Especially this unpleasantness toward *Nancy*." Dottie led Emma's attention toward the water feature and the lone figure staring into it. "He had a soft spot for her."

"Nancy *Davis*?" At Dottie's nod, Emma again took in the stocky build and the salt-and-pepper hair and silently chastised herself for not recognizing the obvious from the start. "It seems to me to be a clear-cut case of spotlight envy."

"Meaning?" Dottie prodded.

"Meaning, Nancy made Sweet Falls look like a million bucks last year. So much so it garnered the accolades of the club's state-level counterpart. And instead of being grateful for the positive press her efforts earned for all of us, jealousy reared its head, as it often does." Emma slid her attention back to the blonde on the other side of the yard, a woman clearly at home in the center of a group. "The fact that it was spawned by someone seen as more important just made it all the more effective. Sadly.

"But you know how it is, Dottie. Far too many people are incapable of leaving the petty jealousy of their high school days behind." Shaking her head, Emma pushed her chair back from the table and stood. "I'll be right back."

With one last glance at Big Max, who'd clearly found a serving tray worthy of a second look, Emma made her way around the smattering of tables to the far side of the extensive patio space. The corner in which Nancy had chosen to sit offered a stunning view of the small garden waterfall that cascaded over a rocky ledge and culminated in a narrow river-like body that meandered its way along the northern edge of the property. Yet, as Emma drew closer to Nancy's table, it was clear the gardening professional saw none of it. Instead, the woman's eyes darted between groups of people, her loneliness seemingly unnoticed or of no concern to anyone but Emma.

"I thought that was you, Nancy—hello! It's nice to see you here."

Startled, the woman looked up. "Oh, hello, Emma. Did you just get here?"

"Ten, fifteen minutes ago, maybe. How about you?"

"I've been here since it started."

She pointed to the empty chair across from Nancy's and, at the woman's nod, lowered herself onto the cushioned seat. "I'm not surprised you picked this spot," Emma said, motioning toward the waterfall. "It's beyond beautiful."

"Thank you."

Swinging her focus back to Nancy, she nodded knowingly. "I kind of figured you had something to do with this."

"Designed it myself."

"Wow. It's really something." Again, Emma took in the water as it cascaded over the ledge and then slowly made its way across rounded stones. "Something like this, in the town square, would be so cool, don't you think?"

"It would. But it won't happen. Not under the new regime, anyway. And if by some miracle they decided to go all-in on the town square with something like this, I wouldn't be the one brought in to do it."

Emma followed the water down to its point of recirculation and then looked back at Nancy. "Regardless, I would imagine your phone will be ringing off the hook after today. From people who see this here and then want you to do something just like it in the backyard of their own home."

Nancy's answering laugh lacked anything resembling joy. "Had this party been a month ago, you would probably be right. But, alas, it wasn't and, therefore, you're not."

"What's changed?"

Sliding her fingertips beneath the bottom rim of her glasses, Nancy kneaded the skin beside her eyes. "Everything that matters."

Emma opened her mouth to ask for clarification but closed it as her gaze—led by Nancy's—came to rest on the impeccably dressed blonde now sitting where Emma herself had sat not more than three minutes earlier.

"I despise that woman."

"Rita Gerard?" At Nancy's slow, yet no less emphatic nod, Emma slanted one last glance at the mayor's wife before settling her full attention on her own tablemate. "I know you said she caused some trouble for you after the state award, but I thought the committee as a whole wised up and brought you back in."

"They did."

"So then I don't get this silent treatment you seem to be getting. What you've done to the town square is literally award-winning. And what you've done here"—she motioned toward the waterfall—"is like something out of a magazine."

Nancy peered over at the waterfall and the near-continuous stream of two- and three-person groups opting by for a closer look. "At one time, that would've been enough for people. But, as I said, everything has changed. No longer is it about beauty for the sake of beauty. It's about being noticed, about climbing ladders, about checking boxes, about getting to the next level of importance, and about making sure you're the person seen as having done all of that."

"It sounds so cutthroat."

"Because it is. Or, at least, the fallout for those who try to fight it is."

"Fallout?"

Nancy's eyes flashed with anger as they lit on Emma. "What else would you call it?"

"I don't know. I don't get the way you're being treated. I really don't." Emma traveled her gaze back to Dottie's table just long enough to confirm her elderly friend was still talking to Rita and then looked back at Nancy to find any and all anger had been replaced by . . . *surprise*? "I mean, how can there be jealousy over something that should've been a good thing for everyone? It seems so counterproductive to me, so short-sighted. But since they clearly came to their senses and brought you back in, shouldn't that mean it's over?"

"It should. And it was. But . . ." Nancy drew in a breath and held it for a beat, maybe two. "I take it you missed the memo, or the letter, or however it was put out there?"

Emma drew back, the answering wobble of her chair against the patio turning more than a few eyes in their direction. "Memo? Letter? I have no idea what you're talking about."

Nancy stared at her for a moment, her gaze one of disbelief. "Huh . . . Wow. Maybe my therapist has been right these last few weeks. Maybe people have just been busy. And for those who haven't been, maybe memories actually *will* fade in time."

Grabbing her purse from its resting spot beside her elbow, Nancy pushed back her chair and stood. "This has been the boost I needed. Thank you for that, Emma. In fact, why don't you stop out at my place sometime in the next few days and you can pick out the seedling of your choice. On the house."

Chapter Sixteen

"I see you had a guest while I was gone." Emma slid onto her chair across from Dottie and took a quick sip of water. "How'd that go?"

Pushing her appetizer plate to the side, Dottie wiped her mouth with a floral napkin. "It was what it always is with the mayor's wife, dear—a photo op."

"It looked to me like you two were talking."

"About the weather? Yes. About the food? Yes. About the turnout today? Yes. About our case and her presence on Mr. Hill's own suspect list? No. As it is, she only stopped at my table because of the many different boxes I fill."

Emma took another sip, inspected the lone piece of food on Dottie's discarded plate, and, at the nod of agreement she sought, helped herself to the bacon-wrapped shrimp. "Meaning?"

"I'm elderly, I'm confined to a wheelchair, I'm the wife of the committee's late founder, and I have a reputation for having deep pockets when it comes to Sweet Falls."

"Wow." Emma polished off the shrimp and sank back

against her chair. "Between you and Nancy, this Rita Gerard woman really sounds like a complete piece of work."

"The Cinderella of Sweet Falls."

"Excuse me?"

The corners of Dottie's mouth twitched with a quick smile. "Alfred had a keen sense about people, that's all."

"Is that something he called Rita? The Cinderella of Sweet Falls?"

"Yes. And that was before Sebastian ran for—and won—the mayoral seat," Dottie mused. "I must say, Alfred would be mighty proud of the accuracy of that name if he were still here, God rest his soul."

"I take it Rita married up?" Emma asked. "At least in Alfred's eyes?"

"From being the town clerk's secretary to being the mayor's wife? You tell me." Dottie fingered the armrest on her wheelchair, her voice taking on a faraway quality. "I miss Alfred's little names for people. They were always so clever, so accurate. But he was an observer. He noticed things in a way few people do—including, at times, myself."

"Did he have a name for me?"

"He called you Emma."

She pulled a face. "That's it?"

"That's it."

"But that's so—so . . . *boring*. So un-special."

"It's what he called you, dear."

"Huh. Well, moving right along . . ." Emma took another sip of her water and chased it down with a bacon crumb she found on her napkin. "My little chat with Nancy earned me a free plant. Woo-hoo!"

"Why?"

"I don't know, exactly. We were talking, I said something, she mentioned something about a memo or a letter and how I clearly hadn't seen it and—Boom!—she was telling me to stop on out at the farm for a free plant."

"What memo?" Dottie asked.

"I don't know. I got sidetracked by the free plants."

Dottie looked daggers at Emma. "Did you get *anything*?"

"Nope, just—wait! Yes, yes I did! She designed that waterfall thingy over there and it's even cooler up close than it appears from over here!"

"There is no denying Nancy's prowess in the garden."

"Yet, somehow, it *was* denied." Emma wiped her mouth with the corner of her own linen napkin. "By enough people—including your little photo-op buddy—that she was actually ousted from her own committee for a while."

Tsking softly under her breath, Dottie waved a server over to the table to collect her empty plate. When the surface was cleared and they were alone again, the woman adjusted her glasses on her nose and leaned forward so as to be heard by no one but Emma. "Did she say anything else? Anything we can use to either take her off our list or move her to the top?"

"You mean, *Nancy*?"

The dagger was back, only this one was even more squirm-inducing than the first. "Yes, *Nancy*. She *is* one of our suspects, if you recall."

"If I recall? Seriously?" Emma took a gulp of water. "I'm the one Brian handed that headache to, not you. You've *chosen* to get involved, Dottie."

"Because a man is dead, dear, and you're clearly out of your element in regard to sleuthing."

"I'm a travel agent, Dottie."

Dottie's eyebrow arched. "Are you?"

"Fine. I *was* a travel agent." Emma drained the last of her glass. "Now I'm—I don't know. A paid friend. To two people. *Three* if you choose to count yourself. But whether you do or don't, or whether I'm actually able to make a go of this"—she cast about for the right word—"*business idea* or not, I know one thing for certain. I am not, nor have I ever wanted to be, a cop. So if I'm *out of my element* as you say, that not only makes perfect sense, it's also fine by me."

"You didn't think my business suggestion would work, either."

She stared at the elderly woman. "And it hasn't. My first client is dead, remember?"

"You have two others and *they're* still alive."

"You mean Stephanie and Big Max? I only have them because you gave them my number and told them I could be their paid companion."

"Yes, and I'm still waiting for my thank-you on that."

Her humorless laugh echoed around them as she grabbed hold of the new water glass that appeared at her elbow and took yet another, even bigger gulp. "You want some sleuthing? Here's some sleuthing for you . . . First, the only suspect list I could imagine Nancy Davis being on would be one in which Mayor Gerard's wife was the victim. Second, Rita Gerard, on the other hand, might be the one we should shift to the top of our list because there was most definitely something there between the two of them."

Dottie leaned forward. "Rita and Mr. Hill?"

"Yep."

"And this is based on what, dear? The fact that Mr. Hill handed you a paper essentially saying as much?"

She lowered her glass back to the table, counted to ten silently in her head, and shrugged. "No, it's based on my *own* investigation."

"Your investigation?" Dottie echoed. "What investigation?"

"The one I started"—she matched Dottie's lean with her own—"on my own the other night."

"You don't know *how* to investigate!"

"No? Then tell me how I know that one of our suspects publicly accused our victim of trying to color people's opinion of her husband? *And* lambasted the *Sweet Falls Gazette* for giving him a place in which to do it?"

Dottie seemed to consider Emma's words only to dismiss them with an emphatic flick of her hand. "That's nothing new."

"Oh? Then how about the fact that, less than a week before his death, Brian did a little calling out of his own where Rita was concerned."

The war between intrigue and ego played out on Dottie's gently lined face, with intrigue coming out on top. "In what way, dear?"

"It took almost a month, but he commented on the on-line version of her public callout."

"How do you know it was Mr. Hill?"

"Because he commented under his own name." Emma reached inside her purse and extracted the slip of paper on which she'd copied Brian's response. "This is what he wrote: *The pot calling the kettle black. How very interesting. Do you want to address that, Rita, or should I?*"

Lifting her gaze back to Dottie, she slid the scrap of paper across the table. "So, while we don't know to what he was referring, I *do* think it's safe to assume they had issues with one another. Maybe even big ones."

"How did you find this?" Dottie murmured, pulling the paper close.

"I did a little searching online."

"On Rita?"

"No. On Brian. In particular, things he may have written or that were written about him prior to his murder. A letter to the editor from Rita popped up." Emma waited for Dottie to stop reading. "I was perusing the comments to her letter when I came across *that*."

Dottie read it a second time, only to look up at Emma again as she reached the end. "This reads like a threat."

"I think so, too."

Again, Dottie looked at the paper, her earlier intrigue segueing into unmistakable joy. "Oooohhhh, this is good, Emma! Really, really good."

"Still think I'm out of my element with this stuff?" she countered.

"Don't boast, dear. It's beneath you."

"Right." Emma scanned the patio and the grounds but came up empty in the top hat department. "Have you seen Big Max?"

"I haven't."

"Should I be worried?" she asked.

"Perhaps." Dottie, too, scanned the crowd and the grounds, her expression unreadable. "Then again, since Beatrice is holding court by the rose-covered trellis, I imagine Maxwell can't be far away."

"Do you think he'll figure it out anytime soon?"

"What? That Beatrice is as blind as she is fake?" Dottie said, only to dismiss her own words, and any answer Emma might give with yet another flick of her hand. "To each his own, dear. To each his own."

"True." Emma took one last look around the grounds before returning her full attention to the woman seated on the opposite side of the table. "Part of me is afraid to keep going with this business idea in light of what happened."

"You must always get back on the horse after you've been thrown."

"But my first and only found-by-me client died right in front of me. *At* the very event for which I was hired to be his plus-one." Leaning back in her chair, Emma ran her fingertip around the edge of her drinking glass. "That's a little defeating."

"Perhaps. But this party today is your *second* job for Maxwell and *he's* still alive, yes?"

"I certainly hope so."

"And you've worked how many times with Stephanie?"

"It was *supposed* to be three, but instead, on day three, we met at your place for breakfast."

"*She's* still alive . . ."

"True. But you found both of them *for* me. Brian is the only one I found on my own and he's the one who's dead."

"The only way to offset that percentage is through more clients, Emma. More *alive* clients, that is."

She knew it was wrong to laugh, but still, she did. "I'll do my best to keep that in mind. Thank you."

"You're welcome. For the business idea *and* the advice."

"Cocktail wiener?"

Startled, Emma looked up to find Big Max, standing beside her chair, holding a tray of cocktail wieners arranged, pyramid-like, atop a . . . *paper plate*? "Big Max? Where have you been?"

"Beatrice said people's pockets are deepest when they are happy and well-fed."

Emma grinned up at Big Max. "The two of you spoke?"

"I wanted to, but by the time I got around the thing with the roses on it, the man in the black pants was gone. And so was Beatrice." Big Max looked down at his tray just long enough to reposition a cocktail wiener that had fallen off the pile. "I checked a few more trays to see if the man in the black pants listened, but he didn't. He just sent out more of the same things. And that's when I decided to help out."

She traded glances with Dottie. "Help out *how*?"

"I paid a young fella who was sitting out front to go to the store and get me a box of these. But he already had one in the freezer at his house." Big Max pointed at a puddle of ketchup on the far edge of the plate. "He didn't have mustard for people to swirl them around in, but that's okay. Ketchup will be fine this time. "

He held the plate closer to Emma. "Take one, quick. They won't last long in a crowd like this."

Chapter Seventeen

With one last look around the kitchen, Emma flipped off the overhead light and ventured into the hallway, Scout close on her heels. Everything that needed to be done was done. Her dinner dish had been cleaned and put away, the leftovers from her dinner-for-one had been wrapped and placed in the refrigerator, and Scout's water dish had been topped off for the night ahead. Yet the normal pull to end her night snuggled on the couch with Scout while watching some sort of hopelessly romantic movie wasn't there. Instead, there was a restlessness, an urge to do or to accomplish something.

When her home travel agency job was what it had once been, such a restlessness would have led to researching new resorts online, or sending follow-up emails to previous clients in the hope it might spark a new booking, or uploading a few client-submitted travel pictures to her website. But those days were over now.

Stopping outside her office door, she took in the floor-to-ceiling bookshelves still teeming with travel books, the bulletin board on which she'd tacked some of her favorite notes from clients over the years, the framed map showing all the places her clients had visited, and the blackened screen of a computer that was no longer powered on twenty-four/seven. She still loved the room, loved the way it reflected her business, but—

"I'm not a travel agent anymore," she said, glancing down at Scout. "Am I?"

Scout's tongue disappeared for as long as it took him to swallow. When it reappeared along with a wag of his tail, he led the way into the office, lay down beside her desk chair, and looked back at Emma expectantly.

"There isn't anything for me to do, boy. No trips to plan. No website tweaks to make. No invoices to send out. And, sadly, no checks to mobile deposit. I was just . . ." She scanned the room again. "I was just looking, that's all. And maybe doing a little remembering.

"Either way, there's no reason for you to be getting all cozy like that. There's nothing I have to do except maybe start perusing the employment ads or looking up names of headhunters I should probably reach out to next week." She pushed at both notions as if they were a weight bearing down on her shoulders. "Neither of which I want to do right now, boy. So, c'mon, let's find something to watch, okay?"

Scout, in turn, nestled his chin onto his front paws.

"C'mon, Scout. It's time to snuggle on the couch."

Lifting his head for a moment, Scout looked back at Emma, dropped his gaze to the hallway beyond, and then rested his chin atop his paws once again.

"You do realize you're killing me, right?" She stepped all the way into the room and stopped in front of the world map. Red pushpins for romantic trips. Blue pushpins for adventure trips. Yellow pushpins for all of the corporate trips that had kept her afloat longer than she might have otherwise been. "So many clients. So many trips-of-a-lifetime booked and executed. And now it's all over."

Sighing, she sank onto her desk chair. "I liked running my own thing, and being my own boss. I was good at it. *Really* good at it," she murmured.

She poked at her pen holder, her desk calendar, and the paperweight a favorite client had given her after a successful safari in Africa before stilling her finger and her gaze atop the stack of business cards she'd so carefully designed just nine days earlier.

A Friend for Hire

For all those plus-one moments

She'd been so excited when she'd come up with the name for her new business. And she'd been equally excited when the tagline had appeared—fully formed—during yet another burst of creativity. Suddenly, the idea she'd found to be so ludicrous at first mention had actually seemed . . . *possible*.

"It could have been so cool. Definitely something I could've gotten some press on." She ran her finger across her own name in the card's bottom right-hand corner and, again, across the email address she'd opened specifically for A Friend for Hire. "I had Big Max . . . I had Stephanie . . . And within hours of putting myself out there all on my own, I had . . ."

Covering her ears against the remembered thud of Brian's body as it hit the stage, Emma willed herself to breathe, to think, to focus on the silence Nancy had mentioned yet she couldn't remember. Maybe Dottie was right. Maybe the best way to offset the whole one-in-three thing was to keep going instead of giving up.

"If Big Max needed me, and Stephanie needed me, and"—she plucked the top card off the stack—"*Brian* had needed me, surely there are others, right?"

Scout lifted his head off his paw, looked Emma in the eye, and wagged his tail.

"You're too much, Scout, you know that?" Leaning over the armrest of her chair, she ran her hand down Scout's back, his love for her every bit as tangible as the collar he wore around his neck. "And I couldn't be luckier to have you."

A quick bark, followed by another wag of his tail, propelled her back against her chair and her fingers toward her computer's power button. Seconds later, she typed the community bulletin board into her search bar and, with a few clicks, found herself staring at the very same virtual notice that had led Brian to call.

A FRIEND FOR HIRE
FOR ALL THOSE PLUS-ONE MOMENTS

NEED A PLUS-ONE FOR THAT WEDDING YOU'VE BEEN DREADING? AN ACCOUNTABILITY PARTNER FOR THOSE RUNS YOU'VE BEEN PUTTING OFF? A COMPANION FOR THAT TRIP YOU DON'T WANT TO TAKE ALONE?

EMMA WESTLAKE OF A FRIEND FOR HIRE HAS GOT YOU COVERED.

CALL OR EMAIL TODAY.

She read the notice a second time and then, on a whim, minimized the screen in favor of her go-to email program and the inbox she'd created specifically for A Friend for Hire. After two tried—and failed—passwords, she got lucky on her third guess and opened her inbox to find three unread messages.

The first, based on the subject line and sender, was from the Sweet Falls town clerk confirming the details of Emma's ad, along with notice of payment received. She opened the message, made sure everything was correct, and then moved it to a folder created specifically for tax records.

Next, she returned to the main inbox and the second unread message.

Need Help.

Intrigued, she read the unfamiliar name in the sender field and opened the message.

Hello.

My name is Andy Walden and I live off Route 15 in Clover-ton. I know this is a Sweet Falls site, but I'm hoping you might consider making the trip out to my place if the pay is right. I'm being sent out of town for work early next month and I need someone who can look in on my dad and make sure he's eating and behaving himself in my absence. He'll be able to reach me while I'm gone, of course, but knowing I have someone actually stopping in and checking on him would reduce a lot of stress for me.

   Please let me know if you'll even consider coming out this way, and if so, I'll need a few references.

Thank you,
Andy

"That's promising." She returned her attention to the top of the email and the date it had been sent and felt her whole body deflate in response. "Well, that's just great . . . Nice going there, Emma. Nothing like blowing an opportunity."
   Positioning her fingers on the keyboard, Emma typed the apology the man was due.

Mr. Walden,

I am sorry I'm just now getting back to you on this. Although my delayed response might indicate otherwise, I am a very reliable person. If you've yet to find someone to look in on your father during your absence, I'd be interested in hearing more.

Again, my apologies.
Emma Westlake

After a second read turned up no misspellings or egregious grammar issues, Emma crossed her fingers, hit Send, and moved on to the final unread message in her inbox, her breath hitching at the sight of the sender's name.

Brian Hill

"What on earth?"

She didn't need to look at Scout to know he'd picked up on the sudden tension in the room. She could feel it, just as surely as she could feel her heart rate accelerating. A glance at the date it was sent had her palms beginning to sweat, as well.

Clicking on the empty subject field, she opened the one-sentence message.

For your records.

"For my records?" she murmured. "What's for my . . ." The question faded into nothing as her gaze fell on the attachment at the bottom.

OPEN MIC NIGHT BOMB

She stared at the words for a minute, maybe more, her thoughts locked in a classic game of *do-I* or *don't-I*. She looked again at the empty subject line, the three-word sentence in the body of the email, the name on the attachment, and, finally, the time it had been sent.

9:33 p.m.

Three minutes after the scheduled start of Open Mic Night . . .

An Open Mic Night that had started right on time, as noted by Brian, himself, as he stood and—

"Just in case."

Rocketing upright in her chair, she revisited the moment the owner of Deeter's came out on the stage. She heard him address the crowd . . . She heard him call Brian's name . . . She saw Brian stand . . . She saw him glance across the table at her and—

"Hit a button on his phone," she whispered as, once again, the last words he'd said to her—words that had made no sense in the moment—filled her thoughts.

"Just in case."

With hands that were beginning to tremble, Emma clicked open the JPG attachment and leaned in for a closer look, the first line of the photographed page sending a shiver down her spine.

> *Look around, look around, here sit those you*
>   *laud,*
> *But soon you, too, will know their fraud.*
>
> *I say it often, I say it now,*
> *Unmasking truth, this is my vow.*
>
> *For far too long you've turned a blind eye,*
> *Their misdeeds hidden by a wink and*
>   *a smile.*
>
> *But it's in seeking the truth that you learn the*
>   *true why;*
> *The laws sidestepped, the roles—*

She stopped, gathered her breath, and continued to read, each new stanza representing another word, another line Brian had been deprived of sharing—until now.

> —they defile.

> The jaw that flaps nonstop revels in the juiciest
>   of stories.
> And is willing to sabotage her own work to prove
>   her worth.

> Avarice and greed, lust for more green.
> In wallet or space, there can be no enough.

> To our own local Lady Macbeth, seeking power
>   by association.
> Good luck washing such guilt from your soiled
>   hands.

> And the one who greased palms for the job he did
>   covet,
> Is now in position to graft it all back.

> Good people of Sweet Falls, join with me today.
> Show them we won't be deceived in this way.

> Consequences will follow for all the misdeeds.
> Let's root them all out, like so many weeds.

When she reached the end, Emma sat back in her chair, exhausted by the power of Brian's words yet at a loss for what they meant. It didn't take a degree in literature or a passion for poetry to know there was a message to be had. But what, exactly, that message was, she had no idea. Sure, it was clear Brian had been determined to prove a point, and that he'd felt it important to make sure Emma had a record of it *just in case*. But without any sort of framework in which to work, the meaning behind his words was elusive at best.

"I'm trying, Brian." A warm lick on her elbow hijacked her attention from the screen to the soulful eyes waiting for some sort of indication things were okay. "Oh, sweet boy, I wish you could talk; I wish you could read this with me and help me figure out what it all means."

A second lick and a head scratch later, Emma looked back at the screen, Brian's words making their way past her own lips as she read the poem aloud a second, third, and fourth time.

"Little did he know I got the only C in my entire high school career in a poetry class," she said aloud, only to realize Scout was no longer in the room. "I know, boy. Trust me, I know. I'm not a fan of poetry, either."

The answering click of Scout's nails in the hallway let her know he was on the way back to her side like the good and faithful companion he was. But instead of the leash she half expected to see in his mouth as he reentered the room, he dropped her phone in her lap.

Chapter Eighteen

‹═══›

Like a programmed robot, Emma plucked the ball from the grass and hurled it down the hill toward the big tree, Scout's immediate departure from her side little more than a blur of fur. She'd come to the park wanting to lose herself in his uncomplicated joy, but, like every other distraction she'd sought out thus far, it was failing. Miserably.

The fact she'd gotten little more than an hour or so of sleep the previous night only made things worse.

The whole amateur sleuth thing had never been on her bucket list of things to do and be in the course of her life, yet, by some twist of fate, she'd been forced into it, anyway. If she could go back in time and refrain from pinning that notice to the town's virtual bulletin board, she would . . . If she couldn't change that, she'd make it so she hadn't answered Brian's call, or that she'd heeded her initial impulse to call him back and cancel the job . . .

But there was no going back in time for her, or for Brian. There was only going forward—a forward that included

Brian's murder and the four people he'd believed wanted him dead.

Nancy Davis.

Rita Gerard.

Robert McEnerny.

Sheriff Borlin.

Four very different people she'd just always assumed were upstanding citizens. But now? After last night?

She shivered as her thoughts returned to the poem she'd revisited again and again throughout the night, her high school poetry teacher's advice to *break it down, break it down* leading her along a series of paths she couldn't ignore no matter how much she wished she could.

Brian was, without a doubt, a pot stirrer. His poem proved that. But he hadn't deserved to die. In fact, if her early interpretations of his words were correct, his pot stirring may have been a good thing. *If* he hadn't been silenced.

But he wasn't silenced. Not completely, anyway. And he'd made sure of that. By giving her the printout and sending her the poem he'd been prevented from reciting.

Now, she had pages and pages of notes, questions she needed to ask, things she needed to find out, and—she shivered again—a road map of sorts in how to go about finding Brian's killer. With or without anyone's help.

Retrieving her phone from her back pocket, Emma checked the time in relation to the doctor's appointment she knew Dottie had and then opened her contacts list. She scrolled down to Dottie's name and—

"His name is Scout."

She stilled her finger atop the screen and looked up to find Jack making his way in her direction. At his side was a miniature version of himself in everything from the shape of his broad shoulders to the smile-spawned dimple in his left cheek.

"Hey, Emma." Jack closed the remaining gap between

them with a few long strides and then dropped his hands onto his mini-me's shoulders. "Tommy, this is Miss West-lake and"—he let go of the boy long enough to shower a newly returned Scout with pets and scratches—"this is her dog, Scout."

"Can I pet your dog, Miss Westlake?" Tommy asked, glancing from Emma to Scout. "I'll be real gentle."

"Call me Emma, and yes, you can pet my dog. What a very smart thing for you to ask." Emma set her phone down on the grass and shifted up and onto her knees. "He likes pets anywhere, but he especially likes them right *here*, behind his ears. Like *this*."

The little boy sat down on the ground next to Emma and Scout, his fingers finding the exact right spot and earning him a giggle-inducing full-face lick of gratitude in return.

"Would you like to play fetch with him?" she asked, retrieving the ball from where Scout had dropped it and holding it out to Tommy. "Because that's his favorite thing to do in the whole world."

Tommy looked up at Jack. "Can I, Dad?"

"Absolutely." Lowering himself to the grass next to Emma, Jack pointed toward the tree at the bottom of the hill. "Try to get it down in that area."

Cocking his right hand over his head, Tommy threw the ball with all his might and, to his obvious delight, Scout took off running, clearly ready to play again. Only this time, Scout didn't have to trek all the way back up the hill with the captured ball because Tommy split the difference. Again and again, Tommy threw the ball. And, again and again, Scout loped after it, eager to catch it and return it to his new friend.

"Thanks for this," Jack finally said, leaning back on his elbows.

"I'm pretty sure it's *I* who should be thanking *you*." She allowed herself the smile Scout's joy demanded and then felt it fade as fast as it came. "Scout can tell when I'm phoning it in."

"Oh?"

Nodding, she rushed to stifle a yawn. "I didn't get much sleep last night."

"Company?" he asked.

"No."

"Late night out?"

"No. Just"—she looked back at Scout and Tommy—"a lot on my mind is all."

"So I guess that's why I didn't see you this morning?"

"This morning?" she echoed.

"At the gym."

"Oh. Right." She yawned again. "Actually, in hindsight, a workout may have helped clear my head a little. But my gym buddy had an early-morning work thing she had to do, so we'll get back to it on Monday."

Silence fell between them—a silence Jack eventually ended with a long, drawn-out exhale. "Tommy can tell when I'm phoning it in, too. Which is why seeing you and Scout just now was just what we both needed."

Something about the change in Jack's tone shifted her thoughts and her gaze onto the handsome deputy. "Are you okay?"

He seemed to ponder her question for a moment as if weighing whether or not to even answer, but he finally did, his voice so quiet she had to strain to hear him. "I think there might really be something to what we talked about last time. About my boss. And if there is, and it leads to . . ."

Jack closed his mouth, shook his head.

"Maybe it's not him," Emma said, looking back at Scout and Tommy. "Maybe Brian uncovered awful things about other people, too."

"Maybe."

Something about the tone of his voice stole her attention again. "You don't sound convinced."

Jack blew out a breath. "Because I'm not."

"Did you find something else?"

"No. But I also haven't found anything about that kid's arrest. I've looked in every folder I can—virtual and otherwise. And it's all gone. Like it never happened."

She thought back to the poem and the section she'd bet good money was about the sheriff. "I can't remember, but did Sheriff Borlin win his reelection easily?"

He nodded. "Surprisingly, yes."

"Surprisingly?"

"He wasn't the front-runner going into that election. Not by a long shot. But at the end, he managed to get a few key councilmen to endorse him and he pulled it off."

She considered his words in relation to Brian's poem, drew in a breath, and went for broke. "Are you familiar with the term *graft*?"

"Sure. It's cop-talk for a bribe." He pulled up a blade of grass and turned it back and forth between his fingers. "Why do you ask?"

"Could that be why you're not finding any records on this young man's arrest?"

"I wish I could give you an unequivocal no. But . . . yeah, if this whole thing with the councilman's son went down the way I'm thinking, that would be an example of graft."

Her eyes followed Scout as he made his way back to Tommy. "Any chance this guy was one of the councilmen who helped your boss get reelected?"

His gaze jumped to hers before lifting toward the sky she knew he wasn't really seeing. "Actually"—he palmed his mouth—"wow . . . Yeah . . . He was. Which means I better make sure my ducks are in a row before I approach him with any of this if I want to keep my job and—"

"The one who greased palms for the job he did covet, is now in position to graft it all back," she murmured.

Was this it? Was this the—

"Excuse me?"

Feeling his eyes on her, she turned and met them, the confusion he wore surely a reflection of her own. "I'm sorry, I think I zoned out for a moment just then. Did I miss something?"

"No. That thing you just said . . . about greased palms. What was that again?"

Like a deer caught in the headlights of an oncoming car, she made a mental dash for the safest ground she could find. "It—it's just a-a poem that went through my head is all."

"I see."

Oh, how she wanted to tell him it was from Brian's poem just so she could have someone to bounce it off of right then and there. But she couldn't. To do so in that moment would only add to the weight Jack was already carrying on a weekend he was supposed to be enjoying his son.

"I probably should get back to the department's family day before my absence is noticed." He nudged his chin and her attention toward a busy pavilion in the distance and stood. "Besides, Tommy's been looking forward to the water balloon toss all week and I don't want to disappoint him by staying away like some sort of coward."

"You're not a coward."

"I haven't moved on my suspicion yet."

"That doesn't make you a coward. It means you're being"—she cast about for a suitable word—"*prudent*. Because while Brian might have stumbled onto something pretty explosive in regard to your boss, that doesn't mean that's the only person he had something on."

His answering shrug held none of the hope she'd intended her words to convey. Instead, the tension oozing off him seemed to only deepen.

"Maybe—just maybe—you're right. But even if you are and *someone else* murdered Brian Hill, that doesn't mean I can turn a blind eye to illegal activity inside my own department. To do so would make me no better than . . ." Again, he palmed his mouth, only to let his hand slip slowly back to his side. "Anyway, I appreciate you listening the way you have. And I appreciate you letting my kid play with your dog. It's good to see him being so happy. In fact, I suspect the highlight of his day isn't going to be the water balloon toss at all. I think it's going to be playing fetch with Scout."

She pushed off the ground and stood beside him, his sudden nearness, coupled with an openness she found infinitely appealing, making her legs feel a wee bit wobbly. "Scout has that effect on people."

"Like owner, like dog, I guess."

Stunned back a step by his words, she watched him make his way down the hill to his son and her dog. When he reached them, he squatted down, gave the now-resting Scout a welcome belly rub, and tapped Tommy on the nose. "It looks like you've made a friend."

Tommy tilted his head off Scout's back and smiled so big Emma felt her breath hitch. "I did!"

"I'm glad. But it's time to go, kiddo. You've got some water balloons to try and catch before Daddy and the other deputies start grilling up all those hamburgers you saw in the coolers."

"But I like it here with Scout," Tommy said.

"And Scout likes you, too," Emma said, joining them. "But Scout and I come here a lot, so you'll see each other again, I'm sure."

Scout didn't budge.

Neither did Tommy.

"In fact, we always come on Saturdays around noon, don't we, boy?"

"*Tomorrow* is Saturday," Tommy said, popping his head back up in tandem with Scout's.

She glanced at Jack to find the same hope she saw in his son's face mirrored on his own. Before she could process it, though, the ring she'd forgotten to mute upon arriving at the park had her reaching into her back pocket for her phone.

"Cloverton?" She looked from the location name on the screen to the unknown number displayed above it and felt the answering tingle of excitement making its way through her body. "I'm sorry, Jack, but I really need to take this call."

"No worries. I understand." Jack held his hand out for Tommy to take. "C'mon, son."

Tommy scrambled onto his feet, his gaze pinning Emma's. "Tomorrow? At noon?"

Nodding, she left father and son to say goodbye to Scout while she stepped away and took the call. "Hello, this is Emma."

"Emma, this is Andy Walden. I sent you an email last week about possibly looking in on my elderly father while I'm away on a business trip?"

"Hi, Andy. I'm really glad you called. My apologies, again, for taking so long to reach out. For what it's worth, I replied to your email as soon as I saw it."

"It happens." The deep, rumbling voice that reminded Emma of her mother's favorite movie star continued in her ear. "I was wondering if you'd have time to come out tomorrow, around two o'clock, so we can talk? See if it's a good fit for both of us?"

She pumped her arm in the air in quiet celebration. "Absolutely! Tomorrow at two will be perfect!"

"Great. I'll send you my address via email and I'll see you then."

"I'll see you then. Thanks, Andy." Returning the phone to her pocket, Emma waved Scout over to her side and wrapped her arms around his neck. "Tomorrow is shaping up to be a very, *very* good day, isn't it, boy?"

Chapter Nineteen

Emma was just pulling the tray of cookies out of the oven when Scout abandoned his post at her feet in favor of a mad dash into the hallway. She set the tray on the stovetop, tossed the oven mitt onto the counter, and followed, the sight of him camped in front of the door—tail wagging—making the knock that came next anticlimactic at best.

"You found us," Emma said, opening the door to the tired face on the other side.

Stephanie's gaze lit on Emma's for the briefest of seconds before she bent down to address Scout. "Who's a good boy? Who? Who? You!"

Scout, in turn, licked Stephanie's cheek, her chin, her nose, her other cheek, and her eyebrow (by way of her eye) before taking a seat exactly halfway between his owner and his new friend.

"He's just the best," Stephanie said, grinning. "You do realize that, right?"

Emma winked down at Scout, laughed at the immediate

wag it yielded, and then stepped back against the open door to allow Stephanie entry. "Come on in. I just took a tray of cookies out of the oven and they're calling our names."

"You made cookies?"

"I did. Chocolate chip."

"For me?" Stephanie asked, stepping into the hallway.

"Put them in the oven as soon as I knew you were coming." Emma closed the door behind them and took point down the hallway and into the kitchen.

Stephanie stopped just inside the kitchen doorway and looked around, her green eyes taking in the wall clock shaped like a daisy, the baking canisters with their daisy motif, the daisy-adorned placemat under Scout's food and water bowls, and, finally, the pair of daisy trimmed dessert plates Emma had set on the table in anticipation of her visit.

"I'm guessing you like daisies, huh?"

"What was your first clue?" Emma motioned Stephanie over toward the table while she transferred the still-warm cookies onto a serving plate. "Actually, in all fairness, I like *all* flowers. Daisies just happen to be my favorite."

Accepting the serving plate from Emma, Stephanie nodded at the offer of milk and sheepishly placed two cookies onto her plate. "This is really nice, Emma."

"What? The cookies? You haven't even tried them yet."

"It's more about the fact you made them. For me. The fact that you even thought to call and see how my meeting with Mr. Evil went blows my mind. But to follow it up with an invite? To *your house*? It's just nice."

Emma carried the milk glasses over to the table and took a seat opposite Stephanie. Helping herself to a cookie, she lifted it—toast-like—and then bit into the warm gooeyness. "Any excuse to make cookies is a good excuse in my book."

Stephanie's answering laugh morphed into a quiet moan as she, too, took a bite of cookie. "Oh . . . Wow . . . This is really good."

"Thank you."

They munched their cookies in companionable silence as, once again, Stephanie took a slow visual tour of the room that culminated on Scout lapping away at his water dish. "I want this. I really do."

"Want what?" Emma asked, placing a third cookie on Stephanie's empty plate and a third one on her own.

"This." Stephanie took a sip of milk. "A kitchen of my own that I can decorate however I want, a pet to keep me company, all of it."

She looked at Stephanie across the rim of her own glass. "So why don't you?"

"Because I have zero time for anything other than work during the week, and on the weekends I have zero desire to move off my couch, let alone actually look for a place to live."

"Better late than never, as they say, right?" Emma quipped.

Stephanie reached for her last cookie. "Trite, but true."

"In fact, maybe we could look through some ads after we meet up at Dottie's in the morning."

"About that . . ." Stephanie took a sip of milk. "What's with this eight o'clock stuff on a Saturday, anyway? Couldn't we pick a time that's more mutually agreeable? Like maybe two or three in the afternoon?"

"But then the day is shot." Emma finished up her own cookie and leaned back against her chair, the move quickly interpreted by Scout as an invitation to approach the table. When he did, she rubbed his neck. "Besides, I'm meeting with a prospective client out in Cloverton at two."

"Ahhh, yes . . . I tend to forget people actually make plans for their weekends."

"Which we can do, too, if you'd like."

Stephanie's eyebrow arched. "We?"

"You and me. I mean, surely we can wrap things up with Dottie by nine, right? That would give us plenty of time to look at the rental ads in the paper and maybe even drive around to see what might be available." Emma gave Scout one last rub and then gathered up their dessert plates and empty milk glasses and carried them to the sink. "If you want to, of course."

"You'd seriously do that with me?" Stephanie asked, hurrying to unhook the dishtowel from its drying spot around the oven handle. "On your Saturday?"

Emma took the dishtowel back out of Stephanie's hand, reattached it to the oven handle, and led her into the living room. "Sure. It would be fun. And maybe, if we get lucky, we can even get into a few places and look around if they're between renters."

"I'm actually thinking about buying."

"Even better." She waited for Stephanie to get settled on the couch and then plopped onto the opposing corner. "We could stop by a Realtor and see if they can take us out."

"If you're serious about going with me, McEnerny Homes has a sales office out in Morehead. Maybe we could check that out?" Stephanie asked.

"Sure. That sounds good."

Stephanie didn't even try to hide her answering smile—a smile so big and so genuine it melted a good five years from her face. "I'd love that! And maybe, just maybe, we can kill two birds with one stone while we're there. Although, the likelihood of the top dog being there on a weekend is probably slim to none. That's what the flunkies are for."

"Top dog?"

Stephanie's laugh echoed around the room. "You might want to count your blessings Dottie didn't just hear you say that."

"Right. Robert McEnerny," she said kneading her temples. "How could I forget? Especially after last night."

"What happened last night?"

"I got an email from Brian."

"Ha, ha. Funny."

"I'm serious," Emma said, kneading harder.

Stephanie laughed for real. "Oh please . . . I realize the use of technology and the need to always be connected has gotten a little out of control, but I'm pretty sure people aren't sending emails and texts from the afterworld."

"He sent it to me before he stepped on the stage at Deeter's that night."

The laughing stopped. "You're serious . . ."

"Deadly." Cringing inwardly at the irony in her word choice, Emma continued, her kneading doing nothing to combat the headache she felt brewing. "I was so thrown by everything that happened that I never thought to check the account I set up for the new business. Then, yesterday, Scout led me into my office. Next thing I knew, I was at my computer, staring at an email from Brian in my inbox."

"What did it say?" Stephanie demanded.

"Just in case."

Stephanie stared at Emma, clearly waiting for more. When nothing came, she rolled her finger. "And? Keep going . . ."

"That's it. That's all it said. *Just in case.*"

"Just in case *what*?"

"Just in case his prediction came true, I imagine." Emma looked around for her phone, spied it on the end table to her right, and quickly pulled up the image Brian had captured. She handed it to Stephanie. "He attached his poem. The one he didn't get to finish reciting."

Stephanie looked between the image on the screen in her hand and Emma. "Can I read it?"

"Of course. That's why I handed it to you."

Emma waited, silently, while Stephanie read the very words that had kept her up for most of the night and inserted their way into her thoughts off and on throughout the day. Every few seconds, she saw the woman's eyes widen or her mouth round in a whispered *Whoa.*

"This is nuts, Emma," Stephanie finally said, looking up. "I mean, did you read this? This guy has—or, I should say, *had*—some serious axes to grind."

"I know."

"I don't get most of it, but that's the way of poetry at first," said Stephanie. "The good stuff requires a little thinking, a little analyzing."

Emma pushed off the couch and wandered over to the window overlooking the street. Scout's eyes followed her, but his body remained stretched across his favorite dog bed. "I was up pretty much all night doing that. Stanza by stanza. Line by line."

"Granted, I'm just now reading this, but it seems pretty clear he thinks our four suspects are hiding things," Stephanie said.

"More like he believes they've gotten away with things they shouldn't." Turning back to Stephanie, Emma leaned against the window. "And that part about the roles they defile? He says that as if it's aimed at all of them, but the only one with a role is Sheriff Borlin. And maybe the mayor's wife. Nancy Davis and Robert McEnerny are just regular people like you and me. They don't have roles to defile, right?"

Stephanie's attention returned to the screen, her lips moving with the words as she silently read them again. When she finished, she set the phone down on the armrest of the couch. "I'm guessing the lust for more green is for the greenhouse lady?"

"Her name is Nancy Davis. And I guess you're probably right," Emma said, shrugging. "But I was thinking she was more the first one because of the jaw-that-flaps-nonstop part. Nancy has a reputation for being a bit of a gossip— although not necessarily in a malicious way."

Again, Stephanie looked at the phone, her eyes moving quickly down the screen. "Okay, I can see that. Especially since he says *her.*"

"Which could be Rita Gerard, as well."

"No. That one is the Macbeth reference. No doubt."

Emma wandered back to the couch but remained standing. "Why?"

"Our *own local Lady Macbeth*?" Stephanie's eyes narrowed on Emma. "C'mon. Think about it, Emma. Our own local Lady Macbeth. Rita Gerard—the mayor's wife. It's poetic, quite frankly. Shakespeare would be proud."

"Shakespeare?" Emma echoed.

Stephanie stared at her. "Yes . . ."

"Ugh."

"I take it you're not a fan?"

"Your take is correct. But the soiled-hand part could refer to Nancy, too, on account of the whole gardening thing."

Again, Stephanie looked at the poem. "True. But if that's the case, what a wasted opportunity with the Macbeth line."

"The one about the greased palms near the end? That one is a total no-brainer."

"Oh?" Stephanie asked, glancing up. "Why is that?"

"Graft is a cop term for taking a bribe." Emma heard Scout yawn and made her way over to his bed. "Jack confirmed that."

"The deputy? He's still following you?"

"He's not following me. He's just . . ." She lowered herself to the open floor next to Scout's bed and began to rub his neck, her thoughts taking her back to the park.

An *uh-oh* from Stephanie pulled her back into the room.

"Uh-oh?" Emma repeated, moving on to Scout's tummy. "What's *uh-oh*?"

"Your smile just now."

She stared at Stephanie. "What about it? I'm petting my dog."

"Oh no. Don't even go there. That smile was about one thing and one thing only and it had absolutely nothing to do with that dog." Stephanie leaned forward, grinning. "*You* have a total crush on that deputy. It's written all over your face."

"No, I don't!"

Stephanie's knowing laugh warmed Emma's cheeks. "Yes, you do."

"No, I don't. If I smiled while talking about him, it was only because I was thinking about his kid, Tommy. He and Scout were like two peas in a pod from the moment they laid eyes on each other at the park today."

"He has a kid?"

Emma nodded. "He's eight."

"Does he have a wife as well?"

"No! He's divorced."

Stephanie's smile was back. "You've got it bad."

"No, I don't. You're nuts."

"In the immortal words of William Shakespeare's *Hamlet*, methinks the lady doth protest too much."

Chapter Twenty

—◦•◦—

"It should be against the law for anyone to wake before noon on a Saturday."

Grinning, Emma pulled up on Scout's leash and turned to find Stephanie exiting her car onto Dottie's driveway in what appeared—from the thirty or so feet between them—to be sleepwear. "You made it!" she said, doubling back. "And on time, no less!"

"Take a picture for posterity reasons as it won't be happening again anytime soon." Stephanie managed a smile—in between yawns—for Scout as he wagged his way over for his first official greeting of the day. "Good morning, Scout. If you were my dog, you'd still be cuddled up in bed."

"No, he wouldn't. He wakes up with the sun. Seven days a week."

Stephanie's lip curled in horror. "Do all dogs do that?"

"I don't know. I can only speak for Scout." Emma traveled her gaze down to Stephanie's feet. "Nice slippers. They go perfectly with your ensemble."

"I'm sensing judgment."

Emma's laugh brought Scout back to her side. "No. No judgment. Though I am looking forward to seeing Dottie's reaction."

Stephanie's still-sleepy eyes slid toward the side yard and the walkway that would take them around to the patio. "She doesn't do pajamas?"

"I'm sure she *does* pajamas. When it's time to sleep. Which it's not, but that's okay." Emma waved for Stephanie to follow and then let Scout lead the way. "The eye roll when she sees you should be epic."

Stephanie stopped. "Should I go home and change?"

"Nah. It'll be good for Dottie—it'll keep her distracted enough by you and your faux pas that she'll miss mine."

Stephanie's green eyes lit on Emma's flowered skirt and eyelet shirt and pulled a face. "Please . . . What on earth could she find wrong with you?"

"Watch and listen." Again, Emma motioned for Stephanie to follow and, when she did, hurried to catch up with Scout at the gate. A peek through the wrought iron posts showed the elderly woman seated at the patio table with a cup of coffee to her left, a plate of something that looked deliciously sinful to her right, and a big manila envelope between them both.

"Hey, Dottie," she called as she unlatched the gate and held it open for Scout and Stephanie. "We're all here."

Turning her head toward the gate, Dottie slipped her reading glasses midway down her nose and, after a momentary hesitation that included a shocked yet silent once-over of Stephanie, pinned Emma with a noteworthy glare. "You do realize Memorial Day weekend is still two weeks away, right, dear?"

"Here we go," she murmured to Stephanie. "Wait for it . . ."

"Because white sandals are wholly inappropriate for the middle of May, Emma."

"I thought that was white pants," she countered.

"No, it extends to sandals, as well."

"Duly noted." Emma closed the remaining gap between them, planted a quick kiss atop the octogenarian's perfectly coiffed hair, and claimed the same spot she'd sat in three days earlier. "And Stephanie? Do you have anything to say to her?"

Dottie pointed the third member of their trio to a chair and then to the serving platter of cinnamon rolls in the center of the table. "Please. Help yourself while they're still warm."

"That's it?" Emma asked. "You comment on my sandals, and you point Stephanie to the cinnamon rolls?"

"You can have one, too, dear." Dottie rolled her eyes.

Emma stared at, first, Dottie. Then, at Stephanie. And, finally, back at Dottie. "You *do* realize she's wearing pajamas and slippers, right?"

"Speaking of your slippers, Stephanie, where did you get them? I must have Glenda pick up a pair for me the next time she's at the mall. They look both sturdy and comfortable."

"They are!" Stephanie sent a triumphant smile in Emma's direction as she plunked a cinnamon roll onto her plate and licked the icing from the tips of her fingers. "Maybe Glenda could pick Emma up a pair, as well."

"Okay . . . Okay . . . I see how this is going to go." Emma, too, helped herself to a cinnamon roll and placed it on her plate. "How did your appointment go yesterday, Dottie? I left you a message—two, actually—but you never called back."

"You knew you were coming here today . . ."

"I did. But I wanted to check on you and I wanted to tell you about the email I found from—"

Stephanie stopped mid-lick and sat up tall. "Oh, Dottie, wait 'til you hear this. It's a doozy."

Uh-oh.

"Tell her, Emma. Tell her what Brian sent you. Or"—

Stephanie took one last lick and then reached for her fork—"better yet, *show* her the same picture you showed me last night."

"Last night?" Dottie echoed.

Emma, realizing her glares were going unnoticed, opted to go the route of an under-the-table kick as a way to silence Stephanie, but to no avail. Stephanie kept right on talking.

"Emma invited me over last night to see the poem Brian never got to finish reading!"

The dagger that was Dottie's glare had Emma scrambling for a glass of water. "You have Mr. Hill's poem, dear?"

"She does!" Stephanie said, forking a bite of the cinnamon roll from her plate. "And boy, was he out for blood at Deeter's that night. The whole thing was one great big callout on each of our suspects."

"Why am I just now hearing about this?" Dottie asked, her voice dripping with hurt-tinged anger.

"Emma got it on Thursday night."

Dottie held Emma's gaze even as she directed her response to Stephanie. "And this is Saturday morning."

"I left you two messages yesterday," Emma said sheepishly. "Remember?"

"You never said anything about the case in either of those messages."

"Because the bigger priority was to check on you. And I figured, when you called back, I'd tell you about the poem *then*."

"Don't worry, Dottie, Emma and I spent a little time last night batting around different parts of the poem, and I think we made some progress." Stephanie turned to Emma. "FYI, that's me you're kicking under the table, not the table post."

In search of an escape hatch, Emma popped her chin up and glanced around the patio for Scout. When her search yielded nothing, she stood, her attention ricocheting between a still-dagger-shooting Dottie and the yard. "Is the screen up in front of Alfred's flowers?"

Dottie took a long, drawn-out sip of her coffee and then carefully returned the china mug to its matching saucer. "It is. I supervised its placement not more than twenty minutes ago, myself."

"Oh, okay, good. Thank you." She sat back down, unfolded her napkin across her lap, and gestured toward the envelope in front of Dottie. "I take it that's it? The autopsy report on Brian?"

Aware of the full and undivided attention of both her guests, Dottie took great care (and time) in turning the envelope over, peeling back the seal she'd clearly opened numerous times over the past two days, and slipping her age-spotted hand inside to reach its contents. "In addition to the coroner's report, my source also included information about Mr. Hill's health in the event that may be of help to us, as well."

"And this source of yours just up and sent these things to you?" Emma asked as Dottie readied the papers for Stephanie. "Isn't that illegal?"

Dottie looked at Emma across the upper rim of her eyeglasses. "We're trying to solve a murder here, dear."

"Which is what the *police* are supposed to be doing, not us."

"If you don't want to be part of this, I'm quite certain Stephanie and I can handle this on our own."

Stephanie took the papers Dottie held out to her and laid them down next to her breakfast plate. "Dottie is right, Emma. We've got this."

"Yes, you just hang back while we work to save your business from the kind of press that could destroy it." Dottie dismissed Emma with wiggled fingers. "We'll be fine."

"Wow. Such guilt . . ." Emma murmured.

"No guilt intended, dear."

Her answering laugh summoned Scout from whatever

bush he'd been sniffing. "Hey, boy," she said, rubbing his head. "Did you find a squirrel to play with?"

"So? Are you in or are you out?" Dottie pressed while simultaneously eyeing Stephanie. "We don't need any dead weight in this investigation."

Emma stilled her hand atop Scout's head. "Dead weight?"

"You and your"—Dottie paused, as if searching for the right word—"*hesitation* about all of this."

"You mean my hesitation about playing armchair sleuth like one of those characters in your cozy mystery novels?" Emma countered.

Dottie's eyes narrowed on Emma again. "There's nothing the slightest bit *armchair* about what we're doing here. If there was, Stephanie wouldn't be looking at a copy of the official autopsy findings on our victim."

"She shouldn't be," Emma said. "That's my point."

Dottie's gasp died along with Emma's sentence as Stephanie looked up from the stack of papers. "Brian came from a long line of pretty extensive heart issues."

"Since when is a heart attack considered murder?" Emma asked.

"It's not."

Emma followed Stephanie's eyes back to the reports. "Then I don't understand."

"While his heart appeared to be in good condition as of his last checkup"—Stephanie flipped back a page, scoured it—"he did have some pretty serious kidney issues that were being watched."

"Okay . . ."

Stephanie returned to the spot she'd been reading and, after a few noises indicative of either intrigue or disgust, looked up again. "There were high levels of digitalis— consistent with the finding of digitalis toxicity—in his body at the time of his death."

"Digitalis," Dottie repeated. "With a family history of heart issues?"

Nodding, Stephanie turned a page forward, and then a page back. "I'm not seeing anything on his lifestyle in terms of activity."

"He ran marathons," Emma offered.

Stephanie's gaze snapped up to Emma's. "Are you sure?"

"Yeah. I came across a few articles about it when I was doing a little research on him after I agreed to meet him for Open Mic Night."

"Interesting . . ." Stephanie murmured, digging back into the reports.

"Interesting, indeed."

Emma turned back to Dottie. "This stuff means something to you?"

"It does."

"I didn't know you were in the medical field at one time."

"I wasn't."

"Then how is any of this making sense to you?"

Again, Dottie peered at Emma across the top of her glasses, a smug smile playing at the corners of her thinning lips. "I read."

"You read *cozy mysteries*."

"You're right, I do."

A flurry of movement gravitated their collective attention back to Stephanie as she neatened the papers into a pile and handed them back to Dottie. "So, from what I'm able to gather, the high amount of digitalis—in conjunction with the kidney issues that lowered his ability to get rid of the toxins through his urine—is what killed him. And since his doctor didn't prescribe digitalis for him, the prevailing thought is that someone introduced it into his system via food or water."

"And it can be fast-acting, correct?" Dottie asked.

"Coupled with his medical history, it can be, yes."

Emma sat up tall, her mind's eye transporting her back to the restaurant and the table as it had looked when she arrived. "He ordered a plate of stuffed mushrooms for us before I even showed up! They were on the table when we walked in from having met outside!"

Dottie's head was shaking before she'd even finished talking. "But you're still here."

"Digitalis doesn't affect everyone the same way," Stephanie said, glancing from Dottie to Emma. "Do you remember any dizziness or lightheadedness at all that night? Any stomach upset? Any—"

"I didn't eat them!"

Dottie straightened in her wheelchair. "You didn't?"

"No. I hate stuffed mushrooms!"

"And all four of our suspects were there when you arrived?" Dottie asked.

Emma considered the question as she followed Brian to the table in her thoughts. "I can't say for sure. But when I opened the folder and looked at the pictures not more than five minutes later—tops!—they were all there. And none of them looked as if they had just arrived."

"So any one of them could've walked by that appetizer and slipped the digitalis into it while Brian was outside talking to you." Dottie plunked her notebook atop the coroner's report and flipped it open. "Do you remember anything specific about the appetizer or its presentation? Did it look particularly different from others you've seen?"

"I'd sooner starve than order mushrooms—stuffed, or otherwise—so I wouldn't know. I just know they looked gross."

Stephanie forked a layer of icing off her roll and deposited it into her mouth, her full attention on Dottie. "I take it, by what you're asking Emma, you're thinking what I'm thinking?"

Nodding, Dottie uncapped her pen. "I am."

"Seems likely to me, as well," Stephanie said.

Emma looked from Dottie to Stephanie and back again, waiting. When neither saw fit to include her in their veiled banter, she shoved her breakfast plate to the side. "Hold on a minute. You two don't get to do whatever it is you're doing right now."

"What are we doing?" Dottie asked.

"I don't know. You're looking at each other like you have some secret code or something. But I will remind you that Brian was *my* client."

Stephanie grinned. "Don't look now, someone is showing interest in sleuthing . . ."

"No," Emma protested. "I'm just . . . Okay, fine. I'm intrigued. So spill it! Why the questions about the stuffed mushrooms and how they looked?"

"Because medication isn't the only thing that can bring on symptoms similar to digitalis toxicity." Stephanie ate the rest of the frosting and then moved on to the roll. "There are some plants that can cause it, as well."

"Plants?" Emma echoed.

Dottie narrated as she wrote in her notepad. "Three, in fact. Foxglove, oleander, and lily of the valley."

"Lily of the valley? As in the plant you screen off when Scout is around?" she asked, pointing around the corner of the fenced-in yard. "It's *that* toxic?"

Stephanie wiped her sticky fingers on her napkin, only to dirty them again by stealing a finger of icing from Emma's plate. "It can be. Those plants contain glycosides. It doesn't matter what part of the plant is consumed. As little as two leaves can prove fatal for young children and pets, but its various parts can take down a full-grown adult, too, if conditions are right."

"Such as a kidney issue and/or a family history of heart issues," Emma mused before moving on to the next most logical point. "If these plants are that dangerous, why would anyone grow them?"

Dottie paused her pen atop her notepad and looked up at Emma. "You remember that smell you commented on a few weeks ago when you came to visit?"

"The sweet one?"

"That was Alfred's lily of the valley in full bloom." Dottie set her pen down, removed her glasses, and rubbed her eyes. "Alfred loved them."

"But—"

"They're inside the gate and it's been decades since we've had any children running around." Dottie looked toward the fruits of Alfred's labor and smiled. "He so loved those flowers. If he could have, he would've put them everywhere. But he knew the dangers and he planned their placement responsibly."

Emma took a moment to absorb it all and to merge it with everything Stephanie had shared from the coroner's report. "So you think someone mixed leaves from a lily of the valley plant into the stuffed mushrooms?"

"It's just a guess—one that could work with the findings of digitalis toxicity," Stephanie explained. "But, as Dottie said a few minutes ago, if it was a plant, lily of the valley is just one of the possibilities. And in any of those cases, it could have been the seeds, the roots, the leaves, the stem, the flowers, any of it. It's all poisonous. And depending on what part was used, or how it was broken down prior to consumption, it could have been sprinkled across the top of the appetizer. If, in fact, the appetizer was the delivery system."

Again, she found her thoughts returning to Deeter's and the appetizer that had been waiting at the table when she and Brian had sat down. "So, if it was a matter of sprinkling, that could've been done pretty quickly, right? Maybe while the culprit was simply passing by the table on the way to the bathroom or something?"

Dottie replaced her glasses, jotted something in her notepad, and then pointed her pen at Emma. "Read me Mr. Hill's poem."

"Oooh, that's right," Stephanie said, giving up on Emma's icing. "Show her the picture so she can read it."

Dottie shot her finger toward Stephanie in a silencing gesture. "I don't want her to *show* it to me. I want her to *read* it to me. So I can hear it the way Mr. Hill wanted the suspects to hear it that night."

Reaching down, Emma retrieved her tote bag from its resting spot beside the front leg of her chair and fished around inside it for her phone. When she had it, she set the bag down and pressed her way into the album. "Okay, here we go . . . Look around, look around, here sit those you laud, but soon you, too, will know their fraud."

"Stop."

Emma looked up at Dottie to find the woman's eyes closed as if she were listening to a beloved song. "What?"

"Read it again."

"Look around, look around, here sit those you laud, but soon you, too, will know their fraud." Emma waited for Dottie's eyes to open and when they did, she offered a shrug. "I think *that* line is easy. He invited them there so he could blow them up in a room filled with Sweet Falls' residents. We know this."

Dottie and Stephanie exchanged glances. "He invited them there?" Stephanie asked.

"Yes."

Dottie waved her hand at Emma to continue and then closed her eyes again.

"I say it often, I say it now, unmasking truth, this is my vow," Emma read. "For far too long you've turned a blind eye, their misdeeds hidden by a wink and a smile. But it's in seeking the truth that you learn the true why; the laws sidestepped, the roles they defile."

Opening her eyes, Dottie jotted a quick note, and then closed them again. "Go on, dear."

"Next stanza: The jaw that flaps nonstop revels in the juiciest of stories. And is willing to sabotage her own work to prove her worth."

"That's Nancy."

It was Emma and Stephanie's turn to trade looks.

"Go on," Dottie said, again.

"But—"

Dottie silenced Stephanie with the same finger she then rolled at Emma. "Go on . . ."

"Next stanza: Avarice and greed, lust for more green. In wallet or space, there can be no enough."

"That's Robert."

"Why do you say that?" Emma asked.

"I take it you've never met him?"

"No."

"You'd understand if you had, dear. But go on . . ."

Clearing her throat, Emma continued. "Next stanza: To our own local Lady Macbeth, seeking power by association. Good luck washing such guilt from your soiled hands."

"Rita, obviously."

Stephanie lifted her fist in the air in celebration. "See, Emma? I told you that one was Rita!"

"Next stanza: And the one who greased palms for the job he did covet, is now in position to graft it all back." Emma looked up. "That's Sheriff Borlin."

When Dottie's only answer came via a nod, Emma kept reading. "Next stanza: Good people of Sweet Falls, join with me today. Show them we won't be deceived in this way. And then for the final stanza: Consequences will follow for all the misdeeds. Let's root them all out, like so many weeds."

Dottie returned her attention to her notebook, her hand gliding the pen across the page with impressive speed. "I used to attend the monthly meetings of the beautification committee in a show of support for Alfred's role as founder. But after his death, I found the meetings to be painfully dry and boring without his sense of humor. So I opted to stay home with my books and let Alfred's generous memoriam be enough. However, the other day at the garden party, I realized that was a mistake. The group appears to have fractured a bit; it's taken on that dreadful middle school pecking order thing as evidenced by the way Nancy Davis sat alone.

"I was sad to hear of her stepping down from her role as committee president in late fall, but I assumed it was a matter of spreading herself too thin. After all, I well remember how much time and effort went in to making Sweet Falls the picture of perfection that it is. However, after the garden party the other day and the way no one approached her at any point, I suspected there was more to the story."

"That's because there is," Emma said.

Setting her pen atop the notepad again, Dottie pinned Emma with her full attention. "Oh?"

"Apparently it stems from the state award the group won last year." Emma called Scout to her side with the click of her tongue and, at Dottie's nod, poured a little water into the travel bowl she kept in her tote. "From what Nancy told me, it sounds as if the mayor's new wife didn't necessarily like the accolades going in Nancy's direction."

"Is the mayor's wife a gardener?" Stephanie asked.

Emma shrugged. "She was part of the committee, so I imagine so."

"Then you'd imagine wrong," Dottie said on the heels of an exasperated huff. "That woman had—*has*—no more interest in flowers than she does anything else that truly makes this town what it is. Alfred's beloved committee was just another way for Rita to infiltrate a group for the sole purpose of garnering votes for her husband. That's it."

Dottie shook her head and drew in a steadying breath. "So she ran Nancy off out of ego? Is that what you're telling me, dear?"

"Yes. Nancy believes Rita was jealous of the press she'd gotten and did her best to stoke the same in the other members. So Nancy stepped down. But it backfired on Rita because the flower beds that won Sweet Falls that award were the true casualties in the end."

Dottie's gasp brought Glenda running. The flick of the woman's jeweled hand sent the housekeeper back inside. "What's happened to the flower beds?"

"You haven't seen them?" Stephanie asked.

"No. I . . ." Dottie looked up at the sky. "I last saw them at the award ceremony, and found it all much harder than I'd expected."

Stephanie wrapped her hands around her empty coffee mug and pulled it close. "They've become weed beds."

"But they brought Nancy back in, so I'm sure it's only a matter of time before they're back to their award-winning selves once again." Emma reached across the table and covered Dottie's hand with her own. "And trust me, when that happens, it'll be a nice slice of humble pie for . . ."

The rest of the thought faded from Emma's lips as another—more chilling—one took its place and sent her scrambling for the picture of Brian's poem once again. "The jaw that flaps nonstop revels in the juiciest of stories. And is *willing to sabotage her own work to prove her worth.*"

"Dottie?" she said, looking up, her mental wheels churning. "Assuming that stanza is really about Nancy, could that second line be implying she intentionally messed with those flower beds?"

Dottie's answering silence quickly gave way to the clink of her cup and saucer as she stacked it atop her breakfast plate. "It could make sense."

"And if you and Stephanie are right, and it was a plant that killed Brian, Nancy would be the likeliest candidate." Emma picked up Dottie's pen, pulled the woman's notepad into writing range, and turned to a clean page. "She probably has all three of the plants you mentioned in her greenhouse somewhere."

Dottie stirred the air above the notepad with her finger. "Yes, yes. Find that out!"

"Wait." Stephanie leaned forward, her brow furrowed. "Assuming you're right about the meaning behind that particular stanza, how—and *why*—would Nancy's bruised ego translate to her wanting Brian dead?" Stephanie asked.

It was a good question. A *very* good question.

"At least we have a starting point where she's concerned," Emma said, earning herself a nod from Dottie in return. "And Steph? Are we still going out to McEnerny Homes now to look at those floor plans?"

"Now?" Stephanie looked down at her pajamas and then lower still, to her slippers. "I kinda forgot we said we were going to do that today. But I want to! I really do! Can I have an hour to get myself a little more presentable?"

"You're building a home, Stephanie?" Dottie asked.

Stephanie slumped back in her chair. "I'm thinking about it. Which is nothing different than I've been doing for the past decade."

"But now it *is* different," Emma reminded. "Because, *now*, you're actually going to take the next step and truly look into it. No excuses, *no pajamas*, no—"

The feel of her phone vibrating in her hand sent her attention back down to the screen and the Cloverton number now displayed where Brian's poem had been. "I'm sorry, I need to take this. I think this is the potential client I'm supposed to be meeting with this afternoon."

"A new client?" Dottie echoed.

"Fingers crossed." Pressing the green button, Emma held the phone to her ear. "Hello, this is Emma."

"Emma, Andy Walden here. Hey, would it be possible to move up our two o'clock meeting to more like twelve thirty this afternoon? There's an outdoor concert going on in town this afternoon that I wasn't aware of until a few moments ago, and I think my dad would like to go to that, if at all possible. He doesn't know about it, so if you can't, it's not a problem. But I figured I'd ask, just in case."

Emma glanced over at Stephanie, mentally noting (yet again) the pajamas, the slippers . . . "Can we move

McEnerny to more like two?" she whispered, lowering the phone to her side and covering it with her hand.

At Stephanie's nod, she returned the phone to her ear. "Twelve thirty will be fine. That'll give me plenty of time to get my dog settled and my references together before I head out your way."

"You have a dog?"

"I do. A golden retriever named Scout."

"Why don't you bring him along? My dad loves dogs."

"I'll do that." She reached her free hand down to the sleeping mound of fur beside her chair and felt the immediate answer of his tail against her foot. "Thank you, Andy. We'll see you soon."

Chapter Twenty-One

There was something about traveling the rural roads between Sweet Falls and Cloverton that Emma loved. Maybe it was the quiet beauty of the tree-canopied road that made up a good five miles of the trip. Maybe it was the large meadow of wildflowers that sprang up on the eastbound side of the road just past the halfway point. Maybe it was the series of horse pastures that filled the gaps in between, or the numerous trailheads closer to her destination that left her wishing she'd donned her hiking boots instead of her wedge sandals. Or, maybe, it was simply the opportunity to get behind the wheel, open the windows, and embrace the feel of the wind on her face the way Scout so loved to do.

Glancing over at the passenger seat, she felt her smile widen at the sight of her steadfast companion. "I love you, Scout, you know that?"

Scout pulled his head back in the car just long enough to lick her cheek and wag his tail before he was back to soaking up every sight and smell his window seat afforded.

"Cross your paws this goes well, okay? Because we need more clients, STAT."

And it was true. Because while she'd made good money each of the two times she'd worked with Big Max, they were isolated jobs. She needed a good half dozen like Big Max every month. That, plus a few more Stephanies and maybe she could really make a go of A Friend for Hire. If not . . .

No. She refused to go down the dreaded *if not* road. Not yet, anyway.

"In five hundred feet, turn left onto Old Hawley Road."

Emma glanced over at the map on her dashboard screen, noted the remaining mileage left in their trip, and then returned her focus to the road in front of them as she let up on the gas. "We're almost there, boy. Almost there . . ."

Again, Scout pulled his head back into the car, eyed her with his usual excitement over any little word that came out of her mouth, and shifted his body to accommodate their turn to the left. The ping of gravel as they left the main road, though, stole his full attention back to the window.

Slowing their pace to accommodate the side road's many ruts and haphazard graveling, Emma looked from the address she'd written down during her first call with Andy to the dash screen and, finally, back to the road. "We're looking for—"

"You have arrived at your destination: 11 Sunnybrook Lane."

She slowed the car to a stop beside a mailbox bearing the same information she'd just heard and then traveled her gaze up the driveway it marked. Tucked away in the middle of a grove of sugar maples was a stunning cabin straight out of the pages of a fairy tale. The home's front-facing exterior wall boasted shingled boards, long dual six-pane windows bordered on the bottom edge by window boxes filled with yellow and purple flowers, and an arched opening that led to the welcoming front door.

"Oh, Scout, it's beautiful," she murmured, transfixed.

Not wanting to miss out on whatever had captured her attention, Scout parked his front paws atop her thighs and stuck his head out her window, his tail going into overdrive as the front door of the house opened and a potential ear-scratcher stepped onto the top of a trio of stone steps.

Even from the distance the driveway afforded, Emma found herself cataloguing a few details about the man she thought must be Andy Walden.

First, he was about her age. If she had to guess, she'd put him at about thirty-six to her thirty-four.

Second, he was tall. Meaning, if the arched mahogany door was a standard six and a half feet from top to bottom, he had about a three inch clearance.

Third, his hair was the color of melted milk chocolate.

Fourth, he filled out his shirt in a way that hinted at a love of physical fitness.

And fifth?

Pulling in a breath, she fairly sank against her seat as, with a gentleness she could practically feel from her position eighty or so yards out, he reached a hand through the open doorway and carefully guided an elderly man with a cane onto the step beside him.

Scout, sensing new friends to be had, licked the air, and then Emma, and then the air again before pelting the center console, the dashboard, and the steering wheel with his tail.

"Okay, okay, we're going." She turned off the car, pocketed the keys, clipped on Scout's leash, and stepped out on the driveway, waving up at the men as she did. "Hi, I'm Emma. I'm guessing you're Andy?"

"You guessed right." Andy said something to the elderly man she couldn't hear and then stepped down off the front stoop to meet her at the top of the driveway, his hand extended. "Welcome, Emma. I hope you were able to find us without any trouble?"

She felt, rather than watched, her hand disappear inside

his as she found herself momentarily mesmerized by the yellow flecks that danced against the sunlit brown of his eyes. "No, no trouble at all."

"I'm happy to hear that." He swept his hand up to the front stoop and the elderly man slowly caning his way down the steps. "Pop? Where are you going?"

"I'm going to welcome our guest."

Andy made haste back to the steps, only to have his offer of a hand brushed away in favor of Emma. "Welcome, young lady. I'm John—John Walden."

"And I'm Emma and this"—she followed the elderly man's eyes to the end of the leash "is Scout. My dog."

At the sound of his name, Scout abandoned all of the new smells along the edges of the driveway and trotted over to first Andy, and then John, his tail going a mile a minute.

"Well, would you look at this fella?" John said, shoving his cane into Andy's hand and then bending over to pet a clearly elated Scout. "He's the spitting image of Rocket— the dog my folks got for my brother and me right before the . . . Eh, don't matter. You're a beauty all your own, aren't you, Scout? Though why that should come as a surprise looking at your momma, here, I don't know."

Emma felt her face warm at the compliment, and then grow warmer still when a glance back at Andy yielded a nod of agreement.

"How old is he?" John asked.

"He's four."

"Had him since he was a pup?"

"No. I got him at the shelter about six months ago."

"Ahhh . . . a rescue."

"I guess," she said, shrugging. "But really, it was more a case of him rescuing me."

John's gaze slid up to hers. "From?"

"Eating alone every night, waking up alone every morning, and living what had become an unhealthy work-life balance."

The elderly man's gaze moved on to his son. "And I didn't even pay her to say that, son."

"Ha-ha, Pop. Well played." Andy's eye roll, while funny, did little to disguise the obvious love between the pair. "Moving on . . . So, should we head inside where we can sit and talk?"

"Of course." She glanced down at Scout and then over at the trees to the side of the house. "Let me just get him situated over there and we can get started."

Andy's head was shaking before she'd even finished talking. "He's welcome inside."

"Are you sure?"

"Absolutely."

She looked back at Scout. "Okay, boy, you're coming in with us."

"And he can come off that leash once we're inside," John said. "He and I can sit on the sunporch and talk dog."

"Talk dog?" she echoed, grinning.

"It's a language."

"Pop . . ."

"Son . . ." John reclaimed his cane, turned toward the house, and held out his arm for Emma to take. When she did, he smiled triumphantly. "You're a good girl, Emma Westlake. I can tell."

"Thank you."

Together, they made their way up the stairs to the front stoop, with Andy trailing them closely. At the top, he stepped around them to open the door, her answering intake of air bringing a smile to John's thinning lips.

"See, son? It's there."

"Pop, this isn't the time to—"

"This is . . . *beautiful*," Emma said, releasing her breath. "It's—it's stunning, actually."

And it was. A million times over.

The entryway, where she'd stopped, looked straight toward the back of the cabin and what was clearly the home's main living space. There, she spied a floor-to-ceiling stone fireplace against a wood-planked wall. Built-in shelves on the wall were filled with books and framed photographs and the kind of knickknacks she knew told stories about the men who lived inside this home. The scattered candles and comfy chairs spoke of evenings spent reading or talking rather than wasted hours in front of a television she didn't see.

To her right, through an arched opening reminiscent of the front doorway, was the kitchen, a cozy nook with cushioned banquette seating around a table that was big enough to seat four yet was clearly appointed for just two. A floor-to-ceiling shelf next to the wall oven held dozens of cookbooks spanning multiple genres of food. "Who's the cook?" she asked, glancing back at Andy.

"That would be Pop." Andy pointed at Scout's leash and, at Emma's nod, unhooked it, much to Scout's delight. "I try, but I'm not even close to him."

"And I couldn't design myself a *doghouse*, let alone a church, or an office building, or a house like this," said John.

She stared up at Andy. "Wait. You designed this place?" she asked.

"He sure did." John beckoned for Emma and Scout to follow. When they did, he led them through the second of two arched doorways off the living room. And once again, Emma found herself looking at the kind of room she'd imagined in every princess dream she'd ever had.

Here, as in the living room and kitchen, cozy found a rightful home alongside stunning in everything from the wall of windows looking down a mountain she hadn't realized they were on, to the glorious sunlight that streamed through them and onto a cushioned settee that spoke to quiet moments of meditation and reflection.

"This is my favorite room in the whole house," John said, settling himself down on the settee and patting the cushioned space to his left for Scout.

Scout, not one to turn down a comfortable spot to sit, jumped into place over the objection she started to give and Andy halted with a gentle hand on her shoulder. "It's okay. Really. I designed this place to be lived in, and nothing gives a house a more lived-in feeling than a dog sitting beside an old man, according to my father, right, Pop?"

"Go on now and leave us be. We'll be fine in here." John rested his hand on Scout's back. Scout, in turn, settled his nose across the elderly man's leg as if he'd placed it there a million times before.

With a nod of satisfaction, Andy guided her back out of the sunroom, across the living room, and into the kitchen. "Would you like a cup of coffee? A glass of soda?" Andy asked, motioning her to the table while he veered toward the prep part of the room. "Pop made up a plate of sandwiches and a little pasta salad for our meeting."

"You didn't have to make a fuss," she said, taking a seat on the part of the cushioned bench closest to the window.

"Pop doesn't know any other way. He hears someone is coming and he makes a beeline for the kitchen. Every. Single. Time." Andy stopped in front of the refrigerator and turned back to Emma. "Drink?"

"Oh. Yes. Sorry. Could I just have a glass of water?"

"Sure." Opening the cabinet to the left of the stove, Andy plucked out two glasses, promptly filled them both from a pitcher of ice water in the refrigerator, and then carried them to the table. He set one in front of Emma, and the other in front of the lone traditional (but still cushioned!) chair, and then headed back to the refrigerator for the bowl of pasta salad and plate of sandwiches. "Despite Pop's occasional mobility issues, he gets around okay and is completely self-sufficient. That's why I'm not looking for anyone to be here full-time while I'm gone, but, rather, stop by for a few hours each day to talk, play a few games, let him cook for you, that sort of thing."

Emma took the bowl of pasta salad from Andy, scooped some onto her plate, and handed it back to him. "You want to *pay me* to let him cook for me?"

"It will be money well spent, trust me." Andy took two sandwiches and passed the plate to Emma. "It was while I was at this same conference, last year, that Pop had a bit of a scare. He was doing something he shouldn't have been doing and fell. Took him thirty minutes to crawl to a phone. Scared me to death when I saw the number for the local hospital come up later that day. He'd broken his hip. He ended up being okay, as you can see, but the crawl to the phone caused added damage that's led to the cane. I've not forgiven myself for that."

"You couldn't know he was going to fall," she protested.

"You're right, I couldn't. But I could have made sure he was better prepared when I left—insisted he refrain from all unnecessary tasks."

"Would he have listened?"

His answering laugh filled the room with a lightness that warmed her from the inside out. "No. But at least now, if he falls, he has one of those buttons he can push that will bring emergency personnel if I'm not around. If you take this job, I'll have your number added to the call list for use during my absence, as well."

At his lead, she forked up a bite of pasta salad and popped it in her mouth, the explosion of flavors on her palate taking her by surprise. "Wow," she said, looking from her plate to Andy. "What is *in* this? It's incredible."

"I have no idea. I just eat whatever he makes and love every bite of it."

She took another bite and another. "If you're worried about him being alone, I could stay here."

"I appreciate it, and I'll keep that in mind for the future, but Pop is good. He's independent. I think you spending a few hours with him every day will be sufficient—that, and being on the call list should something happen again." Andy finished off his helping of pasta salad and hooked his thumb across his shoulder in the direction of the sunroom. "That guy in there is everything to me. I need to know he's okay while I'm gone."

She took a moment to study Andy up close. Everything she'd catalogued from the car still held, but now, sitting across from him, she could see the little things. The fine lines around the outer edges of his eyes when he was deep in thought . . . The faintest hint of a dimple in his right cheek when he smiled . . . The quiet confidence he exuded just sitting there . . . The way his face grew animated when he talked of his father . . .

"You're a good man, Andy Walden."

His amber-flecked eyes lifted from his sandwich back to Emma. "If that's true, it's because of my pop. There's no finer man on earth, in my opinion, than that man sitting in the sunroom right now with your dog. And if you take this job, you'll come to see pretty quickly what I mean."

"Sounds like someone I'd like to know whether I get the job or not." She took a bite of her chicken salad sandwich and, once again, was stunned by its potpourri of flavors. "Wow. Just wow."

His knowing smile called his dimple into action as he sat back against his chair and watched her eat. When she was done, he stacked her plate atop his own and carried it, along with the pasta salad bowl and sandwich platter, over to the counter. "Did you come here from your house?"

"I did."

"Did you happen to notice how long it took, door-to-door?" he asked as he snapped a lid on the pasta salad and transferred the sandwiches into an airtight container.

"Just under twenty-five minutes."

He carried the leftovers to the refrigerator and then

turned back to Emma. "You okay driving rural roads like that at night if necessary?"

"Absolutely."

"I know he didn't when we were outside a little while ago and he was on a leash, but does Scout ever jump on people when he gets excited?"

"Never. He'll lick your knees in shorts weather like nobody's business, but he doesn't jump up on people."

"Okay, good." Andy deposited the dirty plates and utensils into the dishwasher and then returned to his spot across from Emma. "As you can see, Pop loves dogs. So, by all means, feel free to bring Scout with you if you want. I'm heading out next Monday at the crack of dawn and I won't be back until about 8:00 p.m. on Friday. I'm thinking, that first day, you could get here around two? Maybe stay through dinner? And then, over the next four days, you can vary your five hours to encompass breakfast, lunch, or dinner, depending on what Pop wants. Unless, of course, you have a set time with your other clients that might necessitate one here, as well?"

"No, no set schedule except one that has me at the gym with a client at five thirty in the morning on Monday, Wednesday, and Friday." Emma reached over to her bag, plucked out the folder she'd placed inside after returning home from Dottie's, and handed it across the table to Andy. "This is a list of some people who have worked with me in the past and can vouch for my character and my work ethic."

He opened the folder, pulled out the sheet of references, and gave it a thorough read. "This is great. Thank you."

"My pleasure." Looping her bag over her shoulder, she slid her way off the cushioned bench and stood. "I know you have a concert you want to get to, so Scout and I will leave you to your Saturday. You have my number if you need any more information after you speak with my references."

"I'll be back with you on this no later than tomorrow evening." He, too, stood and followed her into the living room en route to the sunroom. "Thanks for getting back to me and thanks for coming all the way out here to meet with us. I really appreciate it."

She paused beside a framed collage of pictures that, upon closer inspection, revealed themselves to be a visual timeline of the building process for Andy's home. "It must've been so incredible to watch your vision coming to fruition."

"It should've been more than it was but"—his shoulders rose and fell in a slow shrug—"yeah, Pop is right, what's done is done. It worked out, in the end."

Shifting her gaze across the collage, picture by picture, she stopped to point at the one in the center. "Oh. Wow. McEnerny Homes built this. I'm heading out to their office today to look at some floor plans with one of my clients. She's looking to build a place with them in Sweet Falls, preferably."

"Wish I could recommend them, but I can't," he said, palming his mouth.

"Oh?"

"I hired him to build this because he's really the biggest name in the game around here. But the guy didn't seem to grasp the concept of the word *no*. As a result, what should have been a fun experience became a bit of a headache, to say the least." He motioned for Emma to follow him to a window overlooking the southern side of the house. "You see that? Trees as far as the eye can see. And the same thing is on the other side of the house. Fifty acres in all.

"Before this, I was living out in Seattle, working for an architectural firm. My parents had plans to build their forever home here on this land—land that had been in my mother's family for generations. But they never actually did it, because they didn't want to be that far away from me. I reminded them of the invention of planes, but . . . they just never did it. Then Mom passed from breast cancer, and I was left this land. It was what she and Pop wanted. They wanted me to have that connection to her past. Anyway, after her death, Pop was lost—absolutely lost. And, honestly, seeing him that way was eating me up even more. So, after a lot of thought, I decided to take my years of experience and strike out on my own, work-wise. Told Pop we were coming here and we were going to design the place together, and we did. I drew it up, of course, but I made sure to incorporate the things we both wanted—the vision we had for our house in the woods." Andy again swept his hands and her focus toward the window. "Once we had the plans set, I did some research on local builders and brought Robert McEnerny in to build it. The second Robert saw the ridge I was building on and the sunsets it afforded, he went full-court press on me. I spent the entire building process telling him—over and over again—I wasn't interested in selling any part of the land. That I didn't want to be surrounded by houses to my left and houses to my right."

"I wouldn't want to, either," she mused as her eyes lit on a mother deer and two speckled fawns making their way through the woods. "It's so peaceful like this."

Nodding, he pointed out a third speckled fawn she hadn't noticed, and then folded his arms across his chest. "It is. But he didn't see that. He saw only the dollar signs possible from building on a ridge like this. Next thing I knew, he was doing title searches and all sorts of stuff to see if there was some sort of loophole that would enable him to get this out from under me. There wasn't, of course, but he sure gave it the old college try."

"Wow."

"Wait. It gets better. This guy actually had his attorney send Pop a letter letting him know he could contest my mother's will and her choice to leave this property to me, as her spouse."

Emma drew back. "Are you serious?"

"Unfortunately, yes."

"What did your dad say?"

"He said nothing, and he advised me to do the same until after the house was finished. And when it was, I told Robert to get off my land, once and for all."

She tracked the third fawn back to its mother and smiled at their sweet reunion. "As much as I hate to do it, I guess I'm going to have to tell Stephanie about this. It's something I'd want to know if I was considering building."

"Me, too. That's why I agreed to speak to that free-lance writer a few weeks ago. The one who died out by you . . ."

Spinning around, she snapped her gaze up to Andy's. "Brian Hill?"

"That's him."

"You—you spoke to him?"

"I did. For an article he was working on about McEnerny. Pop thought I was making a mistake—that I should just let it go—but like I told Brian, when people are entrusting you with something as special as building their home, you should at least pretend to care about the process. McEnerny cares only about money and expanding his empire. He is incapable of grasping the word *no*, and he has absolutely no concept of *enough is enough*."

"Enough is enough?" she rasped, as her mind's eye flew to her phone and the poem she'd read so many times she knew it from memory.

Avarice and greed, lust for more green. In wallet or space, there can be no enough.

"Emma?"

At the sound of her name, Emma forced herself back into the moment—a moment that included a really nice guy sans dimple.

"Are you okay?" he asked, searching her face. "You look a little funny all of a sudden."

"No, I'm fine. But I really should be heading out."

He opened his mouth as if to protest but, in the end, simply led her to the sunroom to collect Scout and say goodbye to John. "Thanks for stopping by, Emma. We'll be in touch."

Chapter Twenty-Two

Stephanie was waiting outside her car when Emma pulled into the lot behind the McEnerny Homes sales office at exactly two o'clock. The fact that Stephanie had beaten her there was a surprise, but so, too, was the number of cars Emma hadn't expected to see on such a beautiful Saturday afternoon in late spring.

"Is there a two-for-one sale on houses or something?" Emma asked as Stephanie approached her open driver's side window. "Because this place is jumping."

Stephanie surveyed the parking lot, shrugged, and then returned her full attention to Emma. "Where's Scout?"

"I dropped him off at home after my meeting with the guy in Cloverton."

"How'd that go? Did you get the job?"

"Let me park and I'll fill you in." Emma pulled into an empty spot three cars over from Stephanie's, retrieved her tote bag from the seat Scout had inhabited less than twenty minutes earlier, and stepped out onto the recently poured asphalt lot. "How long has this place been here? The lot looks new."

"A couple weeks, maybe? I'm not really sure." Stephanie nudged her chin and Emma's gaze toward the makeshift sales office housed in a double-wide trailer flanked by potted trees. "But I'm here, right?"

"You are. And on time, no less."

"Yeah, that won't happen again anytime soon." Stephanie rocked back against the car parked beside Emma's and folded her arms against her chest. "So, go on, I'm listening. Your meeting in Cloverton?"

"His name is Andy and he's a super, *super* nice guy. Absolutely adores his father. He's an amazing architect. And, Stephanie? You should see the house he designed for himself. It looks like something straight out of a child's fairytale—whimsical and cozy and the kind of place where you'd be content to live out your days."

Stephanie's eyes narrowed on Emma. "And this guy wants to hire you for *what*?"

"To look after his father—who, by the way, is a complete sweetheart. Even Scout adored him."

"Hmmm . . ."

"If I get the job, it would start a week from Monday and entail me driving out to Cloverton and spending a few hours or so with Andy's father each day until his return on Friday evening. John is in relatively good shape and thus able to be alone, but Andy wants someone to look in on him on a regular basis."

"Pay good?"

Stephanie's question pushed Emma back a step. "Actually, we didn't talk money."

"You didn't talk money about a job he was interviewing you for?"

"I don't know. I mean, we talked about how often he wanted me to stop by and how long he wanted me to stay each time, but"—Emma shrugged—"I guess I didn't think about it."

"He was cute, wasn't he?"

"Cute?" she echoed. "Where on earth did that come from?"

"The way your eyes lit up the second you mentioned him . . . the way you added that extra *super* to your description of him . . . the way you talked about his profession and his house . . . and the way you only mentioned his father—the one who, by the way, the job actually entails—when I specifically asked."

"I didn't do that, I . . ." The rest of her protest faded into nothing as her mouth caught up with the reality of Stephanie's words. "Okay, fine. Yes, he was attractive. Very attractive, in fact. But that's not why I didn't mention John right away. I mean, if you saw this place, you'd understand."

"Then I'd have talked about the place. Not the very attractive guy who lived inside it."

Emma bit back the argument she knew she couldn't sell and, instead, did her best to take control of the conversation. "Guess who Andy spoke to a few weeks ago?"

"Who?"

"Brian."

Stephanie stared at Emma, her mouth agape. "As in *our* Brian?"

"Yep."

"Whoa. Weird. Why?"

"Well, it seems Brian was doing a little digging on"—Emma hooked her thumb toward the sales office—"our boy, Robert McEnerny."

Stephanie parted company with the car at her back and closed the gap between them. "Okay. Why?"

"Why the digging? Or why did he speak to Andy?"

"Both."

"I'm not sure what Brian was looking for, but he spoke to Andy as a former client of McEnerny."

"I thought you said this guy built his own home," Stephanie countered.

"He *designed* his house. McEnerny built it. And Andy wasn't happy with him at all. Said he spent the whole building process trying to talk Andy into selling some of his fifty acres so McEnerny could parcel it up and build houses on it. And when Andy told him no—repeatedly—McEnerny resorted to some dirty pool to make it happen."

Emma scanned the lot around them and, when she was satisfied no one was within hearing range, lowered her voice and stepped closer to Stephanie. "And get this, Andy said—and I quote—McEnerny *cares only about money and expanding his empire*, that he's *incapable of grasping the word no, and he has absolutely no concept of enough is enough*."

She waited for the lightbulb to go off behind Stephanie's eyes and, when it didn't, she repeated her last sentence. "Andy said McEnerny is incapable of grasping the word no, and he has absolutely no concept of *enough is enough*."

"Enough is enough," Stephanie repeated. "Why does that sound so—wait! Brian says something about that in the poem, right? In the stanza Dottie said is about McEnerny."

"Yep." Emma fished her phone out of her bag and pressed her way to the picture of the poem. "Avarice and greed, lust for more green. In wallet or space, there can be no enough."

"Wow."

Closing out of the poem, Emma nodded. "I know."

"Surely Brian tracked down your guy for something other than just writing two lines of a poem, though, right?"

"Andy said it was for an article. Which got me thinking on the drive back home to drop off Scout. Brian gave me that printout with those four faces on it because he said they all wanted him dead. Which, obviously, begs the question: why? In Sheriff Borlin's case, Brian seemed to be chasing a story involving the sheriff and bribes—a career killer, at the very least. Now, we have Robert McEnerny, yet *another* person Brian was clearly setting out to write unflattering things about. And while we may not know what direction Brian was taking this supposed article he was working on, we do know—*now*—that Andy delivered up a less than flattering example of McEnerny's business tactics. Was it worth killing Brian over? Probably not. But maybe what Andy told him led to something far more damaging— something worth silencing Brian over permanently."

Stephanie's answering silence soon gave way to a squaring of her shoulders. "So what you're saying is that maybe my finally getting off the dime and looking at floor plans is happening at the time it was meant to happen?"

"Maybe."

"Well, alrighty then. Let's get to it, shall we?"

"So apparently, they've called in another sales associate to help and she's due to arrive sometime in the next ten minutes. When she does, she'll sit down with us and go over any questions we might have. So look through the folder and come up with some questions, okay?"

Emma stilled her hand atop the glossy folder bearing the McEnerny Homes name and shifted over on the couch to afford Stephanie room to sit. "This is *your* thing, Stephanie. Not mine. So you need to ask the questions *you* want to ask."

"I don't know what questions to ask. I've never done this. I've lived with my mother since, well, since conception."

"So?"

"So I don't know what I'm supposed to want or ask or any of that."

"Oh, c'mon, Stephanie. You have to have at least an idea of what you want."

"I don't want my mother going on about my biological clock while I'm trying to eat. That's it. That's all I want."

Emma's answering laugh turned more than a few heads in their direction. "Okay, fine. Let's look at this folder and see if anything gets you jazzed."

"I'd like a dog just like Scout. But since I work all day long, maybe I could go with a cat, instead."

"A cat?" Emma echoed. "Seriously? Don't you think maybe you should pick another animal? Something less . . . I don't know . . . curious about windows? Like maybe a goldfish? Or a hamster? Something that lives its entire life in a cage?"

Stephanie pulled a face. "Ha. Ha. Ha. Not. That incident with my roommate's cat, Cuddles, was years ago. People deserve second chances every now and again, you know?"

"I suppose you could be right. But while this is certainly a worthy discussion, how about we focus on what you'd like in the house—feature-wise," Emma prodded, smoothing her hand down the front of the folder. "For now, anyway."

"Fine. A bed. A couch. A TV. I'm easy."

"That's a start, certainly. But let's try and think a little wider, shall we?" Emma opened the folder across their neighboring laps to reveal two pockets' worth of information. The pocket on the left contained a printed list of all the amenities included in a McEnerny home. A second sheet listed the many add-on options people could select.

"That's kind of cool," Stephanie mused, stopping her finger midway down the first sheet. "A planning desk in the kitchen. I like that . . . Oh, and a mudroom off the garage? That's genius. If there's a puddle within a ten-mile radius of wherever I am, I tend to step in it. So having a place to dump off my shoes before entering the rest of the house would be awesome."

Nodding, Emma reached into the pocket on the right side of the folder and pulled out a packet of floor plans: two ranch-style houses, two two-story models, one rowhouse plan, and a one and a half story. Each plan featured four different available exteriors on the front of the page, and a drawing of the interior on the back. "Are you wanting a one-story? A two-story? What are you thinking?"

"I don't know. I just want a house. Of my own. I hadn't really thought about what kind." Stephanie stacked the lists, returned them to their pocket, and then spread the various floor plans across the top of the folder and onto the cushion beside her legs. "But seeing these is kind of fun, you know?"

"It should be. Because it is."

"Excuse me?" In unison, Emma and Stephanie looked up to find a fortysomething brunette smiling down at them with a clipboard. "Miss Porter?"

Stephanie gathered up the floorplans into a haphazard pile, handed them over to Emma, and stood. "That's me. Hi. And this is my—this is Emma."

"Hello, Emma, welcome. I'm Vanessa and I've been working with McEnerny Homes for almost two years now." The woman motioned them toward an open office in the far corner of the room and then led them in that direction. "Have you had a chance to look at your packet and see all of the beautiful homes you can build with McEnerny Homes?"

"We started to. Yes." Stephanie trailed the woman into the office and then waited just inside the doorway for Emma.

Pointing them to a pair of chairs across from her desk, Vanessa took a seat and got straight to business. "How soon are you looking to build?"

"I-I'm not sure. Soon."

"Are you looking here in Morehead?"

"Actually, no. I'd like to be in Sweet Falls," Stephanie said.

"Well, I'll be honest, what few lots we have out in Sweet Falls at this moment are quite limited and rather scattered around. Meaning, we have one lot out on Bruce Road, if you're familiar with that area, another out on Winding Court that can accommodate a walk-out basement, another on Wren Street that can accommodate a side entry garage, and then one more out on Jacob Lane. That one backs to trees, which is a bonus, but it's a small lot at just over a quarter of an acre. I've circled all four of those locations here."

Emma matched Stephanie's lean toward the desk and the artist's rendering of the many streets in and around Sweet Falls, her gaze landing on the circle nearest her own house. "Oooh, I think I've seen that empty lot while out walking Scout a few weeks—"

"What's that?" Stephanie asked.

Following Stephanie's finger to the top right-hand corner of the map, Emma noted a single unnamed road off Route 50 that held a hand-drawn square containing the number *300*.

"I'm not at liberty to share details at this time but . . ." Vanessa lifted her gaze to the door and then lowered her voice to a whisper. "If you'd like to get in on the ground floor of McEnerny Homes' most innovative project ever, there just may be three hundred opportunities opening up very, very soon. And trust me when I tell you, it will be *the* place to live."

Yanking open her top desk drawer, Vanessa plucked out a pad of paper and slid it across the desk at Stephanie. "If you'd like, you can jot your name and number on this sheet and I'll be sure to call you the moment we get the go-ahead to start selling."

"I wasn't aware there was an open tract of land off Route 50 of any kind, let alone one big enough to accommodate three hundred homes," Emma said, looking from the map to the sales associate.

The woman beamed. "On half-acre lots, no less. With room for a clubhouse and a pool, two themed playgrounds, and its very own shopette."

Stephanie added the last digit in her phone number and then pointed at a large hashed-off area in the upper left-hand corner of the box. "And what's that there?"

"That is a private, twenty-acre piece of property that will border the neighborhood, yet have its own private entrance and exit."

"And how much would a lot like *that* set me back?" Stephanie asked. "You know, in the event the lottery ticket I never think to buy, but always dream about, wins somehow."

"It's already bought and paid for."

"Lottery winner?" Stephanie quipped.

"No."

"Foreign dignitary?"

"No."

"Celebrity?"

Vanessa's lips twitched. "I'm really not at liberty to say."

"That's okay. I'm just being nosy." Stephanie drew her information packet to her chest and looked back at the map longingly. "You'll call me at the number I just gave you when this place opens up, right? Because it sounds perfect for me and"—she flashed a grin at Emma—"my soon-to-be cat, Lulu."

Emma tore her attention away from the map in favor of Stephanie. "You have its name picked out?"

"Sure."

"That was fast . . ."

"I'm good with names."

"And if you end up with a boy cat?" she asked.

Stephanie started to stand, paused a moment, and then sank back onto her chair. "I don't know. I hadn't thought about that."

"You've got time." Vanessa stood, a clear signal she was ready to move on to whomever was next in the queue. "In the meantime, if I were you, I'd spend some time looking over the floor plans in your packet. Let yourself dream a little. Before you know it, you'll find yourself narrowing in on the one that works best for you. Once you've done that, you can start making a list of the extra features you might want inside your home. It's also a good time to speak to your lender to find out what you're approved for in the event that factors in on your selection. Because once we announce the opening of our first-ever full-scale neighborhood, I have little doubt we'll sell out quickly."

The woman traveled her gaze out to the waiting room and then back to Stephanie and the folder clutched in her hand. "The best lots will be right here," she said, running her finger along the back edge of the numbered square. "They'll back to trees for that all-important privacy factor—assuming, of course, that's something that appeals to you?"

Sure enough, Emma could almost feel the tug of the proverbial fishing line as Stephanie took the bait. "Oh yes, very much so!"

"Then I'll be in touch. Soon." Vanessa gathered up the various pieces of paper she'd spread across the desk and stacked them neatly into a pile. "I'll walk you out and—"

"Actually, is there any chance Stephanie could have a copy of that map?" Emma asked, rising to her feet beside Stephanie. "The one that shows where this new neighborhood will be if it all goes through?"

The woman's smile grew pinched. "I'm sorry, I can't. In fact, I really shouldn't have shown you that map at all. It's top secret information."

"We understand completely, and we wouldn't dream of showing it to anyone, would we, Stephanie?"

Stephanie stilled her head, mid-shake. "Of course not, but I don't really need to have—"

Silencing the rest of Stephanie's protest with a not-so-gentle squeeze on her arm, Emma looked back at Vanessa. "Being able to look at that will really help with the whole dreaming thing, you know?"

Once again, the woman's eyes traveled out to the waiting

room before settling back on Emma once again. "If you promise not to show it to anyone, you can take a quick picture of it before I put it back in the drawer."

"That'll be great," Emma said, lowering her voice to a conspiratorial whisper as she reached into her tote for her phone. "Thank you, Vanessa. This is all so very exciting."

Chapter Twenty-Three

———◆———

They were barely out the front door of the sales office when Stephanie whirled around, eyes wide. "What was that about just now with the map?"

"I don't know."

"You don't know?" Stephanie echoed.

"It was just a feeling." Emma made her way across the parking lot with Stephanie in tow. "A silly one, maybe, but I felt the need to go with it. So I did."

"You thinking about maybe moving out there, too?" Stephanie asked.

"No. I'm happy with where I am. But it sounds like it could be perfect for you."

When they reached Emma's car, Stephanie leaned her back against the driver's side, and let out a happy squeal. "It does, doesn't it? My own space . . . A clubhouse with a pool . . . A shopette I can hit up on the way home from work . . . It's hard to wrap my head around the notion I could actually live somewhere like that. On my own. Like a real adult."

"You're a real adult, Stephanie," Emma argued. "You're just one who works crazy hours and doesn't have much time to do anything other than work and sleep."

"The way you put that, I don't sound so pathetic."

Emma opened her car door and tossed her tote onto the passenger seat. "You're not pathetic."

"Said the person I've paid to be my friend."

"At the gym," Emma countered.

Stephanie met Emma's gaze, only to abandon it seconds later in favor of a sigh. "Oh, man. Emma, I'm sorry. I didn't even think about it being a Saturday and . . ." She waved aside the rest of her sentence and reached into her own bag for her checkbook and pen. "How about the same rate I give you for a normal gym outing plus a little extra for the gas it took to get out here."

"What? No. That's not what I meant by that, Stephanie." Emma closed the woman's checkbook and wrested it from her hand. "I meant that while you may have hired me to be your friend for working-out purposes, I'm here, looking at houses with you, because I want to."

"You do?"

"Yes. You're . . . *great*. And fun."

"Me? Fun? Ha!"

"Yes. Fun." She tossed the checkbook back into Stephanie's bag and rested her hands on her hips. "And *great*, since you seemed to have missed that part."

"Wow. I don't know what to say."

"That's fine. All you really need to do is *hear*." Lowering herself onto the edge of her seat, Emma pointed at the folder wedged under Stephanie's arm. "And go home and look through all those pictures and dream a little, just like Vanessa said."

"Dream a little . . . I like that."

"Good."

"And you?" Stephanie asked, pushing off the car and

taking a step in the direction of her own. "What are you going to do?"

"I'm going to go home and see my dog. After that, maybe I'll read a little more of that cozy mystery Dottie loaned me."

"Sounds good. See you Monday? At the gym?"

Emma started her car. "I'll be there."

"Awesome." Stephanie took a few steps and stopped, looked back at Emma. "Thank you. For coming today. For including me in that breakfast with Dottie on Wednesday and again today. And for saying what you did a little while ago. It meant more than you can possibly realize."

"Well, I meant it. And other people will, too, once you start putting yourself first and getting yourself back out—"

"Hey!" Stephanie said, doubling back to Emma's car. "I forgot to ask. What did your deputy say about your dress?"

"My dress?"

"Yeah. That's why you got all cutie-d up today, right? Because you were going to see him and his kid today at the park?"

She stared at Stephanie as the woman's words, coupled with a glance at her dashboard clock, struck like a one-two punch to her stomach. "Oh no . . ."

R iddled with a gut-twisting guilt she couldn't seem to shake, Emma pulled off the road just shy of her turn onto Route 50 and dialed Dottie's number.

One ring . . .

Two rings . . .

Three—

"I think I could've told that man you were a serial killer and he'd still decide to hire you."

She took in the name on her dashboard screen and made her way back into the flow of traffic. "Excuse me?"

"That man. Andy Walden. He called to check your references, but I'm not sure why. He seemed fairly taken by you before he ever got around to asking any actual questions as to your work ethic."

"Oh. Wow. I'm surprised he called already."

"So I take it he hasn't offered you the job yet?"

"Not yet. He said he'd call tomorrow. In the evening, I think."

"I see. Well, I suppose there's something to making you squirm a little. But really, Emma? You have the job."

She allowed herself the smile born on Dottie's words as she made the right onto Route 50 toward home. "I'll hope you're right. I could certainly use another client. Or fifty."

"I'm right. As I always am, dear."

Glancing in the rearview mirror, Emma noted the absence of any cars and slowed to a speed that allowed herself a moment to catch her breath, and to get to the reason for her call. "You know your source at the sheriff's department? The one you've been friends with for eons, as you said?"

"Yes . . ."

"Any chance she works on Saturdays?"

"No."

She felt her whole body slump under the weight of Dottie's answer. "Oh."

"But I have her home number. I can reach her on a Saturday just as easily as I can reach her on a weekday."

Her answering flash of hope disappeared as quickly as it came. "This would probably require her to access a work computer, if she even would. Which she probably wouldn't."

"You really have no idea how much money I've given that department over the years, do you, dear?"

"I guess not." Emma took in the homes along her side of the road—a mixture of big and small and varying styles. "Do you think she would be willing to share an address with you?"

"For?"

"An employee. One of the deputies, actually."

She waited through the answering silence in her ear as she continued to take in the long, short, and everything-in-between driveways that branched off the road. One after the other, each leading to yet another family's home.

"I will never understand your generation. In my day, the chasing was for the men. Now, it's the women doing the chasing."

"This isn't about chasing, Dottie. It's about apologizing. To a little boy. That's all." She slowed still further as the line of homes to her right transitioned into rows and rows of Christmas trees, rows and rows of apple trees, and, finally, the dirt road bearing the Davis Farm and Greenhouse sign she dreamed about far more often than she should.

"What's his name?"

"The little boy?"

"No, dear. The employee."

"Oh. Right. Jack. Jack Riordan."

"I'll get back to you on that within the hour. In the meantime though, tell me about your visit out to Robert's place with Stephanie. Did you find anything helpful for our investigation?"

She considered the question as she took in the rows of strawberry plants in front of her, the apple trees and Christmas trees behind her, and the peace and tranquility of the wide-open land on which they all—

Veering onto the shoulder, Emma threw the car into reverse and hit the gas pedal. "Dottie, I-I'm sorry. I have to go. Now."

Chapter Twenty-Four

For the second weekend in a row, the parking lot of Davis Farm and Greenhouse was surprisingly empty. The only other vehicle besides her own and the gardens' van belonged to a young couple currently transferring two flats of flowers from their cart to the trunk of their SUV. Pulling in beside them, Emma looked out over the vast land dotted by trees and fruit-bearing plants and did her best to shake off the growing sense of dread creeping up her spine.

To her right, on a plaque mounted to a fence post separating the lot from the gardens, was a sign that looked as if it was the regular recipient of a good polish.

DAVIS FARM AND GREENHOUSE
FAMILY-OWNED SINCE 1916

She sat for a moment, studying the sign, and then stepped out onto the graveled parking lot capable of hosting as many as fifty cars. On any other day, she'd be as thrilled (albeit surprised) to have the place to herself as she'd been six days earlier. But now, in light of the hand-drawn map Vanessa had pretended not to see Emma immortalizing with her camera's phone, there was no sense of elation, quiet or otherwise.

Nodding hello at the couple now backing out of their parking spot, Emma set out across the empty lot toward the main building, her mind's eye skipping ahead to the woman she knew she'd find standing behind the counter. It wasn't hard to imagine a young Nancy trailing behind her father in the apple orchard, or picking strawberries with her mother, the fruits of their labor being sold to local markets and at the farm stand that once stood where the main building now resided.

So much history resided on Nancy's land—for Nancy, and for the countless families who'd flocked to these same grounds for everything from apples and strawberries to blueberries and Christmas trees over the past hundred-plus years. Surely, its very existence was as much a Sweet Falls staple as the beloved gazebo in the town square, right?

"Only one way to find out," she murmured as she left the graveled lot behind in favor of the concrete floor of the main building.

This time, instead of looking to the right and cataloguing all of the cute gardening accessories or to the left at the seed packets she loved to look at and consider, she continued on straight ahead, her gaze skipping to the counter, the register, and the dozen or so framed photographs lining the wall behind it all.

It wasn't lost on Emma how her footsteps grew heavy as she got within four or five feet of the counter, the anticipation she normally felt at that exact spot simply gone. She wasn't a partier, she wasn't a clothes shopper, and she wasn't one to stay up all night and sleep all day. For her, nonwork hours were all about the simple things. Things like playing fetch with Scout, taking long walks after dinner, sitting on her back patio watching the sun set behind

the church steeple in town, and creating beauty from time
spent digging in the dirt. And Davis Farm and Greenhouse
had been her carrot at the end of many a workweek thanks
to the encouragement of Dottie's late husband, Alfred.

"You're back."

Startled back into the moment, Emma returned Nancy
Davis's smile. "I am."

"Every time I see you here, I can't help but think about
Annabelle and how the only time she ever stepped foot out
on this farm was the day before you came for a visit. She'd
scurry in here, ask my dad what she'd bought for you two
to plant the last time you were around, and then buy the
same thing so you wouldn't know it had died sometime
during the previous year."

"Ha! The truth comes out . . ."

"Annabelle was crazy about you."

Emma blinked against the hint of mist that always came
with a memory of her beloved great-aunt Annabelle. "And
I was crazy about her—even though my lack of a green
thumb can be traced to her, apparently."

"Your thumb is green now."

"True. But I didn't come by it honestly, that's for sure."
Emma looked around the empty room.

"That's neither here nor there," Nancy said, pulling out
her trusty stool. When she was settled on its cushioned seat,
she grabbed a notebook and a pen from the shelf beneath
the register and opened it to a page at about the midway
point. "So, do you know what you'd like? Right now I have
some crape myrtles, magnolias, dogwoods, an eastern red-
bud, a Washington hawthorn, a sugar maple, and some cy-
press."

"All of the above," Emma said, leaning forward against
the counter. "But last week's rosebush is it for me until I
start making a little more money. Sadly."

Nancy stilled her pen above the empty page. "This one
is on the house, remember? For being so kind the other day."

"Oh, right. I forgot about that. But really, Nancy, it's not necessary. Let's just call whatever you think I did *my way* of repaying *you* for never tiring of my crazy questions."

Something that looked a lot like relief sagged Nancy's shoulders and had her returning her notepad and pen to the shelf. "The only way you learn is by asking questions. That's something my dad always said when he was working with customers, and it's a mindset that has proven successful for me, as well. For many years."

"And will for many more years to come," Emma said. "Many, *many* more."

Nancy's answering laugh held no sign of humor. "Not if things don't rebound really fast, it won't. Another few weeks like *this*"—Nancy swept her hand out toward the empty aisles and beyond them to the part of the parking lot they could see from inside—"on top of everything else that's been happening around here and, well, I just won't be able to survive."

"That's what I don't get. Why *has* it been like this these last two weeks?"

"Last *four* weeks," Nancy amended.

"Oh. Wow. I didn't realize." Emma, too, took in the aisles that normally buzzed with activity regardless of the season. "Then I get it even less. This is normally one of your busy times, right? At least in terms of the greenhouse?"

Pinching her mouth closed, Nancy nodded.

"Did the whole town just simply decide not to plant flowers this year? Aside from that young couple I saw when I was pulling in, of course."

Nancy's lips released into the faintest hint of a small, yet fleeting grin. "They were so cute trying to pick out what would look best around the mailbox of their first-ever home together. She wanted something happy and cheerful. He wanted something that bloomed every day, all year long."

Emma's answering laugh echoed in the cavernous room. "Wouldn't we all . . ."

"They were so full of hope and ideas and plans." Nancy ran her fingertip along the wood grain of the counter, her voice taking on a faraway quality. "I remember being just like that when my dad turned over the reins of this place to me. I didn't want to mess with the basics—the apple picking, the strawberry and blueberry picking, or any of that. But I knew I could bring in even more people and highlight even more of what we have here by modernizing things a bit. That's why I made that barrel train for the kids to ride in off the back of my tractor during the fall, and added all of those picnic tables out there for parents to sit at and wave to their kids as they go by. And since I put in tables instead of just benches, it seemed a great time to add apple cider by the paid cup. And the speakers pumping out the Christmas music while people pick their trees every December? I can't begin to tell you just how much that adds to the bottom line every year now."

"Your father would be very proud of you, I'm sure," Emma said. "As would his father before him."

"That might have been the case a few months ago, but . . ." Nancy's eyes glistened with tears she quickly wiped away. "Not now. Not after . . . everything."

"Are you selling your land to Robert McEnerny?" asked Emma, the question, as well as the speed with which it made its way past her lips, surprising her almost as much as it did Nancy.

But unlike the rapid blinking it set off for Emma, it drew a gasp from Nancy that echoed around the room. "Not over my dead body, if I can help it!"

It was Emma's turn to sag in relief. "Phew. You have no idea how glad I am to hear that. This is my place! My—my *mother ship* when I have a few extra dollars to spend!"

"I can't promise I'll be able to keep it going." Nancy slid back off the stool and began an almost aimless pacing that had her moving between the register, the accordion wall, and the picture wall with no rhyme or reason. "But selling to a man who will bulldoze every tree and plant into smithereens is just unthinkable!"

"So he's approached you?"

"He has. Multiple times."

"And you've told him no?"

"Each and every time. But that was before . . ." Nancy pushed the rest of her words away with splayed hands and a groan of frustration. "I keep waiting for time to work its magic, but it's not. And every day that goes by before it does is another nail in the coffin of my family's heritage."

Emma flashed back to Brian's poem and the stanzas that Dottie was convinced were about the woman standing in front of her now. "Why did everyone ignore you the other day? At that party? I thought the members of that committee had seen the error of their ways when your work—your *award-winning* work—took a complete dive in the wake of your removal."

"They did."

"Okay . . ." Emma prodded. "But no one came near you the whole time I was there."

Nancy's only answer was a shrug, followed by an almost manic straightening of the framed photographs tasked with telling bits and pieces of the Davis' family story.

"Did *you* kill those plants in town?" Emma asked in the wake of a steadying breath. "As a way to prove your worth to all your naysayers?"

The straightening slowed, sped up, and then slowed again before finally stopping altogether. "It was *my* work that won that award," Nancy finally said, her voice a rasped whisper. "Mine. You don't get to win a statewide award by stopping by once a week and plucking a few weeds. It's an ongoing dance of weeding and watering and feeding and grooming and, most importantly, time. *I* did that. *Me*. Not Stacy. Not Jane. Not Linda. And most definitely not Rita

Gerard. Stacy *knew* that. Jane *knew* that. And Linda *knew* that. But they all seemed to forget it when Rita started making more of the award and the press that invariably came my way because of it. Then, and only then, did they all jump on her bandwagon and push me out with their coldness.

"I knew they couldn't keep it going without me. I knew it. But I was also afraid it was going to take a while and I missed being in the know about things like I was when I was in that group. So I thought I'd just speed it up a little, that's all." Nancy ran her finger across the image of her parents and then dropped her hand to her side. "Running a place this big is hard work—time-consuming work. It leaves little time for friends, let alone an actual relationship. Sure, I get to talk to people when I'm ringing up their purchase or making sure they find what they need. But in those conversations, I'm always standing on the outside, hearing about their plans and their projects. I'm never actually a part of any of it."

"The committee was different, though, wasn't it?" Emma prodded.

"It was. There, I was part of something. And I was appreciated."

"Until Rita messed it up."

Nancy's nod was slow, yet definitive. "That one is so starved for the spotlight that the thought of someone else getting even a sliver of it for a day or two enrages her."

"Which, in this case, was all the press the state award garnered for you, right?"

Another nod. "I didn't submit us for that award. It wasn't even on my radar. I just wanted to be part of a group where I truly fit, and one devoted solely to gardening seemed like the perfect match. Granted, I fussed with the beds in the square outside committee time, but that's just the way I am with plants. *Rita* is the one who put us in for that award. Because she was trying to get her name known in the months leading up to the mayoral race. And once we actually *won* it and it came with publicity that highlighted me more than her, she got angry and jealous and spiteful. Because she's someone in this town, and I'm not supposed to be. Ever."

"But you already *are* someone in this town," Emma protested. "You run this place—a place that's beloved by so many people."

Nancy's eyes left the pictures, traveled around the empty room, and came to rest on Emma. "It's not feeling all that beloved anymore. But I was going to fix it—I really was. I-I just wanted to be appreciated for what I'd done. I tried to make that awful little man understand that, but clearly he didn't give me the chance to make it right. Because people stopped coming here after that."

"By 'awful little man,' do you mean Brian Hill?"

"Yes. He showed up here about three weeks before his death with a picture of me. Taken at night. In the town square."

"What *kind* of picture?"

"A picture of me sabotaging everything I'd done in those plant beds along the town square." Nancy kneaded the skin beside her temple. "I fell apart when he showed me that picture. Not because he'd caught me, necessarily, but because it made it so I had to face what I'd done. In the moment, when I was dousing the plants with a toxic spray, I was so hurt and so angry I wasn't thinking straight. But later, when he showed me that picture of myself—a picture he had the gall to deny taking—the only thing I felt was disgust. At myself. I told him I would make it right. I begged him to keep from making the picture public the same way the stuff that's happened here on my property hasn't been made public. But even though I never saw the picture in the paper after that, he clearly did something with it because it was right after that when my business dropped off to nothing."

"Wow. I had no idea. About any of this."

"Clearly. Otherwise I'm sure you wouldn't have come last week, you wouldn't have been so nice to me at the garden party, and you wouldn't be standing here now. But, Emma? Why is it that what *I* did can cause *this*"—again, Nancy swept her hand and Emma's gaze around the room—"yet the damage *I've* been dealing with for close to six weeks now doesn't even warrant so much as a mention in the paper?"

"Damage?" Emma echoed. "What damage?"

"Someone keeps cutting the deer fence I have around the property. The first time, I didn't notice it until the deer had destroyed nearly one whole row of plants. When I finally found their access point and saw that it had been cut, I called Sheriff Borlin's office. A very nice deputy— Riordan, I think—came, took a report, and then sent the sheriff out for a look. Sheriff Borlin checked it out, gave me his personal number, told me to call him directly if anything else came up, and then left, promising to be in touch. Which he wasn't.

"A week later, I came across another cut in the fence. This time, there was fairly significant damage in the apple orchard. So I called the sheriff directly, just like he told me to. He came. Took a report. Left. And again I heard nothing. No follow-up call . . . No added patrols in the area that I could see . . . And not a single mention of either call in the *Sweet Falls Gazette*'s police blotter."

"Have you complained? Or followed up on your own?"

Nancy tapped her way into her voice mail, scrolled down the page, and stopped on one from Tim Borlin. Another tap and she held the phone out to Emma.

"Nancy. I got your messages." Her gaze lifted to Nancy's at the sheriff's clipped, almost biting, tone. "Do not call Jack Riordan or any of my other deputies about the incidents at your farm. I will look into it as I said I would. In my own time."

At Nancy's mouthed "Keep listening," Emma pulled the phone tighter against her ear.

"Don't mess with me on this, Nancy."

At the end of the message, she handed the phone back to a teary-eyed Nancy. "I-I don't know what to say."

Shrugging, Nancy took the phone back from Emma.

"His tone, his words, his *threat* . . . And you listened?"

"I thought about reaching out to Deputy Riordan anyway, especially in light of how stunned Brian was when he realized something was happening in this town that he hadn't known about. But after he left, and I really thought about what I'd done, I realized I had no right to complain." Nancy yanked open a drawer behind the counter, plucked out a bottle of headache medicine, and downed two capsules. "Because really, how could I? I should just be glad I haven't been brought up on vandalism charges of my own."

Emma did her best to take it all in, processing what she could in the moment and saving the rest for later. But still, there was one last question she needed to ask. "Did Brian really invite you to Open Mic Night at Deeter's that last night?"

"He did."

"Why?"

"Brian was all about shock value. It's why he wrote the kind of articles he wrote . . . why he stirred up the problems he did . . . why he argued everything . . ."

"So why would you accept an invitation from him for anything?" Emma asked. "That doesn't make any sense to me."

"It was one of those e-invite things. On the subject line it said: 'An Ode to Your Deception, a poetry reading by Brian Hill.'"

"An ode to your deception?" Emma repeated. "Seriously?"

"Yes."

"But from what you just told me, your business was already declining before that night. So why go if everyone already knew what you'd done?"

"Because three other people were copied on that invite. And, right or wrong, I wanted to hear what he had on them, too."

Chapter Twenty-Five

———

Armed with a litany of restless thoughts, a clearly oblivious Scout, and the text with Jack Riordan's address, Emma made her way down one street after another. She tried to be present in the moment, to really notice each house they passed as she normally did on their walks, but it was as if everything was cloaked in a thin layer of fog.

"How did I let myself get talked into this?" she asked of Scout's back as he stopped to sniff every tree, every rock, and every mailbox along the way. "I didn't play cops and robbers when I was a kid. I didn't read mysteries. I didn't even own a magnifying glass. Yet now—*ugh*. Ugh. Ugh. *Ugh*."

More than anything she wanted to call Dottie and Stephanie, tell them she was giving up on the whole sleuthing thing, and just focus her full attention on the new business. Yet when she'd passed Dottie's street on the way home from Nancy's, she'd kept on going, her mind unable or unwilling to completely disengage from the mess Brian had laid in her lap.

It was an intriguing mess, no doubt, but a mess none-theless.

At the next street, they turned left, Scout's delight in the longer-than-normal after-dinner walk evident. She tried to lose herself in his uncomplicated joy but, every time she got close, another question, another possibility, reared itself inside her head.

Brian had indisputable evidence of Nancy's misdeeds. Nancy knew this . . . Nancy was angered by it . . . Nancy's livelihood was suffering because of it . . . And if Dottie and Stephanie were right and it was a plant that had killed Brian . . .

Shaking the troubling thought from her head, Emma willed herself to focus on something, *anything*, else. Nevertheless, every unusual flower that caught her eye, every tap of a hammer in the distance, and every glimpse of a Realtor's sign in someone's yard ripped her thoughts right back to Nancy Davis.

At the next street sign they came to, Emma glanced down at Dottie's text, compared the road name in front of her with the one on her phone, and turned left, her gaze immediately skipping ahead to the third house on the right—a tiny, cute bungalow-style home. The black shutters—paired with a maroon-colored door—gave the medium-hued gray house an inviting pop of contrast. The empty front porch begged for a cushioned swing or a pair of wicker chairs on which to sit and enjoy the sun's slow farewell to another day.

As they approached the house, Emma looked up the driveway to the black midsize sedan parked in front of the single-car garage. On the back of the car was a bike rack with two bikes—one adult, and one child-sized—held into place by a black rope and a lock.

Pulling in a breath, Emma held it for a moment and then released it slowly, summoning Scout's full attention in response. "Well, boy, we're here. Finally."

She gathered the excess leash in her hand and set their

pace up to the door at slow and steady. Once on the porch, she allowed herself a moment to visualize the space as she might decorate it, and then knocked, the curiosity as to what might come next dividing Scout's attention between Emma and the door.

The second the door opened, though, Scout's tail went into wag-overdrive as he took in the face looking back at first him, and then—more warily—Emma.

"This is a surprise," Jack said, his tone clipped.

"I know. But I wanted to apologize for not being at the park today." Feeling suddenly foolish, she stepped back. "In case you brought Tommy there to see Scout."

"Had him there at noon just like you told him."

Guilt drove her gaze to the wooden slats beneath her feet. "I'm sorry. It . . ." She looked up at Jack and squared her shoulders. "Honestly, it got lost in a last-minute schedule change."

"Daddy?"

Tightening her grip on Scout, she followed Jack's eyes through the narrow opening in the door. There, just beyond him, peeking toward them from an interior doorway, was the little boy who'd stolen her dog's heart.

"I'll be with you in a minute, son."

"Who is it?" Tommy asked.

She reached out, rested her free hand atop Jack's arm, and lowered her voice to a whisper. "Please. I'd like to apologize to him if that's okay?"

"I don't think that's—"

Scout's whimper claimed the rest of Jack's protest and pulled Tommy more fully into the room. "Daddy? Is that a dog?"

"Please," she repeated.

"Fine." Stepping back, Jack pushed the door open the rest of the way, and motioned his son to come closer. "Someone is here to see you, pal."

"Scout!"

In a flash, Tommy was at the door, Scout's ready licks igniting a series of happy squeals from the little boy. Emma, in turn, felt her guilt only deepen.

"Hi, Tommy!"

Looking up, the little boy grinned at her over the top of Scout's head. "Hi, Miss Westlake!"

"Emma, remember?" She squatted down, rubbed Scout's head, and locked eyes with Tommy. "I am so sorry we weren't at the park like I said we'd be. Scout and I were both looking forward to it very much when we woke up this morning. But some work stuff got switched around and I lost track of time. It's not an okay excuse—I was wrong, and I own that—but it's what happened, and I'm very, very sorry."

Tommy looked from Emma to Scout and back again, the set of his jaw as he considered her words reminiscent of the man looking down on them now. "That's okay!" Tommy said, burying his face in Scout's side. "Me and Scout can play fetch now, right, Daddy?"

She looked up at Jack. "I'm game if you're game."

"Please, Daddy? *Please?*"

"Okay. But only for a little while. It's getting close to bedtime."

Tommy stood, darted his attention out to the yard and the lone rubber ball resting beneath a dogwood tree, and then looked back at Emma. "Can you take that off him?" he asked, pointing at the leash.

"I can. But you need to stay in the yard so Scout doesn't get in trouble, okay?"

"Okay!"

Together, Tommy and Scout raced to the tree while Emma lowered herself onto the porch step. The click of the door at her back was followed, moments later, by the sound of Jack's approaching steps. "Thanks for this."

"What? The play time?" She scooted over to the far edge of the step as he sat down beside her. "It's the least I could do."

"The play time *and* the apology," he amended.

"I owed it to him, and to you, as well. I really had been looking forward to it." She smoothed the bottom half of her flowered dress across her bent knees and released a quiet sigh. "But a prospective client I was scheduled to see at two called and asked to move it up to twelve thirty. Something about the change in time threw me off and the next thing I knew, it was after two and I was out at McEnerny Homes with Stephanie when I realized what I'd done—or, rather, what I'd forgotten. And that was being at the park at noon so Tommy could play with Scout."

Jack pointed her attention to his son and the ball the boy was in the process of throwing for Scout and shrugged. "Clearly, his disappointment has been forgotten."

"I hope so. And, again, I'm sorry. Truly."

"Did you get the client?" he asked, resting his elbows on his knees and turning his full attention to Emma.

"I don't know yet." She thought back to Andy and his father and the warmth she'd felt there, and turned to meet Jack's eye. "I hope so. It would certainly help."

"Then I hope you get it."

"Thank you." Swiveling her body so the porch upright was at her back, she studied him closely, the decreasing natural light casting shadows across his tired, yet oh-so-handsome face. "Hey, can I ask you a question?"

"Sure."

"What makes some crimes end up in the *Gazette*'s police blotter, and some not?"

He scrubbed at his face with his hand. "Are you kidding? If someone sneezes the wrong way it ends up in the blotter. Always has. It's par for the course in a town the size of Sweet Falls."

"The stuff that keeps happening out at Nancy Davis's farm hasn't. And it's caused a lot of damage."

"You mean the fence that got cut a month or so ago?"

"Times four," Emma said, nodding.

His hand dropped to his leg. "Come again?"

"Someone keeps cutting her deer fencing. It's caused all sorts of damage to her trees and plants—costly damage. Yet, according to Nancy, there's been no mention of the vandalism in the paper and no follow-up from your department on any of it."

"No follow-up?" he echoed, pushing off the step. "I handed that incident off to the sheriff when it happened. At his request. He said he'd take care of it. Yet now you're saying he didn't?" Jack stood and began to pace from one end of the porch to the other, looking out at his son every few steps. "And that it's happened again?"

"It's happened four times. In four different places."

"I had no idea," he said, doubling back. "And you're saying the sheriff never followed up with Nancy?"

"He's come out each time. Taken a report each time. But then that's the last she sees of him until she calls him back out again. And the last time she called him for a status update he was nasty, at best. And threatening, at worst."

Jack stared at Emma. "And you know this because . . ."

"Nancy played me a message he left her on the phone. He told her *not* to reach out to you the way she mentioned doing in her message to him. He said he was handling it and not to mess with him on it." Emma returned a smile and wave from Tommy and then looked back up at Jack. "That said, is it normal for the sheriff to be handling vandalism reports? Isn't that something you or one of the other deputies would do?"

He stopped, looked out at his son and Scout, and palmed his mouth. "It absolutely is. But I figured he took the first incident from me because he's known Nancy for years. I didn't know he was going to drop the ball like this. Or that he told her not to contact me again."

"And the police blotter?" she asked. "Why is it not showing up there?"

Jack's sigh was long, labored. "Because, for whatever reason, it's not making it into the log book," he murmured.

"Why not?"

"That's a very good question. One I'm going to have to track down tomorrow. After I drop Tommy off at his mom's, and after I pop in on a poetry group that's meeting at the library."

"Poetry group?" she echoed.

"In case Brian was a part of it." He dropped his hand to the porch railing. "If he was, maybe one of them might be familiar with the poem he was going to read that—"

"You were right, Daddy!"

Together, Emma and Jack turned their attention toward the lawn and the little boy making his way in their direction with Scout close at his heels.

"About what, son?"

"Emma really does like flowers! See? She has bunches and bunches of them on her dress!"

Surprise had her following Tommy's pointed finger down to her dress. Confusion had her lifting her gaze back to Jack. "What's he talking about?"

"Tommy wanted to bring a little surprise for—"

"It was *your* idea, Daddy," the little boy corrected, earning himself a set of widened eyes—and Emma a sheepish look—from Jack in return. If Tommy understood his father's unspoken plea for silence, though, he was completely undaunted. "Daddy thought it would make you happy."

It was hard not to laugh at the quiet thud of Jack's head hitting his hand. It was even harder when the sound was followed, seconds later, by a low groan.

"Are you okay there, Jack?" she teased, winking at Tommy.

"Yup. I'm good."

"Please, Daddy? Can I give it to them?"

Lifting his head, Jack met and held Emma's gaze for a moment. "Of course. Why don't you go in and get it, son."

"Okay!" Tommy turned to Scout and held up his hands in true crossing-guard style. "Stay right here, okay, Scout? I'll be right back."

Scout, clearly sensing something momentous in the works, sat and waited, his tongue lolling.

"I'll be right back," Tommy repeated, running up the steps and into the house.

Seconds later, he was back, his hands hidden just out of sight, his mouth stretched wide with an anticipatory smile. Crossing over to Emma, Tommy extended his hand to reveal a dog bone wrapped with a big flowered bow. "The bone is for Scout. But Daddy said you like flowers so the bow is for you."

Chapter Twenty-Six

S he was woken from the first dreamless stretch of sleep she'd managed to catch all night by a quiet yet persistent ring. Rolling onto her side, Emma rubbed her eyes into the open position and stared at the source of the racket.

"Go away," Emma whimpered. "Please. It's too early for this."

Surprisingly, the ringing stopped. Not surprisingly, Scout bounded into the room and jumped onto the bed.

"No, no, no, boy." She repositioned her pillow, dropped her head squarely in its center, and closed her eyes. "It's not time to wake up yet."

Seconds later, the ringing was back, this time followed by the warm, sticky sweetness that was Scout's overeager tongue. Rolling onto her side once again, she grabbed the phone, read the name on the screen, and held it to her ear.

"Dottie? Did something happen?" she asked, struggling up onto her elbow. "Are you hurt?"

The beat of silence that had her swinging her legs over

the edge of the bed didn't last long. "Of course not, dear. I'm fine. Why?"

"Because it's morning? And you're waking me up?"

"Good heavens, Emma, the early bird gets the worm in life. Tell me you know this."

Sighing, Emma threw her upper body back onto her mattress. "It's still the weekend, Dottie. The early bird is allowed to sleep past seven every once in a while."

"It's nine o'clock, Emma. It's time to wake up."

Her gaze flew from the ceiling above her bed, to the clock on her dresser, to Scout. "Oh, Scout, I'm so sorry. I'll take you out now, boy."

The answering wag of Scout's tail returned her to the edge of the bed and the slippers she'd staged at its base. "I can't believe I slept this long. I never do this."

"Late night?" Dottie asked as Emma made her way out of the bedroom and into the kitchen.

"More like a lot of bizarre dreams that made it so I didn't sleep all that well." Emma opened the back door, stepped aside for Scout to pass, and then followed him onto the back stoop. "I need to show Jack the poem."

"Why?"

She lowered herself onto the top step and breathed in the morning air, the fog of sleep slowly beginning to recede from her brain. "I would think that answer would be obvious."

"Then why haven't you given it to him yet?"

"Because he was with his son both times I wanted to. And I didn't want to ruin that for him by . . . I don't know. Maybe I *shouldn't* show it to him." She tracked Scout around her postage-stamp-sized backyard until he reached a suitable place for emptying his bladder and then stood and waved for him to follow her back inside. "If I do, the sheriff will probably stonewall it, anyway. Maybe even take it out on Jack if Jack shared it with him."

"I see."

Emma dug the metal scoop into the bag of dog food on the floor of her pantry closet and deposited it into Scout's bowl. "I think solving it on our own is the only way."

"And we have the poem."

"Unfortunately or fortunately, depending on how you look at it." She returned the scoop to the bag and shut the closet door, her mind's eye rushing ahead to the cup of hot cocoa she was suddenly craving.

"Stop it, Emma! This is fun!"

"I really need to get you out more, don't I?"

"No. What you need to do is answer my question regarding the little excursion you and Stephanie took out to Robert's place yesterday."

"You asked me about that?"

"I most certainly did. Yet, despite you practically hanging up on me, I still tracked down that deputy's address you requested."

Bypassing the stove, Emma wandered out of the kitchen and into her office, all thoughts of cocoa suddenly gone. There, nestled inside her tote bag, was the bow Jack had affixed to Scout's new bone—a bow he'd specifically picked out for Emma based on a comment she didn't even remember making at the park.

"Emma?"

She fingered the edges of the bow as her thoughts traveled back fourteen hours—

"Emma, did you hang up on me again?"

Shaking herself back into the moment, she pulled out her desk chair and sank onto its vinyl cushion. "Right. About yesterday . . . First, thank you for the address. I was able to rectify a mistake that needed rectifying. And second, yes, the visit out to McEnerny Homes was illuminating, to say the least."

"I'm listening, dear."

"Actually, if you're free and Stephanie is awake, could we meet up at your place around noon?" She stood, made her way back into the hallway, and veered off into the living room. "I've got stuff Stephanie needs to hear, as well."

"I'll have Glenda make sandwiches."

"Perfect. I'll call Stephanie." She waited for Dottie to end the call and then dialed Stephanie's number. Stephanie, surprisingly, answered on the first ring.

"Hey."

Emma grinned. "You're awake."

"Not by choice."

"Oh?"

"My mother has decided the downstairs television should be heard from every room in the house."

Emma's answering laugh stirred a sigh in her ear and a lick on her wrist. "Hey, Scout! All finished with breakfast? Good boy!"

"Man, I want my own place," Stephanie murmured.

"And you will have one. Soon. I have faith."

"Thanks, Emma."

"Hey, are you free by any chance today? Around noon? We need to bring Dottie up to speed on the McEnerny stuff. And I've got some new stuff to share with you, as well."

"Stuff having to do with another one of our suspects?" Stephanie asked.

"Two of them, actually."

"Then I'll be there. I may be deaf when I arrive, but"— a swell of noise in the background of the call was momentarily muffled—"at least I won't be here."

"Just a little longer."

"Emphasis on *a little*, I hope." Stephanie groaned as the noise in the background grew even louder. "You *can* hear that, right?"

"Hear what?" she asked.

"Ha ha."

Searching for and finding the remote control, Emma let the jingle on Stephanie's end of the call lead her to the correct channel on her own TV. "I'll see you at noon at Dottie's."

She set the phone down on the end table to her right and patted the sofa cushion to her left. "Sit with me, Scout, while we see if there's anything new on Brian's case."

"Good morning, everyone, I'm Mike Lemper and I'm your host for *Sweet Falls This Week*. On today's segment, I'm sitting down with Mayor Sebastian Gerard and—later in the show—his wife Rita for a behind-the-scenes look at his first ninety days in office. So grab your coffee and your morning pastry, and we'll see you right after this break."

Three minutes later the host was back, only this time he was joined on set by a man she recognized from the countless political signs that had dotted the town's landscape in late winter, as well as from a smattering of town-wide events that had followed his election. Like the image on those signs or in the pictures she'd glimpsed in Dottie's newspapers, the new mayor was, indeed, young. Just shy of thirty-six when he was sworn into office three months earlier, Sebastian Gerard was almost movie-star handsome with his full-wattage smile, chiseled cheekbones, and boyishly long eyelashes framing emerald-green eyes. Yet, despite an outward appearance that made one feel that a part was being played, everything that came out of his mouth carried a sincerity that was undeniable.

Cuddling up next to Scout, she turned up the volume a smidge.

"Thank you for sitting down with us this morning, Mayor Gerard. Welcome."

"Thank you for having me."

"So, Friday marked your ninetieth day in office here in Sweet Falls. How would you say it's going?"

"I'm enjoying it, that's for sure. But really, the true mark of my success or failure comes down to what the residents of Sweet Falls think. Because I'm here to serve them and their wants and needs for their town."

"We asked our viewers for their thoughts via a poll on Friday and we will share those results later in this half hour. That said, I want to remind viewers that you grew up in Sweet Falls, didn't you?"

The mayor smiled. "Born and raised."

"Did you always have political aspirations?"

"Actually, all through college, I fancied myself a sports announcer, truth be told. After college, I lived on the East Coast for a few years, working as a sports reporter for a small newspaper. But it was while filling in for one of the beat reporters who was out on maternity leave that I discovered my passion for being a political servant. When it became clear that was what I wanted to do with my life, I came back here—to the town where I was born and raised, and set about the task of learning everything I could about the Sweet Falls of yesterday and today, as well as the possibilities for it in the future."

The anchor looked down at the sheaf of notes in his hand and posed his next question. "I understand it was during that process of familiarizing yourself with the inner workings of our town that you met your wife Rita?"

"I did, indeed. From the moment I saw her sitting behind that desk in the clerk's office, I was smitten. Fortunately for me, she understands my drive and my passion for this town. She's also much better looking than I am." Sebastian paused and chuckled. "And she has a real gift for helping me fine-tune my thoughts when it comes to my speeches."

Mike's eyebrow lifted. "She writes your speeches?"

"She takes my words, my ideas, and my plans, and makes them sound more eloquent." The mayor's laugh was warm and endearing. "In other words, she helps me cut to the chase so I don't put everyone to sleep."

"I see." Mike shuffled through his papers for a moment, settling on one that had been closer to the bottom. "Since you brought up your speeches, I'd like to ask you about the one you gave on the night you were elected."

The anchor looked off-screen. "Roger, can you roll the clip of that speech, please?"

Seconds later, a clip Emma vaguely remembered seeing bits and pieces of—while finalizing a client's trip, clipping Scout's nails, and talking to her mom on speakerphone three months earlier—filled the screen.

In it, a clearly exuberant yet also surprisingly humble Sebastian Gerard stood behind a podium. Beside him, in a royal-blue dress that perfectly complemented the newly elected mayor's tie, was his wife Rita. Quieting the cheers with his hands, he cleared his throat, looked down at the podium, and began to speak.

"It is my promise to all of you, tonight, that the next two years will be a true renaissance for Sweet Falls. The time for being just a sleepy little town is behind us. Ahead of us is a vast ocean of growth and change that will make Sweet Falls one of the safest and most sought-after zip codes" he looked over at his wife, her smile as bright as the flash-bulbs reflecting off her brooch as she nodded for him to continue—"country-wide."

"I see. Well, we have to cut to a break, but after that, we'll bring out your wife, chat with her for a few moments, and then reveal the results of our viewers' report card for your first ninety days in office."

Mayor Gerard smiled. "I look forward to it."

Emma stretched her arms above her head and yawned as the screen went to commercials. Scout, in turn, yawned and then nestled his chin against her leg once again. "As soon as this is over, boy, I'll get showered up, take you for a real walk, and then we're off to Dottie's, okay?"

She gave some thought to actually turning on the kettle for the hot cocoa as she'd intended some twenty minutes earlier, but dismissed the idea in favor of the television as the anchor returned to the screen.

"For those of you just joining us, we're talking with Mayor Sebastian Gerard. In a little while, we'll reveal the results of our phone-in poll regarding his first ninety days in office. But before we get to that, I'd like to welcome the mayor's wife to our discussion. Rita, hello, thank you for being here with us."

The camera zoomed in on the petite blonde, clad in pink, seated next to the new mayor. "Thank you for having me."

"How do you feel your husband has done these first three months in office?"

"He's done an incredible job. And he's just getting started. We are on the cusp of being able to expand our parks and our trails without raising taxes. And, likewise, our schools and our roads will benefit from the influx of new residents those amenities will bring."

"Without raising taxes?" Mike repeated.

"That's right. The kitty grows in many ways, Mike. Asking for more isn't the only way." Rita turned her winning smile on the camera. "And while crime has never been a huge problem in our little town, a look at the police blotter over the last month or so shows my husband's commitment to making Sweet Falls a desirable *and* safe place to live is already proving true."

Emma pulled a face. "Actually, the blotter thing is more about the sheriff being lazy, but whatever . . . Who's counting, right?" she murmured as Rita droned on.

"I have no doubt that, with my husband at the helm, Sweet Falls can and will be a tremendous draw. The kind of place where even some of the country's brightest stars can live the American dream—the perfect blend of old and new, quaint and modern, close-knit and private."

Mike looked from Rita to Sebastian and back again. "Sounds like something that, if successful, could have you—Mayor Gerard—commanding a much bigger ship in the future . . ."

"One thing at a time, Mike, one thing—"

Rita stopped the rest of her husband's sentence with a hand on his arm. "And when that happens, people will look to Sweet Falls and his record here as an example of what he'll do for our state and, perhaps, even our country as a whole one day."

"*Our country?*" Emma echoed. "Slow down there, lady, he's the mayor of Sweet Falls, Tennessee. That's all."

"Nothing like aiming for the stars," Mike said, turning his attention back to the camera. "We'll be back with the results of Mayor Gerard's viewer-graded report card in just a moment."

"Have fun with that." Emma powered off the TV, planted a kiss on the top of Scout's nose, and stood. "C'mon, Scout. Let's make some hot cocoa and go for a walk."

Chapter Twenty-Seven

———◆———

She was just readying her hand to knock when the door opened, revealing a clearly distraught Dottie. "They beat us to it!"

"Who's they?" Emma waited for Scout to get in his welcoming licks on Dottie's hand and the footrests of her wheelchair, added her own peck on top of their hostess's head, and followed him into the hallway to find a grim-faced Stephanie. "And what did they beat us to?"

"The sheriff's department," Stephanie said, bending down to scratch Scout. "Apparently they're on their way to make an arrest."

Lowering her tote bag off her arm, she turned back to Dottie as the woman wheeled her way into the living room. "Is this true, Dottie?"

"Unfortunately, yes. My friend Rhonda just called me not more than ten minutes ago." Dottie made a beeline for the middle of the ornately decorated room and engaged her brake with a sigh of disgust. "The police weren't supposed to solve the murder! We were!"

Emma looked back at Stephanie, noted the woman's dejected expression, and spread her arms wide. "That's exactly who *is* supposed to solve the murder, guys! The cops. It's what they do."

"No, they're *supposed* to bumble along, following go-nowhere leads . . . or go off fishing . . . or blindly focus on the main character or one of her sidekicks. But they're absolutely *not* supposed to solve the crime." Dottie lifted her gaze to the framed photograph of her beloved Alfred and shook her head. "It's against the cozy mystery rule."

Emma couldn't help it; she laughed.

Likewise, neither Dottie nor Stephanie could help from pegging Emma with the death glare she got in return.

"Look, I get that you love the cozy mystery genre, Dottie. I really do. They're cute." She swung her attention onto Stephanie. "And you, with your TV shows, I—"

"Cute?" Dottie echoed, her voice shrill.

Stephanie looked down at the floor. Then back at Emma. And, finally, back at the floor with a wince.

"Okay, sorry." Emma said. "Poor word choice. They're clever, they're engaging, and"—she looked to Stephanie for help she didn't get—"hard to put down."

Dottie's answering sniff of indignation would've been grin-inducing if Emma hadn't known better. "I couldn't agree more."

"Okay, good." Crossing to the Victorian loveseat across from Dottie's chair, she lowered herself onto one end and motioned for Stephanie to take the other. "So, how did they figure it out?"

"The medical examiner's final report pointed to oleander," Dottie said. "And apparently an anonymous tip led them to Nancy Davis's doorstep."

Emma drew back so hard and so fast, she smacked the back of her head against the sofa's wooden accent. "Nancy Davis? Why?"

"Rhonda wasn't privy to all of the details, but what she

did know was that Mr. Hill had caught Nancy sabotaging the flower beds in the town square and it was impacting her business."

"So why kill him when the damage was already done?" she asked, rising to her feet.

"Revenge killings are very common, dear."

She walked to the window, fiddled with the edge of the curtain, and then looked back at her friends as she tried to make sense of the unsettled feeling in the pit of her stomach. "What about killing to keep someone from exposing something the guilty party doesn't want exposed? Are those common?"

Dottie and Stephanie nodded in unison. "They can be."

"Nancy wasn't the only one on that sheet."

"Nancy knows plants, dear." Dottie removed her glasses. "Nancy's business was suffering because of Mr. Hill. And she was present in the room where he ingested the poison that killed him. It's an open-and-shut case."

"Is it?" Emma asked. "Because the damage was already done to Nancy when Brian was murdered. And Nancy was by no means the only person he had something on."

"She owns a greenhouse," Stephanie countered.

"So? Dottie has *lily of the valley* growing right outside her kitchen window—a plant you both said is every bit as dangerous as this oleander stuff. Surely other people can grow those kinds of plants, too."

Stephanie's shoulders rose and fell in a shrug. "Unadvisable, but yes. They can."

"And"—she nudged her chin at Dottie—"they do."

"Don't look now, dear; you're thinking like a real sleuth."

Was she? She didn't know. What she *did* know, though, was that the thought of Nancy as a killer wasn't sitting right.

"I don't think it's her, Dottie. I really don't. I . . ." She stared unseeingly out the window, her mind's eye visiting a very different view and a very different possibility. "I think she's being set up."

Dottie's answering gasp was echoed by Stephanie. "Framed?" they said in unison.

"Framed . . . set up . . . It's the same thing, isn't it?" She paced her way over to the fireplace, the framed photographs that dotted the mantel little more than a blur in her head. "On the way home from McEnerny yesterday, I ended up stopping out at Nancy's. Because it dawned on me that the only tract of land on Route 50 big enough to accommodate a community like Vanessa mentioned is Nancy's farm."

"*That's* the land?" Stephanie said on the heels of another gasp.

She turned around. "It's the only land it can be."

The click signaling the release of Dottie's brake stole Emma's attention off Stephanie and back onto the octogenarian. "What community, dear?"

"Apparently, Robert is on the verge of announcing a whole McEnerny neighborhood with more than three hundred homes, a clubhouse and swimming pool, an on-site shopette, and two or three playgrounds with different themes. And in the far corner of this supposed community, there's a hashed-off area that's a good twenty times the size of any other lot."

"In a community of half-acre lots, try *forty* times," Stephanie corrected. "With its own private access road out of the development."

Dottie signaled with her hand for Stephanie to stop talking and rolled her way over to the fireplace and Emma. "Nancy wouldn't sell her land. It's been in her family for generations. It's all she has outside her love for gossip."

"And, according to Nancy, she *wasn't* selling."

"Then where else is that kind of land along Route 50?" Stephanie abandoned her seat on the couch to take one on the hearth instead. "I can't think of any."

Emma held Dottie's gaze while she answered Stephanie's question. "You can't think of any, because there isn't. Nancy's land is the only land capable of handling a community of the size Vanessa spoke about."

"But you just said she wasn't selling," Stephanie protested.

"Robert approached her. Many times, in fact. But Nancy was determined to fight the odds as long as humanly possible. In fact, when I first asked if she had plans to sell to Robert, she said *not over her dead body.*"

Intrigue pulled Dottie forward in her chair. "Odds? Like the loss in business she was experiencing because of this supposed picture Mr. Hill had?"

"Sure, I guess. Though I have to ask, Dottie, did you ever see a picture in the paper of Nancy pouring weed killer over the town's flower beds?"

"No."

"Might you have missed it?" Emma prodded.

"No. I read every issue of the *Gazette*. Cover to cover. If there had been a picture of Nancy doing something so shameful, I would have had her head on a silver platter."

"Word got out *somehow*, it seems." Emma took two steps away from the fireplace, only to retrace her steps back to the mantel and a spot on the hearth beside Stephanie. "Which means, between that and the ongoing vandalism, selling her property might be the only option Nancy has."

Dottie's eyes narrowed on Emma. "Vandalism? What kind of vandalism?"

"The deer fencing around the apple orchard and her Christmas tree farm has been cut four different times, in four different places. In all four instances, she suffered some pretty significant damage to her crops."

"So much for Mayor Gerard's falling crime rate," Stephanie mused on the heels of a snort.

Emma slanted a glance at Stephanie. "You watched that program this morning? The one with the mayor and his wife?"

"Not by choice, but yes. I saw it."

"It's possible they don't know about the vandalism because Sheriff Borlin never filed the reports. And, according to Jack, the police blotter in the paper is based on the report log each week."

"Sheriff Borlin doesn't take calls like that, dear," Dottie corrected. "Those are the kinds of calls the deputies go on."

"You're right. In fact, Jack is the one who responded to Nancy's call the first time the fence was cut. But when he got back to the station and Sheriff Borlin heard about what had happened, he told Jack *he'd* talk to Nancy and file the report. Only, for whatever reason, he didn't. And Nancy, not knowing he'd dropped the ball the first time, called him directly each of the next three times the fence was cut."

Stephanie leaned back against the bricks at her back. "I repeat, so much for the mayor's decreasing crime rate."

"If the reports aren't logged, the public can't know," Emma said. "That's not on the mayor, it's on Borlin."

"Which begs the question, *why*?"

Emma gave Dottie her full attention. "Why what?"

"Why wouldn't Tim log those reports?"

"Because no one is going to tell the top dog how to do his job?" Stephanie said. "I mean, can you imagine some rookie cop walking into the sheriff's office and saying, *Dude, do your job*? Yeah, that wouldn't happen in a police station any more than it would happen in my department at the VA."

Holding up her finger, Dottie looked around the room. "Emma, dear, do you see my notebook and pen? I need to sketch this out."

Emma pushed back off the hearth, scanned the various surfaces around the room, and located the book on the end table beside Alfred's favorite chair. When she returned with them, Dottie snatched both from her hands.

Turning to the first empty page she could find, Dottie uncapped her pen. "So he isn't reporting the vandalism. Why?"

"He's lazy?" Stephanie offered. "Overpaid? Waiting for his minions to do it? He's losing it? He's sleeping on the job? He doesn't *want* people to know he's sleeping on the job?"

Emma laughed.

Dottie looked up from the series of boxes and lines she was furiously drawing and pointed her pen at Stephanie. "Good! Yes! That one!"

Stephanie preened.

Emma stared at Dottie. "Wait. What one?"

"Think about it, dear. Tim forgets to file one report; inexcusable, of course, but it could happen. He forgets to file four? No. That doesn't happen. Not for a man at Tim Borlin's level."

"So you're saying he's *deliberately* not filing them?"

"Yes."

"But . . ." And just like that, the failure to report multiple acts of vandalism on Nancy's property formed an image in her mind that was so clear and so disturbing she actually shivered.

"You're cold?" Stephanie asked, eyeing her closely.

She was pretty sure she shook her head. She meant to, anyway. But really, in that moment, all she knew for certain was that she needed to read Brian's poem again.

"Listen." Emma reached into her back pocket, extracted her phone, and began to read. "And the one who greased palms for the job he did covet, is now in position to graft it all back . . . *That's* why the sheriff took that first vandalism report off Jack's hands! And had Nancy call him directly for each subsequent case! He's in cahoots with Robert McEnerny to drive her off her land!"

It was Stephanie's turn to stare. "By not logging a few fence cuts?"

"By not logging four costly fence cuts, and by taking a screenshot off a town camera that showed Nancy dousing those plant beds and then making sure to get it in Brian's hands!"

"I don't know, Emma, that sounds—"

Dottie snapped the rest of Stephanie's protest away, her own eyes shining with excitement. "Yes, yes! Now you're getting the hang of it, dear! Keep going . . ."

Like a Tetris game, the pieces of the puzzle began to fall into place—pieces she kept spouting and Dottie kept track of with more odd little boxes and arrowed lines leading between them. "Robert McEnerny stood to make a lot of money if his proposed development went through. *A lot* of money. Nancy refused to sell. Which would be a pretty big problem if you're Robert. So now he only has two options. Give up, or find another way. And based on that little map Vanessa showed us yesterday, he hasn't given up. Not by a long shot. So he finds another way, one that makes it impossible for Nancy not to sell."

"By sabotaging her orchards," Stephanie says, earning a nod from Dottie.

"Exactly. And if Sheriff Borlin is on the take, as it's clear he is from both Brian's poem and the stuff Jack has been uncovering on the sly, the promise of a hefty payoff if Robert gets his land might be worth"—Emma shot her fingers in the air, quote-style—"*failing to file* a few reports."

Stephanie pointed at Dottie's notebook. "And we know that he took the report of the first fence incident away from Jack under the guise of taking care of it himself!"

It was all falling into place.

Every last piece.

And boy, did it feel good . . .

"Tim—or Robert—sends the picture to Brian. Brian does exactly what they knew he'd do. And bam! Nancy starts to unravel. But still, she's resisting the notion of selling," Emma mused aloud.

Stephanie wasted no time in picking up the baton. "Which is kind of a problem, considering he's already taken money for a twenty-acre lot on property that isn't even his, you know?"

"How do you know that?" Emma asked.

"Vanessa said it."

"When? I don't remember that."

Stephanie shrugged. "You were totally fixated on the map."

"I was trying to figure out where that land could possibly be."

"Well, that's what you missed. That huge hashed-off area on the left-hand side of the development—the one with the private entrance—is already bought and paid for."

Bookending the sides of her face with her hands, Emma looked from Dottie to Stephanie and back again. "We've got it! This is it! Robert had to get that land and he couldn't wait Nancy out anymore! So he pulled out the big gun! He killed Brian by way of a plant—thereby framing Nancy!"

"And no one would question it because everyone knows Nancy would do anything to keep her family's legacy alive," Dottie added.

Stephanie pumped her hand in the air in victory. "And with her entire livelihood coming from that property, a murder charge and everything that comes with it would make it so selling was a given."

"My thoughts exactly," Emma said, nodding.

Slamming closed her notebook, Dottie smiled up at Emma and Stephanie triumphantly. "Nice work, team! We did it! And by week's end from the moment we took on the case!"

Chapter Twenty-Eight

———

Emma glanced over at the face peering back at her from the passenger seat and grinned. "Right about now, Scout, justice is being served and it feels mighty good knowing we made that happen."

And it was true. It did.

Talking everything out with Dottie and Stephanie . . .

Laying it all out on the phone for Jack . . .

Knowing that Nancy would soon be back where she belonged, on a farm she owned . . .

It was all so very satisfying. As a job well done tended to be.

Sure, she still had some measure of disappointment over having to shutter what had once been a very profitable home travel agency. But just as the decision to adopt Scout had been for the best, maybe following Dottie's advice and trying her hand at something new would prove to be, too.

Time would tell, as it always did. Just as truth always found a way to reveal itself.

The sound of her phone ringing sent her eyes to the

dashboard and the Cloverton number. Hitting the green button, she took the call.

"This is Emma."

"Andy Walden here. Am I catching you at a good time?"

"Absolutely. I was hoping you'd call. How was the concert?" she asked. "Did your dad enjoy it?"

"He did, as I knew he would. He loves any band that promises ukulele music."

"Really? That's funny. Another one of my . . ." She stopped, then tried again, the mere thought of Big Max with his rubber band ukulele making her smile. "One of my clients loves the ukulele, as well."

"Then he would have loved this concert, too, I imagine."

Her mind started to wander at the notion of Big Max at an outdoor concert but returned to the car and the call she'd been waiting for as Andy continued. "I checked your references, Emma, and they were more than a little impressive. I also spoke with Pop, who is clearly smitten by you. So, if you're still interested and available, we think you're the perfect person to look in on him while I'm gone. Scout, too, if he's free."

She looked over at Scout, the wag of his tail as much of an answer as the smile she felt spreading across her face. "He's free. And so am I."

"Fantastic. How about I give you a ring at about this same time tomorrow and we can iron out all the details?"

"That's perfect. And Andy?" she said, letting up on the gas as her turn approached. "Thank you. I'll take good care of your dad while you're gone."

"I'm counting on that."

The call over, Emma turned onto the graveled lane that was the entry point for Davis Farm and Greenhouse. Today, like far too many days before it, the parking lot was empty. But that wouldn't always be the case. This land was as much a part of Sweet Falls as was its owner. Treasured memories would bring people back. Just as the true story of what happened to Brian would bring Nancy back from what Emma could only imagine had been a terrifying experience involving police cars, handcuffs, and little time to think, let alone make sure the various outbuildings were locked and secure.

Had Nancy been wrong in how she'd chosen to deal with her ouster from the garden committee? Of course. Sabotaging her own work to prove her worth, as Brian had said, had been shortsighted. Holding her head high and waiting would've been the better choice. But that didn't mean she wasn't a good person. Quite the contrary, in fact.

Scout's tail wagged hard and fast as she pulled to a stop beside Nancy's van, his eagerness for whatever Emma had planned for their evening predicated on nothing but his complete and unwavering trust. It was a heady feeling knowing she was that person for someone.

"Okay, boy, we're only here to make sure everything is locked up. That's all. So don't get too cozy in any one place, you hear?" Leaning forward, she planted a kiss on the dog's nose, ruffled the hair beneath his chin, and opened the door for their dual exit.

Together, they made their way across the parking lot to the main building. The lights inside were on, but the door itself had been locked. They moved on to the large, cavernous shed in which the animal train—fashioned from old barrels and mounted atop wheels—lived in anticipation of the birthday parties and fall fun days Emma was confident would bring children by the hundreds again soon.

A check of the door had her securing it with the large wooden two-by-four she found leaning against an outer wall. Once it was in place inside its bracket, she stepped back, her eyes scanning the area for her missing pooch.

"Scout?" she called. "You're supposed to be helping me, boy. Not exploring on your own."

When he failed to come waltzing out from behind a nearby tree, she tried again. "Scout? Come!"

Still nothing.

"Scout, come! *Now!*"

The slow creek of a door hinge from the vicinity of the greenhouse had her turning in that direction. "You better not be eating—oh no!" Taking off in a sprint, Emma navigated the hard-packed earth and occasional rut from a tractor wheel like the runner she wasn't and never would be. "Don't eat any plants, Scout! Please, please, please don't!"

Sure enough, the door to the greenhouse was slightly ajar, its opening just big enough for a curious Scout.

She pushed the door open wider and stepped inside the warm, almost sticky air, her heart pounding with worry. "Whatever you've found, Scout, drop it! Drop it right now!"

The immediate clang of something being dropped sent her running for the back of the greenhouse. Her heart pounding, Emma made her way down the main aisle and toward the back corner. There, sitting next to a DANGER, DO NOT TOUCH sign, was a head-cocked, tail-wagging Scout.

"What part of *Don't get cozy anywhere* did you not . . ."

The rest of her words fell away as her gaze fell on the object he'd clearly dropped at her command—a small, round, shiny object that left her grabbing Scout by the collar and running for her car.

It took less than a minute to find the address on the Sweet Falls home page. And it took a little less than that to throw on her seatbelt, order Scout to sit, and start the car as Big Max's verbal confirmation replayed itself in her head again and again.

"We were so close," she murmured as she turned the key in the ignition and started the car. "So, so close."

Throwing the car into reverse, she backed out of her parking spot and headed toward the main road, her thoughts running a mile a minute.

The framing part was right . . .

The method of poison was right . . .

Her phone ringing brought her eyes and, then her finger, to the dashboard screen. "I still can't believe we did it, Emma! That we actually solved a real—"

"Stephanie, we were wrong."

"What?"

"We were wrong. About all of it. Or"—she pushed down on the gas—"at least some of it. The biggest part of it, anyway."

"What are you talking about? Did you just talk to Jack or something?"

"No. Big Max."

"Who's Big Max?"

"A friend . . . I mean, client . . . I mean, friend."

"Okay . . ."

"Scout found her brooch!"

"Come again?"

"Her brooch! The one she always wears! It was in the greenhouse! Back by the lily of the valley and the oleander and the other dangerous plants! She must've dropped it there when she was taking what she needed to frame Nancy!"

"She? Who's—"

Stephanie's quiet gasp let her know they were finally on the same page of music, enabling Emma to move forward with the rest. "It all makes even more sense now. Not reporting the vandalism on Nancy's property . . . The way the speeches she writes keep talking about growth and change and offering more amenities without raising taxes . . . Three hundred new homes with three hundred new families living inside them brings more property tax revenue!"

"And a celeb living in Sweet Falls?" Stephanie added. "Think about the press that would bring this town and her husband!"

"Celeb?"

"When Vanessa described the big, fancy lot and said it

was already purchased, I asked if a lottery winner had bought it. She said no. I asked if it was a foreign dignitary. She said no. But when I asked if it was a celebrity, she grinned, and said she wasn't at liberty to say. I didn't think she was serious, but now, I'm not so sure."

Emma thought back on the television program she'd watched just that morning, the things Rita had said falling in line, one behind the other. "If you're right, and it was purchased by some sort of celebrity, can you imagine the press this town would've gotten if it turned out there was no land to be purchased? Sweet Falls would've found its way into every celebrity and lifestyle magazine—not to mention news publication—across the country."

"Have you told Dottie yet?" Stephanie asked.

"No. Not yet."

"You call Jack. I'll call Dottie."

Chapter Twenty-Nine

It was just after seven thirty when, after sitting on hold for Jack during the entire drive, Emma and Scout pulled into the dimly lit parking lot on the outskirts of the town square. Up ahead and to her left was the old converted one-room schoolhouse that served as a gathering place for Sweet Falls' various committees and civic groups. Tonight, according to the town website, it was scheduled to play host to the Sweet Falls Beautification Committee's monthly meeting, a meeting she knew from past conversations with Dottie tended to end around this time.

"Come on, Jack, pick up. Please, please pick up," she murmured again and again to no avail.

She considered hanging up and trying again, but the moment she saw the mayor's wife heading toward the only other car in the lot, all thoughts of Jack took a back seat to her anger over Brian's senseless death and the attempt to frame Nancy Davis. Instead, she pulled into a spot a few over from Rita's, told Scout to stay, and stepped out of the car.

"Rita?"

Like Scout when his name was said, the woman turned, her megawatt smile at the ready. "Yes, I'm Rita. Are you here for the beautification committee meeting?"

At Emma's half nod, half shrug, Rita tsked softly under her breath. "I'm sorry, but that ended about fifteen minutes ago. However, if you'd like to give me your name and email address, I'll have our secretary reach out with information on our next meeting as well as our upcoming projects. The more folks we have helping to spit shine our town, the better."

"Actually, I'm not here about the meeting," Emma said, stepping out from the shadow of a nearby tree.

Rita leaned forward, recognition widening her eyes. "I know your face! You were at the garden party on Thursday! Dottie Adler pointed you out as her guest! Only you were sitting with that—that *criminal*, Nancy Davis, and we didn't have a chance to meet."

"I'm Emma. Emma Westlake. I live in this town—have for a few years, actually." Emma tried to clear her throat of the anger she heard in her voice, but she couldn't, and that was okay. "I found something of yours and figured you might be looking for it."

Rita tilted her head and narrowed her gaze on Emma, waiting.

"I imagine it's special since you wear it all the time." Lifting her closed fist into the space between them, Emma slowly opened her fingers to reveal the brooch Scout had found in Nancy's greenhouse.

"My brooch! I've been looking all over for that! Did I drop it at the party?"

Emma shook her head. "No. You weren't wearing it at the party."

"Oh, that's right. I lost it before that!" Rita stepped forward, only to pull back in surprise as Emma closed her hand over the brooch once again. "What are you doing?"

"I'll get to that. First, though, I thought you might like to know where I found it."

A wariness was coming over Rita. It was as real as the purse on her arm and the gardening book in her bejeweled hands. "Fine. Where did you find it?"

"At *that criminal's* farm."

It was fast, and it was fleeting, but there was no denying the woman's flinch. "But—"

"Inside her greenhouse," Emma added.

Rita's throat moved as she swallowed. "Her greenhouse?"

"That's right." Anger propelled Emma forward a step. "Back by the oleander plants you used to kill Brian Hill."

Like a snake shedding its skin, Rita's wariness gave way to understanding and, moments later, the kind of simmering rage that had Emma taking one backward step after another until she bumped into her own car.

Scout, in very un-Scout-like behavior, began to bark. Loudly. Angrily.

"Sorry, little fella, can't help mommy when you're inside and she's outside, can you?" Slipping her hand inside her designer purse, Rita pulled out a revolver and pointed it straight at Emma. "Thank heavens I was able to protect myself from the crazy lady waiting to do me harm in the parking lot, yes?"

"No one who knows me will believe you."

"Of course they will. I'm the mayor's wife, remember?" Rita cocked the hammer on the revolver and leveled it at Emma's chest. "I'm somebody. You, on the other hand, are *who* again? Because I've already forgotten."

Scout's barking grew louder and wilder as everything else around them grew silent. "Please," Emma begged. "Whatever you do, please don't hurt him. He has nothing to do with—"

"Police! Drop the weapon! *Now!*"

Chapter Thirty

——◆——

It was close to midnight when Jack was finally able to spring her from the aftereffects of what had to be one of her dumbest decisions in life. And, surprisingly, he waited until they were safely inside his car before giving her the stare-down she more than deserved.

"What were you thinking, Emma?" he asked. "If, in fact, you were even thinking at all?"

"I was angry."

His eyebrow rose nearly to his hairline. "Angry?"

"Yes. She killed Brian, and she tried to pin it on Nancy!"

"You didn't track *McEnerny* to an empty parking lot and you thought those same things about him . . ."

It was a valid point. But . . .

"I don't know. Seeing that brooch in front of Scout? Thinking about the awful way Rita had treated Nancy when it was *Nancy's* work that won that state award?" Emma blew out a breath. "And . . . I don't know. We'd been so sure it was Robert—and the pieces had fit so well for it to be him—that when I realized it wasn't, I felt doubly duped."

"Doubly duped?"

"Yes!"

The beginnings of a smile she thought she detected in the corner of his mouth disappeared as quickly as they'd come. "You could've gotten yourself killed. You do realize that, right?"

"I do now," she murmured. "And I did in the moment when I was terrified she'd shoot my dog after she shot me."

"Your dog . . ."

"Did you not hear him in that car? He was like a caged animal! There's no way she wouldn't have shot him, too."

"You were more worried about *Scout* than *yourself*?"

"Of course!"

Slanting his gaze through his front windshield, Jack shook his head, pulled in a breath, and released it in conjunction with a groan of frustration. "I don't know what to say right now."

"That's okay. I get it."

He turned back to her. "You do?"

"Yes. I was careless. I'm not a cop. But please know that I *tried* to call you after I found that brooch and Big Max verified it as being Rita's. You just didn't pick up."

"And?"

"And what?"

"And what else do you get?" he asked.

"I should've told you about the printout sooner than I did."

"And?"

She looked at the car's ceiling. "I should've given you the poem."

"You were careless, Emma. And you're right, you're not a cop. You should've come to the station or called dispatch rather than driving over to confront Rita yourself. And last but not least, yeah, the poem might've been helpful information to have." He palmed his mouth, then let his hand drop to his lap. "She could've killed you, Emma."

Something about his tone, coupled with the memory of

his soothing embrace in the wake of Rita's attempt to kill her, only deepened the guilt she couldn't shake. "I didn't hold that back from you because I didn't trust you. I held it back because the timing was wrong, and you were already in such a bad position that"—she sighed—"I don't know, I thought maybe I could see if I could figure stuff out about the others?"

"Is that a question?" he asked.

"The whole sleuthing thing was more my friend Dottie's idea. And Stephanie's. But I ended up getting caught up in it, too. We were so sure Robert was the one. But—"

She suddenly remembered a very important question she'd forgotten to ask. "How did you know where I was? That it wasn't Robert?"

"We'd barely put him in the car and he started singing like a canary. Told me about his ties to Borlin, the kids he'd paid to cut different sections of Nancy's fence, the real estate paperwork he'd doctored so he could sell land he didn't own to some young celebrity couple adamant about raising their future kids in small-town America, and, finally, how Rita asked him to keep watch while she sprinkled what she said was a pulverized laxative of some sort on Brian's appetizer." Jack blew out another breath. "When Brian's death was ruled a homicide, Robert put two and two together but stayed quiet out of fear he'd be charged as an accomplice. I was on the way out the door to track Rita down when I got a call over the air telling me a Dottie Adler needed to talk to me that very minute. I told my dispatcher to take her number and the next thing I knew, my cell phone was ringing."

Emma laughed. "Dottie?"

"Yes! I don't know this woman, nor do I have any idea how she got my number!"

"She's Dottie—Dottie Adler. *That's* how she got your number." Emma looked out at the streetlamps lining Main Street as she thought about the various faces on the paper

Brian had given her. "So what does this all mean for your department?"

Jack ran his finger around the edge of the steering wheel. "You mean in terms of the sheriff?" At Emma's nod, he shrugged. "I imagine the mayor will order a thorough investigation into Borlin's actions."

"Think they'll fire him?"

"Either that or he'll resign."

"Maybe *you* could be sheriff," she said.

"Uh . . . no. I'm good where I am." A quiet, comfortable silence settled around them as he started his car. "I imagine you want to go see Scout?"

"I do. But first, I want to thank you. For saving my life, for saving my dog, and for letting me call Stephanie to come and get him from the parking lot of that meeting hall."

"Of course." He paused his hand on the gearshift and held her gaze with his own. "And just so you know, I would've hung around to meet you at the gym that first day even if you hadn't mentioned Brian to your cat-killing client."

She didn't need the rearview mirror or the side-view mirror or any other sort of mirror to know the shy smile making its way across the deputy's mouth was a near-perfect match of her own. "I believe you mean my cat killing *friend*."

Acknowledgments

It was during the early days of the pandemic that the idea for this series was born. Emma and Scout revealed themselves to me quickly and without any second-guessing—something I took to be a good sign as I sat down at the computer each day. Their antics proved a wonderful escape for me during such an uncertain time and reinforced (at least for me) the importance of friendship, and creativity, and a positive attitude.

That said, you know the saying. It takes a village. And this book, this series, has a whole village of people behind it who are deserving of recognition.

Kathleen and Bill. For providing a safe place for me and my daughter at a time when my first-responder husband had to be in the thick of things.

My daughter, Jonny. For being the best of companions during such uncertain times, as well as a ready and able sounding board for the aha moment that became this book and this series.

My husband, Jim. For stepping in with his poetry ability when I was at a loss. A poet I am most definitely not . . .

My longtime editor, Michelle Vega, and the entire team at Berkley/Penguin Random House. For always believing in me and my stories, and for giving me a place to tell them.

And, finally, my agent who just so happens to share my name. For making me feel seen and appreciated, and for believing I'm worth the extra mile.

Keep reading for a sneak peek
of the second Friend for Hire Mystery
by *USA Today* bestselling author Laura Bradford

A Perilous Pal

Coming Summer 2022!

Exhausted, Emma Westlake slid the paperback mystery across the wrought iron table and slumped back against her chair. "Part of me wants the next one in the series, and part of me wants to refrain just so I can get to sleep before 3:00 a.m."

"You can sleep when you're dead, dear." Dottie Adler reverently ran her age spotted fingers across the book's detailed cover. "It was a good one, wasn't it?"

"My favorite one so far."

A smile that rivaled the afternoon sun spread the octogenarian's thinning lips wide as she reached for her Limoges teacup atop its matching plate. "You've got five more to keep you busy over the next few weeks."

"And then?" Emma asked, ricocheting forward against the table's edge. "Tell me she's writing more."

Dottie's sage green eyes disappeared behind heavy lids for a moment before returning to meet Emma's across the rim of her cup. "I wish I could."

"But what do I do then? How do I know what's going on with these characters you've gotten me attached to?"

"You reread. And you pray."

Emma plucked a cookie from her plate, broke off a piece from the top, and held it below the table's edge, the answering wetness across the tips of her fingers . . . and her palm . . . and her wrist stirring a smile of her own. "Pray for what?"

"A series reprieve." Dottie took another sip of her tea, followed it up with a bite of her own cookie, and narrowed her gaze on Emma. "I have to say, dear, aside from the raccoon circles under your eyes, your incessant yawning, and the fact that you really could stand a lesson or two in ironing, you look content."

Emma's laugh echoed in the still summer air. "Um, gee . . . *thanks*? I think?"

"Of course, I had nothing to do with your decision to leave your house without applying concealer or consulting a mirror. However, in regard to the content part, you're welcome." Dottie wiped the edges of her mouth with the cloth napkin from her lap and then summoned the third member of their weekly tea party out from under the table with another cookie. "The career path I've set you on is proving quite ingenious, isn't it, dear?"

"Your off-the-cuff suggestion as to something I might consider as a job has led to some work, yes."

Dottie bent forward, nuzzled her nose with Scout's, and then released the brake on her chair's wheel and rolled a few inches back from the table. "I wasn't aware that coming up with an idea, pushing a person to try it, and procuring said person's first two clients was akin to an *off-the-cuff suggestion*, but that's okay, I'm not looking for credit."

"Cue the martyr music." Grinning, Emma pushed her own chair back from the table, gathered their empty cups and plates onto the serving tray she'd set off to the side, and made her way around the table to plant a kiss on top of the woman's snow-white head. "A Friend for Hire is showing promise, yes. A *lot* of promise, in fact. And while I may pretend otherwise just to yank your chain a little, I'm very aware of the part you played in making it happen."

"The *part* I played?" Dottie echoed.

"Oh. Right. My mistake. I'm aware of your starring role." Emma left the patio just long enough to set the tray inside the kitchen for the woman's housekeeper to attend to, and then returned to the patio and her chair. "Funny thing about my new business, though? I'm becoming real friends with everyone who's hired me thus far. Which makes it a little hard to take a check from them, you know?"

"You didn't make friends with Mr. Hill . . ."

She stared at Dottie. "Brian Hill *died*."

"While you were in his employ," Dottie drawled.

"Gee, thanks for the reminder." Propping her elbows on the table, Emma dropped her head into her waiting hands and shuddered. "Because, you know, I *have* been meaning to put that little fact on my website . . . Maybe even add a testimonial from the grave or something . . ."

"There's no need for sarcasm, dear. It's most unbecoming."

Emma popped her head up in favor of a shrug and a sigh. "Sorry. That whole thing still wigs me out a little. But the good stuff that's happened so far? That makes me feel a little weird sometimes, too. Just in a different way."

"Weird how?" Dottie transitioned her finger-scratching to more of a petting motion, much to Scout's tail-wagging delight.

"I don't know. I think it's what I just said. Taking money for what essentially amounts to being nice feels wrong somehow."

Dottie nudged her chin at Scout. "It's enabling you to keep feeding this one, right? And it's also allowing you to remain your own boss, yes?" Answering Emma's nod with a shrug of her own, the elderly woman continued.

"Besides, you've been accepting money from me for the same thing for more than eighteen months, so what's the difference?"

"I really wish you wouldn't go there about this." Emma spread her hands wide to indicate both the table and the teapot she'd forgotten to add to the tray. "It's about tradition more than anything else."

"A tradition you get paid handsomely to continue, compliments of my dear Alfred's estate, I might add."

"Semantics."

Dottie's left eyebrow arched, followed closely by her right. "Oh?"

"I mean, technically, yes. In the beginning I came because Alfred arranged for me to do so."

"And he paid you."

"Yes. But over time, I've come to look forward to our Tuesday afternoons because of this . . . The friendship we've built."

"A friendship for which a sizeable deposit is still made into your checking account each week," Dottie mused.

Emma shifted in her chair. "Would you stop saying that? Please?"

"Why? Is that not the truth?"

She shifted back against her chair, then forward against the table, and, finally, back against the chair once again. "Yes, Alfred's attorney sends me a check for being here every Tuesday and has since Alfred passed. And yes, in the beginning, that was why I came—that, and because I knew how much you missed him. But"—Emma glanced across the table at Scout's face lying atop the armrest of Dottie's wheelchair—"so much more has come out of this than I ever imagined."

"Such as?"

"Well, for starters, Scout has become quite partial to the dog treats you slip him under the table while I'm getting things ready each week."

Dottie pulled a face. "I don't know what you're talking about, dear."

"O-kay . . . So the whole *Shhh, don't tell* that always precedes the sound of Scout crunching something with his teeth while I'm making our tea is what? My imagination?" Emma rolled her eyes. "Please. You two are anything but sly."

"Fine. So it's the fact you get a check and I feed your dog that makes our teas valuable for you?"

Emma's laugh brought Scout to her side, tail wagging. "I thought you didn't feed my dog . . ."

"Oh, and we mustn't forget they've also made you *literate*," Dottie said, plucking a crumb off her shirtsleeve.

"I knew how to read, Dottie."

"But you didn't."

"Because I was working morning, noon, and night," Emma argued. "Or, rather, I was until people started booking their own travel instead of having me do it."

"Still, a thank-you is surely in order."

Oh, how she wanted to remain silent if for no other reason than to watch the normally calm, cool, and collected octogenarian turn six distinct shades of red, but she couldn't. Because so much of her life *had* changed because of their Tuesday teas. The three biggest things being Scout, her new business venture, and maybe even the first thing resembling a grown-up relationship she'd had in a very long time.

"You're right, Dottie. I *do* owe you a thank-you—you *and* Alfred," Emma said, her voice growing heavy with the same emotion that was beginning to take over Dottie's face. "To *Alfred* for asking me to continue these teas with you after his death. And to *you* for pushing me toward the animal shelter that gave me Scout . . . For coming up with this crazy business idea that shows signs of actually working . . . And for the people that same crazy business idea has brought into my life in just the last few weeks."

Blinking against the misty sheen clearly brought on by

Emma's words, Dottie cleared her throat once, twice. "By *people* do you mean Deputy Jack Riordan?"

"Perhaps," she said on the heels of a swallow.

"You're blushing, dear."

"It's summer. It's hot. We just drank tea."

"Has he taken you on a proper date yet?" Dottie prodded.

"He's a single dad, Dottie—a *working* single dad. And, hello? His department is just now on the backside of its first murder investigation and everything that brought with it." Emma buried her growing smile in Scout's fur for a few moments and then gave up and put it on full display for Dottie to see. "*But* he dropped soup off on my doorstep last week when I was dealing with a cold, and he set a dog treat next to it for Scout."

"That's not a date."

"But it's a sign that he's thoughtful."

"It's not a date."

Her smile fading, Emma pinned her tablemate with a little well-deserved irritation only to stifle it in favor of her phone and the chime signaling a new email. "Do you mind if I check this real quick?" she asked, pointing at the still-lit screen at her elbow. "It's my inbox for A Friend for Hire and it could be a potential client."

At Dottie's nod, she keyed herself into her mail service and noted the bold name and subject line of the lone unread message.

I have no life!

Intrigued, Emma opened the email and began to read . . .

Ms. Westlake,

I've started and erased this inquiry half a dozen times in the past forty-eight hours after seeing your ad in the *Sweet Falls Gazette* on Sunday. The writing was out of desperation, the erasing was out of embarrassment. But it appears the desperation may actually win out this time around.

I always thought I had friends. But they were really just friends by way of my kids. And now that my kids have both graduated college and are off doing their own thing (including forgetting to call every day like I always thought they would!), those friends have fallen away. I have no hobbies, no career, and no interests. My hobbies and interests were my kids' hobbies and interests. And the traveling I thought I might do at this point? Well, that went out the window when my husband of thirty years announced he was leaving for a newer, hipper version of me.

You're probably wondering why I'm telling you all of this. And, honestly, I'm not sure. If my daughter would just come around to the fact that one call a day isn't enough, and my son's new live-in girlfriend didn't have such an issue with me dropping in on occasion, and my husband would wake up and realize that I look the way I do because I devoted my life to him and our children, everything would be fine. I would be fine.

But none of those things are happening, and I just feel completely rudderless. Maybe hiring you as my friend would help. If nothing else, it would give me something to think about besides my poor, pathetic existence, and my overwhelming desire to murder my husband.

I have no schedule, so if you're interested in possibly taking me on as a client, you can email me back or call me at 555-2324. Maybe we can meet for coffee and see if I'm someone you'd even want to take on.

Friendless & more than a little pathetic,
Kim Felder

"Wow," Emma murmured. "This is absolutely heartbreaking—this poor woman sounds so sad, so alone, so . . . *pitiful.*"

"Oh?"

"Yeah. Her whole world has just imploded. Her kids have graduated college and flown the nest, leaving her at a loss for what to do with her time. Her husband of"—she looked back at the email, skimmed her way down to the second paragraph—"*thirty years* up and dumped her for a younger woman. And it sounds as if she doesn't have any real friends with whom she can vent."

"Or plot the louse's demise."

"And then there's that," Emma murmured as she reached the end of the email once again. "I feel so bad for this woman."

"Then what are you waiting for?"

Glancing across the table, Emma met Dottie's pointed gaze across the top edge of the woman's glasses. "*Waiting for?*"

"We're done with our tea for the week, yes? So call this woman, or email her, or do whatever you do to sign a new client in this day and age."

"Are you sure?" Emma asked. "I was planning on staying a little longer . . ."

At Dottie's nod, Emma returned her attention to the top of the email, read it silently a third time, and then pushed back her chair and stood. "You're right. If there's anyone who needs my services, it's this Kim Felder."

Ready to find
your next great read?

Let us help.

Visit prh.com/nextread

Penguin
Random
House